GOODNIGHT LYDIA

GOODNIGHT LYDIA

E. M. JONES

LAMPPOST PUBLISHING

Published 2026

Hardcover ISBN: 979-8-9910106-6-5

Paperback ISBN: 979-8-9910106-7-2

E-ISBN: 979-8-9910106-8-9

Logo design by Kim Taylor Creative

Cover design by Stuart Bache

ALSO BY E. M. JONES

THE DARLING KILLER

THE READER'S RESORT

For Mom and Dad

1

Lydia opens her eyes to complete darkness. She can't move her arms or legs, and when she goes to turn her head, a heavy blanket smothers her face.

Something is holding her down, suffocating her.

There's an overwhelming stench of earth, mixed with sweat and blood. She screams, and dirt trickles inside her mouth. Granules of soil are trapped beneath her eyelids, scraping her with every blink. The dirt in her throat makes her gag, but if she throws up, she'll drown in her own vomit.

She can't breathe. There's dirt in her nose, ears, and under her clothes.

It's everywhere.

She's going to die.

Now, Lydia can't help it; the guttural cry comes from her chest, and she begins to choke. She blinks rapidly, her eyes burning like hot stones.

She's going to die like this.

Flexing her hands and feet doesn't help; the earth is too heavy. She's too far down, she keeps choking, and she's out of options. Out of time.

She tries to slow herself down. The harder she breathes through her nose, the more dirt she inhales.

How much time does she have? How long can someone survive underground?

She can't panic. There *has* to be a way out.

Concentrating, she slowly shakes her head, jostling the dirt above her until she's facing her right shoulder. She breathes through clenched teeth, preventing dirt from falling inside her mouth and nose. There's more air here than she would've guessed, but it won't last.

Breathe in, breathe out.

Where was she before this? At the restaurant! Yes! She had dinner with Eddie, and that's her last memory.

She remembers the bland food, the overly loud music, the stab of guilt she felt when he awkwardly dropped the engagement ring back inside his pocket.

She remembers breaking his heart.

But what happened *after* that? What did he do to her?

Arching her back, she feels the dirt shift beneath her. That's it! She rotates her arms, forcing more dirt under the small of her back. Then she flattens her spine, pressing the earth down, and arches it again, repeating the process.

It's like the fable of the Crow and the Pitcher, where the crow is thirsty and can't reach the little bit of water at the bottom of a pitcher, so he slowly fills the pitcher with pebbles, bringing the water to the top so he can drink.

I'm the water, she thinks, clawing at the dirt like an animal, hysterical laughter bubbling inside her chest.

Where is Eddie? Did he take her home after dinner, or did they stop somewhere? Did he leave her at the restaurant? After what she's done, he has every right to hate her.

Lydia's lungs are burning. How long does she have?

The soil loosens; it ripples around her like a thick liquid. She thrashes her arms and legs, knowing she doesn't have much time left. Her limbs are going numb, and all she can see is Eddie's stupid, upset face.

Where is he?

Why is she here alone?

What happened to her?

There's a brush of air on her fingertips, and she punches out of the dirt, freeing her entire right hand. For a second, she doesn't know which way is up, and it feels like she's about to fall. She claws with her left hand now, breaking through the ground like something undead. Her eyes are on fire, and beams of white light are shooting through her vision.

Then her face is free, and she's lurching up and rolling on her side, where she vomits all the dirt, bile, and laughter onto the damp ground. Her eyes are clenched shut, and she's afraid of what'll happen if she opens them.

Pressing her cheek against the cold ground, Lydia breathes in the fresh air. It smells like pine needles, and there's a symphony of crickets and bullfrogs surrounding her. She's in a forest, at night, and close to water.

Is she in the nature preserve? They would've passed it on the way home.

The crickets and the bullfrogs suddenly quiet down, replaced by the sound of footsteps in the woods.

She knows it's not a random stranger; it's the person who put her in this grave.

They're coming back because they heard me, she thinks. *Oh God, where do I go? I can't see anything!*

Lydia shuffles on her hands and knees, feeling the soggy earth collapse beneath her, and a sharp terror pierces the inside of her chest.

She holds her breath and slides back into the grave, where the loose earth is now cold and grimy against her skin. She sinks down, kicking dirt over herself like a crab in a sand dune.

It's not enough; they're going to find her.

She lies perfectly still and plays dead.

A car door slams in the distance. A voice calls out, but Lydia can't make out the words, whether it is a man or a woman, or if they say anything of value.

The footsteps move away from the grave, a second car door closes, and a vehicle drives off. She must be near a road.

The crickets and the bullfrogs perk back up, and the forest resumes its natural rhythm.

Why did her attacker come back? Did they hear something?

Lydia tries to stand, but the grave shifts under her, making her slip. She catches herself, and her hand strikes something blunt. Blindly, Lydia feels for the object. Her fingers close around a gaping mouth with sharp, wet teeth. Someone is staring up at her, and they aren't breathing.

Shaking, Lydia covers her mouth to stop from screaming, because she's not alone in these woods.

And she's not the only one in this grave.

2

Lydia scrambles off the corpse and slides down a short hill.

She still can't see. She feels her way along the forest floor, ramming her fingers into roots and tree stumps until she stops and realizes her mistake.

There is a very small chance she was buried with a stranger, and she hates the idea, but she should go back and check. What if it's someone she knows? What if it's Jack, and he's dead because of her?

Before she can move, she hears a faint cough. There's a rush of tiny echoes, like plastic beads spilling on the ground. It's the sound of falling dirt, and footsteps staggering toward her, the smell of earth strong enough to turn her stomach.

The cough is now continuous, and it sounds like a man. He's rustling through the woods, gagging and spitting. His hands rasp against his clothes as he frantically brushes himself off.

It's the other person in the grave.

Lydia crawls away from him, praying she doesn't make a sound.

She stops. He's gone dead quiet.

Is he looking at her right now?

She rubs her eyes again, biting the edge of her shirt sleeve. She still can't see, and maybe he can't either.

Should she say something? She wants it to be Eddie so desperately that she almost says his name. But the last thing she remembers is telling Eddie she doesn't want to marry him, and what did he do after that? Oh God, why can't she remember?

If it is Eddie, he would help her piece together what happened. But she's sprawled out on the dark forest floor, unable to see, defend herself, or escape. Staying quiet right now could save her life. There's still a small chance it's not Eddie or Jack or anyone she knows, and that makes her hesitate.

Then, without a word, he takes off through the woods like a big animal, making too much noise until Lydia can't hear him anymore. He must've been able to see well enough to run, but he didn't notice her on the ground, in the dark.

The crickets and bullfrogs had paused their chatter, reluctant to resume after all the interruptions. In the quiet, she hears a trickle of water.

Lydia scrambles toward it, scratching her arms and legs against honeysuckle bushes, tangling her hair in briars and low branches.

Footsteps echo behind her. Lydia bumps into another tree and slides around it, lying on her stomach and pressing her face against the earth; it smells like death.

The footsteps stopped when she did. She tries to hold her breath long enough to listen, but there's nothing else to hear. Maybe she imagined it. Or they're very patient.

She quietly slides toward the sound of water, crawling with both hands extended until her fingers find the edge of the riverbank. She swings her legs around and lowers herself feet first, holding onto what feels like a large, exposed tree root. Her shoes touch a slanted bank, and she lets go of the root and trips on her own feet and lands on her backside, her hands plunging into the soggy river floor to catch herself. The water is shockingly cold, but she's not complaining.

She plunges her face into the river, rubs her eyes in the water, and comes up for air. The forest is dark and blurry, but she sees moonlight streaming through the trees, and a sob of relief builds inside her chest.

She cups water in her palms and washes her face. Then she takes a sip, knowing she shouldn't, but it soothes her throat.

There are footsteps again, closer this time, right down the riverbank.

It could be the man in the grave, or their attacker, or something else entirely.

In these woods, there are worse things than people.

The moon is nearly full, and the woods have a soft, ethereal glow to them. She's sitting in Moon River, where the rapids meet the main channel, in a nature preserve five minutes from Hope, her hometown. She knows this forest well, as does her family and anyone who volunteered to find her baby brother.

A stick snaps in the dark.

Something's out there. The wildlife is quiet again.

She sinks into the river and swims to the other side, searching the woods behind her, seeing only shadows.

We found him curled up beneath a tree. He died two days later from a fever.

Her earliest memories are rushing back. She can't stop them.

She climbs up the far riverbank and scans the forest she just left, her heart battering her ribcage. Is this how Sammy felt when he was lost in these woods twenty years ago?

The townspeople blame the preserve for every bad thing that happens in Hope, including Sammy's death. Some said the woods made Sammy sick. Others said the Reaper cursed him. Lydia's classmate in second grade, a dopey boy with a crooked haircut, once looked her dead in the eye and told her Sammy was haunting these woods.

Those old stories are hard to ignore right now.

She finds a trail along the river and starts running like she's five years old again, staring through a wide-open cabin door at a gravel driveway filled with vehicles. The adults are freaking out about the open door, passing the blame before rushing into the night and beginning the search.

Lydia follows the trail while keeping an eye across the river. She knows something is there. On her left, a long, jagged rock face travels for miles, quietly trapping her down this path.

We found him curled up beneath a tree.

Lydia sees little two-year-old Sammy in every shadow, tears rolling down his face.

She can't get him out of her mind. His tiny casket lowering into a grave.

The memories circle like vultures.

It's not a coincidence, she thinks. *Burying me in the same woods where Sammy got lost.*

Whoever did this is someone in her life.

Someone she knows.

She doesn't hear footsteps anymore, and as she listens and scans the woods across the river, the night erupts with the sound of scraping metal.

3

The sound is coming from the parking lot across the river, next to Route 4. She's deep enough in the woods that no one standing in the lot should be able to see her, but she kneels on the ground anyway, out of breath.

Across the river, a dark shape moves through the parking lot, dragging a piece of metal behind them. They get inside a parked car and start the engine. Yellow headlights shoot through the woods on her left.

It's them, she thinks. *They must've come back for something. Or there are two of them, and one never really left.*

She waits for the car to move. The stranger is just sitting there, maybe on their phone.

Lydia shuts her eyes as a furious headache blossoms inside her skull. The darkness in her mind rolls across her vision like heavy clouds. And there's something else, a black moon eclipsing the sun, the same event Lydia had watched with her family in April of 2024. But this solar eclipse is so clear in her mind, it can't be a memory; it's currently *happening*. The eclipse is only covering a quarter of the sun, but it's moving toward totality, and there's a great roar in her ears that reminds her of a hot fire whirling inside a wood-burning boiler, like her grandparents used to have.

Lydia opens her eyes, her vision peppered with spots. She's afraid to close her eyes again or even attempt to understand what seeing an eclipse inside her mind could mean.

The car in the parking lot hasn't moved. If she can get closer, she'll see who her attacker is and get the license plate number.

The headlights are shining on her left, stretching through the woods and across the wooden bridge, the only access to this side of the river. She slowly moves toward the bridge. She'll cross it when the car begins to turn.

Behind her, the ridge stretches for miles, and there's no easy way around it unless you can climb. Every local climber has attempted the tallest point, where the cliff slopes outward to create an impossible overhang they call the Reaper.

Lydia hasn't managed to summit the Reaper yet; she falls every time. Something about the overhang makes her squeamish. Even now, coming up on the Reaper in the dark, she sees that curved beak at the top and it sends shivers down her spine. The headlights are pointed directly at it, but with the winding path and trees in the way, only small pockets of light touch the Reaper's dark robes.

She stands in its shadow and sinks into the darkness. She can partially see the car through the trees. It's on the edge of the parking lot. A small, normal-looking car. No make, model, or color is visible. She needs to get closer.

Crawling on the ground, she keeps the wooden bridge directly between her and the vehicle. The bridge has a small arch that hides her from the stranger's sight. The headlights stream overhead, inches away. Every few seconds, she feels the Reaper's eyes on her, and she looks over her shoulder.

It's called the Reaper because of its shape. Silver anchors travel down the rock wall like a knobby spine, reflecting the moonlight. The crevices make a blockish square, curving upward into a pointed overhang that looks like the Grim Reaper's outstretched hood. In that darkened pit, she sees a monstrous face leering down at her. Maybe that's why she falls at the overhang; it's like she's climbing inside the Reaper's gaping mouth, and it's bothered her since she was a child. Since the night they lost Sammy.

The headlights slowly twist through the forest. The car's backing up.

Lydia jumps to her feet and sprints across the bridge.

The car turns onto Route 4, a hunched shape sitting behind the wheel. Lydia stops at the edge of the parking lot in disbelief.

That's *her* car.

She apparently drove here on her own volition, and now someone's erasing the evidence. She can't tell who it is, but she feels a crawling shiver as the dark shadow drives toward Hope. There's no reason to go that way unless you live there, and Lydia knows every single person in that tiny village.

There's a creaking sound from the green Porta-Potty nearby; the door is loose and shifting in the breeze. Is someone inside, watching her through the crack in the door?

She can't decide if being in the woods is worse than staying close to the road. The attacker is clearly gone, and if someone else drives by, maybe she can signal for help.

Lydia stands in the middle of the road, checking both directions. Going north on Route 4 will take her to Blue Hill and deeper into the nature preserve, but she might as well follow the direction of her attacker and her home by walking south. She can stay within the tree line so no one sees her, at least while it's dark. The glowing ember of dawn is on the horizon, but she'll deal with that soon enough.

Then up ahead, coming from Hope, white headlights appear around the bend.

4

Michael is sitting in the back room of his church, finishing his daily prayer, when a strange noise comes from the sanctuary.

On weekdays in the summer, he leaves the front door propped open while he cleans and talks with his Maker. This way, anyone is free to commune with him, and the whole church smells like fresh grass clippings, flowers, and melting blacktop. The breeze is strong today, and the wind is carrying the distracting hum of lawnmowers and passing cars into his church. But this noise is different.

It happens again; it's the sound of his door stopper, a five-gallon bucket filled with tools, being pushed across the concrete stoop.

The front door slams shut.

In a heartbeat, the church is quiet, cut off from the outside world.

Michael tries to peek into the sanctuary, but he can't see anything from where he's sitting.

Someone's entered his church and closed the door behind them.

He stays glued to his chair. He's always known they'd find him eventually. It hovers in the back of his mind every time he unlocks his apartment, prays for a miracle, or drifts off to sleep.

Light footsteps echo through the sanctuary, coming closer. The floors are wooden, and they sound a hundred years old, which he prefers for two reasons: no one can possibly sneak up on him unless they come through the back door, and there's a lot of character in the way someone walks. Their intentions, confidence, and guilt bleed through the squeaky floorboards.

Listening to footsteps was ingrained at an early age, when his dad would walk up the stairs. He can still hear the steady *thump-thump-thump* of heavy boots on worn boards, the belt already in hand. Michael had prayed for a miracle even then and was always denied.

"Pastor Michael?"

He knows that voice. Eddie West never visits him during the week. What could he possibly be doing here in the middle of the afternoon?

Michael walks into the sanctuary. Eddie is standing rigidly between the old-fashioned wooden pews, hands tucked inside the pockets of his athletic shorts. His eyes are fixed on the cross above the altar.

"Everything all right, Eddie?" Michael asks. Considering Eddie shut the front door, this must be important.

Eddie shakes his head. He's tall, somewhere in his late twenties, and normally ablaze with charisma. This is the most subdued Michael's ever seen him.

"Is something wrong?"

Eddie has a look on his face that Michael can't decipher. Is it fear? Exhilaration? Dread? Or something in between? Eddie glances at the pews. He's too scared to move, to even sit down.

Michael knows this song and dance.

He sits on the first pew, right on the end, and pats the seat next to him. He's not Catholic, never has been, but he's always respected the confessional box and has tried to recreate it here. He even polishes the pews himself. After the last church went belly up, no one cared enough to clean it out. Bibles were left to rot, tools left to rust. Michael had to inspect, clean, and reutilize every item. He doesn't blame the former congregation for washing their hands of it all. He would've done the same thing under the circumstances.

Eddie sits beside him, finally clearing his throat. "You ever seen someone die, Pastor?"

Together, they stare at the cross on the back wall, which holds a statue of Jesus in his dying state, three days before his resurrection. Before the *miracle*.

"I have," Michael says. "Once."

"How'd it happen?"

He doesn't hesitate. "Oh. Well, he was an old man with cancer. It was quiet, just the two of us in his living room. He hated hospitals and chemo. He wouldn't waste time on them. I prayed with him, and for him, every day. Then he finally knew, I don't know how, but he knew this day would be his last. He called me, and I came over early. He died ten minutes after we prayed. Very quiet, like I said."

Eddie crosses his arms, his fingernails digging into his bicep, as if in pain. "Did you feel anything when it happened? Like, were you calm? Or bitter? Being a Pastor and whatnot, I figured you've, you know, been exposed to this stuff before. Maybe a lot. I don't know."

Michael isn't actually a Pastor, although he spent time in seminary. It's astounding what people will believe with enough sincerity and a few fake certificates. Hope only has two hundred and twelve residents stubbornly living in the shadow of a much larger town, Blue Hill. For Michael, Hope was the perfect place to start over; the perfect place to hide. Not once has someone questioned his authenticity as a Pastor.

"I felt sad for him," Michael says, thinking of the old man's final breath, the way his frail body jerked beneath the water. Eddie doesn't need to know the real story, but bits and pieces are harmless. The best lie is mired in truth, and the stuff about the cancer and the quiet come to Michael so naturally, he almost forgets he's telling a fabricated tale.

"After he passed, I felt very sad for him. He deserved better. So I begged God for a miracle." Michael prayed when he held the old man down. Maybe the hardest he'd ever prayed in his life. "I asked God for a *resurrection*."

Eddie slowly turns to him, his eyes lighting up. "And did he live?"

"He did not."

"Holy shit—sorry, Pastor, it's just. I didn't expect you to pray for something like that."

"Why do you have these questions, Eddie? I'm guessing something serious is going on, with you bringing this up."

The young man pauses, not fully committed to spilling his guts. "If I tell you something confidential, will you keep it between us?"

Something in Michael hungers for the dirty secrets of others, and this causes him to sit up straight and lean in, gently patting Eddie on his muscular shoulder. "You can tell me anything, Eddie, and it will stay between us."

"Even if it's a crime?"

"It depends. Are we talking petty theft or grand larceny?"

"Ha. If only."

Michael frowns. This isn't what he expected. "Did someone hurt you?"

There's a definite twitch on Eddie's face. Michael is onto something, but he won't ask again.

"You said you prayed for a miracle, for that old guy. You believe in miracles?"

Every day since his mom died, Michael has prayed for a miracle.

He was nine years old when they diagnosed her with cancer. It took two years to finally claim her. And every day for those two years, he prayed that God would heal her.

Well, He didn't, but Michael keeps it up to this day, at forty-nine years of age. Instead of praying for his mom, he prays for a miracle of any kind. He wants to believe in God, and yet one thing continues to stop him: proof. One miracle, and he'll believe. Is that too much to ask?

His hunger for miracles and secrets comes from a little beast inside his stomach. Every time a church member confesses their sin, the thing in his stomach wakes up and swallows it. It's hard to say when he first noticed its presence. Sometime after Darling, maybe. He can really feel it paying attention now, like it's cracked one eye open.

Eddie, oblivious to the turmoil inside Michael's head, takes a long time to respond. Michael suspects Eddie's weighing the pros and cons of telling him this secret.

It's most unfair, always counting on other people to provide the miracle, when Michael, a willing vessel, is perpetually overlooked. His prayers always went unanswered, back when the footsteps were worse than the beatings.

Finally, Eddie reaches a decision. His eyes are bright blue and lined with tears. "Do you have your phone on you?"

"I do."

"Can you put it in the back room? They listen to us. I know it's dumb, but please?"

Michael tries not to look worried. "Of course," he says. He sets his phone on the little table in the back room and shuts the door behind him. He's sweating, and the lack of AC isn't helping. Is it a mistake to leave his phone behind? Eddie's never acted like this.

"Good enough for you, young man?"

"Yes sir."

Michael sits again, crossing one leg over the other and folding his hands. "If you want my undivided attention, Mister Eddie, you have it."

Eddie nods in appreciation. He clears his throat, and somehow, they both realize he's about to cross a line, and Michael's partly afraid of what'll happen next. Especially when Eddie says, "I have some questions about miracles, if you can help me. You know Lydia?"

The thing in Michael's stomach twitches happily. "As in your girlfriend, Lydia Pratt? I know her a little. Why do you ask?"

Genuine fear fills the young man's eyes. "Something bad happened to her."

5

It feels like Lydia is drowning. Eddie's faint, distorted voice is somewhere above the surface, shaking her shoulders hard, his fingernails digging into her skin.

She jerks awake and sits up in bed, greeted by sunlight bursting through her windows. Her head feels like it's splitting in half. Falling back into her pillow, Lydia rubs her eyes until she has blurry spots and swirling colors in her vision.

Eddie brushes the hair from her face. His fingers make her flinch. "Good morning, Lydia," he whispers, pausing for a long time. "Scary dream?" He's lying on his side in his usual pajama pants and a plain white T-shirt. "I honestly thought you were going to punch me."

Lydia stares at the ceiling where she used to have a *Twilight: New Moon* poster. She had forgotten all about that. "What happened?"

"Which part?" There's a small frown on his face, as if he's trying not to cry.

"What's wrong, babe?" she asks.

He hasn't shaved in a few days, and there's a shadow on his cheeks. It actually looks good on him. His hair is a mess, and he combs it with his hand instead of answering her.

She's too groggy for this. "Is everything all right?"

He nods. "Yeah, just feel sick."

Lydia sits up again, her stomach heaving. At least her eyes are finally adjusting to the light. "Shit, what did I drink?"

"Your head hurt?"

"I can hardly think right now." A wave of nausea rolls through her. "Oh my. I overdid it, whatever I did."

"*We* drank way too much Fireball."

There's an empty bottle on her dresser, along with two Gatlinburg shot glasses. She pinches his arm. "I have work today!"

"Not anymore," Eddie says. "I stole your shift. I already texted Kevin."

"That's sweet of you." Lydia glances at her childhood bedroom. Her bed is shoved into the corner, facing a second-story window with a view of the garage's slanted roof. As a teenager, she used to sit out there with her friends, back when that *New Moon* poster was socially acceptable. She hasn't done that in a long time. She's twenty-six now; Eddie's twenty-seven. They're still young enough to live with her parents, but maybe she's been naïve about that. Here she is in the same bed she's used for fifteen years. The wooden headboard was painted bright white and has a little shelf along the top, where she keeps a lamp and a pile of books she hasn't touched since high school. In the opposite corner of the room is a small desk she's had since her seventh birthday, and beside that, a white dresser with pink trim holds an old TV and a landfill-sized pile of jewelry, hairbands, and half-used lotion bottles. It all looks childish now. What changed?

"Are you okay?" Eddie asks too intently, like he's studying her.

"Mmhm, my head hurts."

"Shots will do that, hence why I'm taking your shift. You need a rest day anyway. You've been working too much."

"How can you tell?"

He peels the covers back, exposing her bare legs, and points to a large purple bruise on her left thigh. "That's a new one. It's almost as big as the others." She has half a dozen bruises on both legs, all in various stages of bloom.

"Stop it. I bruise easily."

"Yeah, because you're not a gentle climber."

Lydia's heard that for years. First from her parents, then Eddie. They said she rock climbed like a cat holding on for dear life, and as a result, her legs took a beating. But the bruises were never ugly in her eyes.

Has she been working too much?

Something catches her eye—a red scratch down his chest, barely visible beneath his shirt. She reaches for him. "Babe, what happened?"

He pushes her hand away. "So you *really* don't remember last night?"

"*I* did that?"

"No, my mistress did." Eddie smiles, but his eyes are twitchy.

"I think I blacked out."

"You think?"

"Come on." She pats his chest. "I'm just confused now. Let's eat breakfast. My parents are probably waiting. And I'm sorry I did that to you, but I doubt you are."

Lydia gingerly climbs out of bed, wobbles over to the dresser, and changes into a matching pair of sweatpants and a sweatshirt.

Eddie stares at the room with a blank expression. "We should've moved out a long time ago."

Why is he so weird today? He's never like this. "So let's move out then," she says.

Eddie sits up, his shirt pulled tightly against his chest. He has the body of a climber, and that was one of the first things Lydia noticed about him. His face is telling her something, but she's not sure she can handle a serious conversation right now.

Oh. Oh no no no.

Lydia freezes; it's coming back.

On her dresser, near the empty bottle, is a small black jewelry case. *Oh no, what's wrong with me?* she thinks.

"Why would you say that?" Eddie asks.

"I know, I know." She sits on the edge of the bed. "I know."

"Why'd you say we should move out? You don't want to marry me."

"Babe, can we talk about this later?"

"You said no, Lydia, and you wouldn't tell me why." His voice cracks. "Do you remember *that*? Why are you acting like that didn't happen? Was the dinner that bad? Was my proposal that shitty?"

"No, no, Eddie, I just, I'm still waking up, and I feel like shit. I'm so sorry."

She can't tell him the truth. What would that do to him? She closes her eyes to stave off the dizziness and lies on the bed, hoping this all magically goes away.

The bed shifts as Eddie comes closer, and it makes her skin crawl. She's never felt uncomfortable around him before, but maybe rejecting his proposal changed more than she would imagine.

I have to break up with him, she thinks. She'll break his heart all over again. *I have to do it tonight, before Eddie discovers anything, and it all goes to hell.*

Eddie's hand covers her own. "Lydia?"

It feels like he's holding her down. Between the alcohol, her stomach, and the jarring memory of rejecting him, her body finally catches up with her.

"I need to throw up," she says calmly. She leaves the bed, walks out of the room, and makes it to the bathroom before vomiting all over the tile floor.

6

Lydia dashes off the road as the vehicle speeds toward her. She can't decide whether to seek help or hide. If the attacker is circling back, she's giving them another chance to kill her... and she doubts she'll survive a second time.

Or, if it's a helpful stranger, they'll take her home.

She sinks into the tree line as the vehicle approaches; it's an SUV. Is it her imagination, or is it slowing down? She decides to show herself. She'll know if the driver is shocked to see her, right? She'll know right away, and if she doesn't trust it, there's a whole nature preserve right here. They won't catch her.

She steps up to the road. The SUV is close now, and she starts to raise her hand when it zooms past. It's not a random bystander, either, but a cop. The officer is staring down, and there's a glow on his face.

He's on his phone. Lydia knows him: Sheriff Alex Lee, one of the only law enforcement officers who patrols Hope and the nature preserve, and an old friend of the family. She can't be sure, but she's almost positive he glanced at her. His eyes, lit by his cell phone, flicked in her direction as he drove past.

Why would he not stop?

He didn't actually see me, Lydia thinks. *I was standing still.* And if Alex had been the one who put her in that grave, he'd be backing up right now and running her over. He's only driving away because he didn't see her.

But how? She saw his eyes!

Lydia walks onto the road, watching his taillights disappear around the bend.

Maybe he *couldn't* see her.

What if she didn't crawl out of that grave? What if her body is still there, and she's not a survivor after all, but a ghost?

"I'm not dead," she whispers to the empty road, just to hear her own voice; it doesn't help. Her words dissolve in the gentle breeze, and the woods' nocturnal stirrings continue without her.

Am I even alive?

She weaves through the woods and back to the grave. The glow on the horizon keeps expanding, but she finds it difficult to care. If she's actually dead, she can watch the sunrise for another thousand years; she can watch Eddie summit the Reaper without her. Maybe with a new woman by his side, one who can make it to the top.

Running along the river, she has no trouble finding the grave, gaping at the sky like a black, rotting mouth. She's terrified her corpse will be in there, and then what? What does a ghost *do* in these woods all alone? She wishes she hadn't thought that.

Why did Sammy have to walk out that open cabin door?

Why does her last memory of him have to be his casket lowering into the earth?

Lydia's back in the grave for the third time tonight. She claws through the broken soil, bracing herself.

Her body's sinking, the earth swallowing her again. The dirt tugs on her arms as she worms her fingers deeper and imagines taking hold of her own lifeless hand, and brushing the dirt out of her own dry, frozen eyes.

She touches a cold finger and jerks back, her body slipping into the center of the grave. She reaches in again, holding her breath, and from the earth pulls out a long, severed root.

Crawling away, she drops the root and breathes an aggravated sigh of relief.

"I'm really here," she says, clinging to the sound of her voice. "It's okay, breathe. You're alive."

It won't take long for people to realize she's missing, right? Twenty-four hours or less, depending on what she told her family last night and if they expected her to be home or not. That gives her a single day's head start on whoever did this to her. Providing the man from the grave doesn't somehow alert everyone. What happened to him? Is he okay? Not that she can be of help.

She has zero resources. How can she check on everyone in her life when she has no car and no phone?

Her only advantage is the element of surprise. The attacker thinks she's dead, and that's useful. They won't expect her to be alive and actively pursuing them.

Would going home put her parents in danger?

She would normally trust her parents and Eddie with her life... but things are complicated. What happened feels like a direct reference to Sammy's death. How could it not be?

It's these woods.

And although her parents would never hurt her, if Lydia's hunch is correct, someone they all know is responsible for this. Going to her parents right away might not only rob her of this head start, but it could also alert the attacker.

As for Eddie, now *that* is a problem. She doesn't think he'd ever hurt her either, but it's no coincidence that this happens after she turns down his marriage proposal.

"Oh Eddie," she says. "What did you do?"

Going straight to the police feels like the right step, but after Alex sped past her earlier without stopping, something doesn't sit right. Why was he driving by the preserve this early? So close to where she was buried?

There are no coincidences. Alex being nearby means something. These woods mean something.

But there are too many unknowns and variables. And if she wants to use being "dead" to investigate her own murder, then what? How can she move through a very tiny town unnoticed by everyone? Or go home without being seen? If she tries to pursue the would-be killer, where would she, an average person, even begin? She still lives with her damn parents! She can't even climb a small, tricky cliff without falling!

"Start with the grave," she tells herself. *One thing at a time. Start at the beginning.*

Talking out loud helps her think. "I woke up, and I got out. I was... coughing. I threw up. And someone was in the woods, walking toward *me.*"

Lydia circles the grave, finding a range of broken plants and trampled weeds. What about footprints? She carefully picks her way around the forest, trying to find a single shoe print. "Okay. But I heard them coming, and I hid again. They walked away. What else?"

She looks at the woods. "Two car doors slammed shut, with different sounds. Like a trunk and a side door. Then they drove off. Wait, no. They yelled. While I was in the grave, someone was talking."

She wants to believe two people were out here conversing, but given the solo conversation with herself right now, she can't rule out the possibility of a single, talkative attacker. Besides, picturing one person is bewildering enough, let alone a pair of them.

She heard one vehicle drive off. Then a few minutes later, after she crossed the river, a dark figure walked to her car and drove away.

Could it all have been the same person? First, they drove down Route 4, turned around for some reason, and stopped in the parking lot. They looked around, found nothing, and left again. It's possible, but so is the idea of a second attacker.

The person drove her car toward Hope, where she lives. If she can find out where her car is *now*, it would give her something to work with. But that will have to come later.

Lydia walks a straight line toward the road, finding more plants bent in half, but no shoe prints. There are too many leaves and pine needles on the forest floor.

She pushes through a cluster of honeysuckle shrubs and steps onto the dirt road that sits between Route 4 and the woods. It stretches from the parking lot with the Porta-Potty, all the way down to Wiggins, the road off Route 4 that cuts into the heart of the preserve.

She glances up and down the dirt road in both directions. Even with the improving light of dawn, she can hardly see the parking lot in the distance. But they must've come this way to bury her.

Jumbled shoe prints cover the dirt road, but that's hardly useful. Hope residents often walk through here. There must be a dozen different prints. There *are* tire tracks, but what is she supposed to do with that? She can't take a picture of them or remember their exact squiggle. She's completely helpless.

So, she sits down to study the tire track, hellbent on memorizing it and proving her brain is worth something.

"Lydia?"

She trembles and turns around to see a lone figure stepping out of the woods and onto the dirt road, a tackle box in one hand, a fishing rod in the other. The short, stout person is wearing a heavy jacket and waterproof overalls tucked into their boots. There's a bucket hat on their head, with tufts of wild gray hair poking out from the edges.

"Lydia?" the person says again, dropping the tacklebox and fishing rod in the dirt. Lydia knows her. How did she miss it the first time?

"Kathy?"

"The one and only," Kathy LeGrand says, walking closer with her palms open. "You look like you've seen a ghost. What the *hell* are you doing out here, girl?"

Lydia imagines how this looks: with her sitting in the dirt in dawn's early light, intently staring at a track in the road. She doesn't need a mirror to *know* she looks like a freshly unearthed worm, and she doesn't even care.

She had forgotten about Kathy's morning fishing routine, and at the sight of her, every determined thought about doing this solo melted away.

She jumps into Kathy's arms and suffocates her with a bear hug. The dam breaks inside her, and she cries on the woman's shoulder, unable to get a single word out. This is how it feels to be alive, and it's incredible to be held by someone after what she's been through.

That's all she can think about until she hugs Kathy tighter, and her stomach presses against the distinct outline of a gun strapped to Kathy's belt.

7

Lydia steps away from Kathy, even though it feels wrong. Kathy's a longtime family friend, like a second mom. What does she have to be afraid of?

"Lydia," Kathy whispers in bewilderment. "What's wrong?"

"Why do you have your gun?"

Kathy pulls her jacket aside, showing off the holster and small pistol on her belt. "Oh. I take this everywhere."

She knows Kathy has her concealed carry, but for some reason, it feels unnatural here. "Why are you wearing it now?"

"Because I live alone, and I fish alone, out here in the middle of nowhere." Kathy chuckles and smooths out her jacket. She smiles awkwardly. "It's never bothered you before."

It's only Kathy. Why is she afraid of someone she's known her whole life? Someone who can help her out of this nightmare.

Someone who knows about Sammy.

Kathy crosses her arms. "Why are you out here so early? Where's your car?"

"I don't have a car... someone left me out here."

"They left you out here *alone*?"

"Sort of. Yes."

Kathy looks around. "Okay, care to explain?"

"That's the problem. I don't remember." Lydia hates to admit it, but there's something very wrong with her brain. She refuses to close her eyes again because in her mind, she'll see that solar eclipse slowly inching toward totality. Even a long blink brings the burning sun and the roar of fire.

Bending down, Kathy picks up the tackle box and fishing rod from the ground. Her eyes are unfocused, as if she's trying hard to solve an impossible problem. "Why don't you come to my place? I have extra clothes, coffee, whatever you need. Then you can tell me what happened, whatever you can remember, if you want. Or we'll call the police."

I didn't mention a crime. Why would she assume we need the police at all? Lydia thinks.

"Do you want me to take you home?"

"I don't know."

"Did someone hurt you?"

Lydia forces a small nod. Why does she feel guilty? As if she somehow deserved to be buried alive?

The way Kathy looks at her makes it worse. "Then maybe it's best you don't go home yet, not until I hear what happened and can judge for myself. We'll get this sorted, Lydia, I swear. But not until I know I can keep you safe. If you're okay with that."

Lydia wants to believe her, but there are no coincidences. "Are you always here around this time?"

Kathy cocks her head. "Of course. Why else would I be here?"

A dreadful image crosses her mind: Kathy with a shovel in hand, smiling down at Lydia while spilling fresh dirt over her eyes. It's too horrible to imagine.

"But why now, at this exact time?"

This seems to amuse Kathy, and she suppresses a smile. "Because the fish don't expect me."

Kathy turns away as if the matter is settled. Was she too quick to assume that Lydia didn't want to go home? Would Kathy have a reason to keep her away from her family?

She thinks Eddie's involved, Lydia tells herself. *Why else would she hesitate to take me home?* Which reminds her.

"Wait! Can you take a picture of these tracks?" Lydia points at the dirt road. "I'll explain everything, I promise."

Kathy frowns. "Those are mine, sweetie. I drove through here and parked up the way, close to Wiggins. I was already in the woods when I saw you over here."

Lydia glances at the tracks, her heart sinking.

Kathy leads her down the dirt road, not saying anything while Lydia checks behind them, catching glimpses of the parking lot on the other end and the Porta-Potty door drifting in the wind.

At the end of the dirt road, where Wiggins Street branches off Route 4, they climb into Kathy's SUV. It's incredibly clean inside, especially the leather seats that Lydia's dropping dirt all over.

"I don't fish quite as much anymore," Kathy says, swinging the SUV around and heading toward Hope. "You're lucky today's fishing day."

Nothing about this situation feels lucky. The familiar woods and road signs are glowing red in the sunrise, and everything looks the same as always, except Lydia has changed. She's an outsider in her own world like Jimmy Stewart in *It's a Wonderful Life*.

They drive in silence to the edge of town, where Kathy takes a lonely side road with a yellow sign at the entrance that says DEAD END. A crow is perched on the sign, cawing fiercely at the two of them. Lydia watches its little head swivel in her mirror, its beady black eyes following her as if it knows something she doesn't.

Kathy checks her rearview mirror. "They give me a lot of trouble, those birds."

"They're mean creatures."

"You got that right. Tiger wants to eat 'em, and I'm inclined to allow it."

"How is he doing? I haven't stopped by in forever."

"Oh, he's the same," Kathy says. "But he's very old now, and meaner than the birds."

Lydia remembers all the times she tried to pet Tiger when she was younger, only to end up with long red claw marks down her arms and hands. *You shouldn't declaw an animal*, Kathy used to say. *Claws are all it's got.*

They pull up to the quaint, one-story, two-bedroom home, where Kathy's lived for a thousand years, and Lydia's come over with her mom more times than she can count. Her mom and Kathy always drank tea while Lydia read books, played with dolls, or chased poor baby Tiger around. Lydia asked her mom once why Kathy never married or dated anyone, and she said it's because Kathy dislikes ninety-nine percent of people, and that was the only time Lydia brought it up.

"Lydia?"

She snaps out of the memory and looks at Kathy.

"Are you remembering something?"

Lydia shakes her head. Is she doing the right thing? Is she safe here? There are no close neighbors, and only one way in and out. She doesn't know these woods well enough to get home without using the main roads.

"Hey." Kathy's hand brushes Lydia's shoulder, and she pretends it didn't make her jump. "You have nothing to worry about, Lydia. We'll get this sorted, I promise."

Lydia nods; she doesn't trust herself to give a convincing reply.

They step out of the SUV, and Lydia swipes the dirt off her seat before following Kathy inside the house. She kicks off her shoes on the welcome mat, scattering dried chunks of dirt and pebbles.

Kathy glances at the mat, then at Lydia. How many questions are racing through her head? Instead of lingering, Kathy disappears into her bedroom and gives Lydia space to breathe.

The inside of the house hasn't changed much. Same living room setup, even the same coffee table and TV stand from Lydia's childhood. Only the couch is different. God knows what Tiger did to the last one.

"Would you like a shower?" Kathy appears with items from her room. "Here's a towel, some sweatpants, underwear, and a shirt." Kathy hands them to Lydia. "You can use my soap if you like. There's an extra towel on the shelf above the toilet. Just make yourself at home. I'll brew some more coffee. You need anything?"

"Water, please."

"Oh, right." Kathy pulls a plastic water bottle from the pantry. "You have anything on you? Purse? Phone?"

Lydia shakes her head, chugging half the bottle before making herself stop. "I don't know where it all went."

"That's okay, we'll figure this out. Get cleaned up and take all the time you need."

"Won't this..." Lydia looks at herself. "Won't a shower wash away evidence?"

There's a flicker of annoyance on Kathy's face. "You told me you didn't want to go home or call the police."

Did Lydia say that exactly?

"So, if you want forensics, we need to call nine-one-one, sweetie." Kathy clears her throat. "Were you raped?"

"I don't think so."

"Any visible marks, scratches, scars?"

"No. I don't know how they thought I was dead unless it's something in my system. Like poison."

Kathy shrugs. "A shower won't change that. We can still get you to the police if that's the direction you want to go, and they can run tests. You have some bloodstains here, on your shoulder."

She looks down. "It's not mine." *Was it from the man in the grave? she wonders.*

Kathy doesn't respond. Maybe she's waiting for Lydia to tell her more of the story. "What would you feel comfortable doing?"

Lydia doesn't know what to think at this point.

"If we want to be discreet," Kathy says, "we can call Alex. He should be working today."

There are no coincidences, Lydia thinks and feels her stomach about to heave. "No, that's okay, I'll just shower for now."

She wants to get away from Kathy, if only to be alone in the bathroom. Kathy and Alex were co-workers for years before Kathy retired. It shouldn't feel intentional for her to bring him up, but Lydia can't shake it.

Something's very wrong about this.

She hugs the clothes to her chest, feeling more dirt fall from her jeans as she walks down the hallway. "I'm so sorry."

Kathy's already pulling the broom out, waving a hand. "You have nothing to be sorry for. I'll get it."

Lydia tiptoes into the bathroom and goes to shut the door. Kathy's sweeping the floor in the living room, and behind her, underneath the couch, a pair of pale green eyes study Lydia from the darkness.

Keeping the door half-open, Lydia kneels on the tile and holds out one hand. "Hey Tiger, here boy."

Kathy stops sweeping and looks curiously from Lydia to Tiger's hiding place. The pale green eyes don't move, but a low hissing comes from the shadows, and a pair of white fangs flash in the low light.

Kathy shakes her head. "I told you he was meaner. Don't worry, he'll warm up to you." She smiles at Lydia, but her eyes are far from joyful. She's looking at Lydia like she's a broken thing; something no one could ever warm up to. Maybe Kathy's onto something.

Lydia closes the door and tries to calm her brain down.

Everyone in Hope is deeply connected, especially her parents and their friends. Kathy worked as a Blue Hill dispatcher for twenty-five years. She knows policing; she knows crimes and victims. She also knows Alex, who may or may not have seen Lydia on the side of the road and kept on driving.

Why wouldn't he stop if he saw her?

Lydia gently turns the bathroom lock. It sends a loud click throughout the quiet house, and she hopes Kathy understands.

8

The sanctuary is dead quiet.

Michael misses the distant lawnmowers and passing cars. He can hear his own blood pumping through his body.

"Eddie? Look at me. What do you mean, something bad happened? Where's Lydia?"

The fear is still in Eddie's eyes, and his voice quivers. "It's complicated."

Michael fights the urge to scoot away from the young man. Did Eddie lock the front door? He feels like he's trapped in his own church.

"Are you going to tell me what happened to her?"

"I want to..." Eddie trails off.

But then I'll have to kill you, Michael imagines Eddie saying, finishing the classic joke. It doesn't feel very funny now.

Michael wants his phone back and the front door open again. This is becoming something he isn't prepared for.

"Are you afraid because you think I'll judge you?"

Eddie wipes his eyes with his sleeve. "Once I tell you, there's no going back. And I can't promise you'll be safe."

Michael's on high alert now. The thing inside his stomach is wakeful, like it needs to stretch but can't get enough room. "Safe from who?"

Eddie looks around the church like he's scared of being overheard. "Explaining this will take time. What's your afternoon look like?"

"It's free."

"That's good." Eddie stares at the clock on the wall and watches it tick. "We have enough time then. I need to ask you a few questions before I go any further."

This feels like a twisted sort of interview, but Michael doesn't understand what for. "Is there a reason you're so hesitant?"

"To be honest, I don't think you'll believe me."

"Why not?"

"Because it's hard to explain. Almost impossible. That's why I asked you about miracles."

There it is again! That little hint. Michael is ready to run for his life, but the thing in his stomach is growing curious, so he stays put.

"I told you, Eddie, I believe in miracles. I believe in the supernatural. Isn't that good enough?"

Eddie leans forward, the way some people do in church when they're about to gossip. "So you believe in evil?"

"Of course, but what's that got to do with Lydia?"

There's a dark look in Eddie's eyes. "How do you know if it's a miracle, or... something worse?"

The thing in Michael's stomach twitches; he's very interested now. He can tell Eddie is deathly serious. This is no exaggerated theater; he truly believes what he's saying. Of course, Michael's learned to be wary of what people say. Humans are famously biased, unreliable, and prone to lying. Michael knows this better than anyone.

"Just tell me what happened," he says gently, always the empathetic pastor. "I know a thing or two about evil. You'd be surprised."

Eddie licks his lips. He seems content for now. "How well do you know the Pratt family?"

9

Lydia *hates* throwing up.

She assumes everyone does, but for her, the anticipation is a nightmare. This time, however, her body feels relieved, and she wipes her lips with a hint of déjà vu and satisfaction.

Eddie rushes into the bathroom like he'd heard a bomb go off. Rather than reprimanding her for throwing up two feet from the toilet or finding a way to continue their horribly awkward conversation, he swoops in, almost shoving her aside. He uses his bath towel to clean up the mess, even though he could've gone downstairs for paper towels. Maybe he doesn't want her parents to know that she barfed after drinking too much, as if he'd be held responsible.

She doesn't want his help, but he hands her a stick of gum, and she can't say no to him. They clean the bathroom in awkward silence, because throwing up is a great conversation killer.

When Eddie's done, Lydia rips the gum down the middle and hands him the smaller half. It's their special rule: you have gum, you share.

"Thank you," she says.

He takes his half-stick quietly, and she leaves before anything about marriage is brought up. But now she gets to face her parents, who are expecting a big announcement. Last night seemed to have ended cordially enough between her and Eddie, so her parents may be assuming the best.

Will they be disappointed?

Maybe not right away, but after she breaks his heart tonight, she imagines they'll want to know why. Same with Eddie. But as long as the truth doesn't come out, she can smooth everything over. Eddie will come around eventually.

She heads downstairs and into the kitchen, where her dad is standing in his pajamas beside the black coffee maker.

"Hey honey," he grins, holding an empty Cincinnati Reds mug. His hair is grayer these days, and the lines on his face seem to have deepened since he stopped working last month. He retired too early. All he talks about is the squad: the firefighters and paramedics he once worked beside. He visits the Blue Hill fire station almost every day.

"Sleep okay?" he asks.

"Sort of. What are you up to?" She opens the medicine cabinet, removes a bottle of painkillers, and takes three tablets. Hopefully, this offsets her hangover and magically fixes the rest of her problems. So far, her dad's acting completely normal. But that's how he is, regardless of the situation. He never cries, yells, or does anything out of character. His level of consistency should be studied

"This thing's making a weird noise." He swings his mug at the coffee maker. "I think it's shitting the bed."

Lydia laughs. "Eddie's covering my shift today, if you wanna do something later." She takes a long drink of water and hopes it'll wash the taste of bile away.

"Sure. You up for target practice?"

"I'll throw; you shoot."

"Deal."

Her mom emerges from the bathroom and immediately hovers over the kitchen counter, poking a homemade muffin with a toothpick. She also retired too early and recently closed the bakery she owned and managed for twenty years and now works part-time at a florist shop. Everyone in Blue

Hill wept the day she shuttered the bakery's doors. Twenty years of feeding every cop, firefighter, paramedic, and nurse bought her something close to legendary fame. Not to mention the normal folk who were addicted to her donuts, or the kids at Blue Hill's community college who pushed her to stay open later.

But right now, she declines to even acknowledge her daughter standing in the same kitchen as her.

Sharon Pratt was known as a fair and generous boss, but never to Lydia. Even after Lydia graduated from high school and told her parents she was skipping college, her mom refused to give her a job at the bakery. She didn't want to tie Lydia down to a family business. So, instead of helping, Lydia would sit on the stools at the bar and be a fly on the wall of her mother's empire. People would chat with her mom all day long and say goodbye to Lydia on their way out. She had some good memories there, like when her mom would talk to her between customers or give her deformed pastries. Whatever *that* signaled.

Now, Lydia almost expects her mom to remove the ugliest muffin from the fresh batch and hand it to her, as if to say, *This is what you get for ruining a good thing.*

She feels sick to her stomach. Her parents already know what happened, and now they're waiting for her.

Her mom's wearing a sweater Lydia recognizes, leggings, and her hair tied in a messy bun. It bothers Lydia that her mom is twenty-one years older and yet wears the same clothes as her. Every few months it feels like Lydia's aging while her mom looks younger, fitter, and has more energy.

Is she really going to ignore Lydia all morning? "Mom, that's my Ohio State sweater!"

She glances at Lydia and shrugs, a steely determination in her eyes. "It's actually Eddie's."

Eddie bounds down the stairs, dressed in shorts and a long-sleeved shirt. "Morning, everyone."

Dad turns around and salutes Eddie with his raised coffee mug. "Coffee's almost done. If it survives the trip."

"Thank goodness." Eddie squeezes past Lydia and picks out a Universal Studios mug.

Sharon ignores them and sets the table. Lydia and Eddie secretly call her *Karen* when she's not around, and Lydia wants to bring that joke up to Eddie now, but under the circumstances, she stays quiet. Her mom finishes the table and sets steaming plates of eggs, sausage, and bacon in the center. They always do breakfast this way, and Lydia's asked a million times if her mom needs any help, and much like with the bakery, she does not.

But the way she's acting right now, she *has* to know Lydia said no. Is that what she's so angry about?

They all sit: Eddie opposite Lydia, Mom opposite Dad, who prays for the food.

As they eat, no one talks.

Lydia glares at Eddie, but he's not looking at her. Can't he own up to *his* part of this situation?

"Lydia and I are shootin' clays after this," Dad says with a dopey smile, proud of himself for shattering the stalemate. "If anyone wants to join."

"I took Lydia's shift," Eddie mumbles. "I'm out."

Her dad nods across the table. "Sharon?"

Sharon makes a face like it's the dumbest idea she's ever heard. "No thanks." She looks at Lydia and goes back to her plate.

"Just us." Her dad winks and sips his coffee. Lydia knows he prefers it that way, and she wonders if he chooses activities the rest of them dislike just so he can take her on daddy/daughter dates like they used to.

Eddie clears his throat. "Kevin wants to set a new climbing route this week."

Lydia takes a bite of her food. Talking about work is better than nothing. "Did he ask you?"

"He asked *you*."

"Umm, he never asked me."

"Well." Eddie sips his coffee. "Maybe he told me in passing, you know? Like I'm supposed to convey the message or something."

"Not sure why he'd do that." Lydia pours herself a cup of coffee, feeling like Eddie's covertly fishing for something here. "Should I come in today then?"

"Nah, I'll do it." Eddie smiles at her, but it makes Lydia feel worse. Every passing second expands the rift between them and magnifies the unresolved proposal hanging over their heads. "Kevin thinks you're better at route setting than I am, and this is my chance to show him."

"You'll *actually* do it yourself?" she says,

"Yeah. Right after you stop in later and tell me what to do."

Her dad laughs, wiping his mouth with a napkin.

Eddie raises his hands. "What's the big deal? Kevin doesn't need to know I had help."

"We'll see. You gave me a free day, remember?" Lydia sits back down. "I could use some time off."

"Sorry, excuse me." Her mom bumps the table as she stands. She walks down the hallway and into her bedroom, closing the door softly.

Eddie and Lydia stare at each other until her dad stands as well. "Better check on her."

When the bedroom door closes again, Lydia frowns at Eddie. "Why the hell did you tell them you were proposing?"

"That's a normal thing to do, babe. Give me a break. Are you ready to talk about it now? Your mom's probably upset because she knows you said no. And here you are eating breakfast and making plans with your dad and acting like it's not a big deal. Well, I think it's a big deal to them."

Lydia can't believe what she's hearing. "Don't pretend you know what's important to my parents and I don't."

"You said you couldn't even explain your answer. What am I supposed to do with that? Just move on and try again later? At least give me a reason! That's why I'm upset. It feels like you're hiding something from me."

"I don't know why, Eddie," Lydia yells. "I don't feel normal. No one is acting normal today, except for my dad! I've been awake for less than an hour, and I'm hungover. I mean, can you please give me a minute here?"

He can't look her in the eyes anymore. "Is it someone else?"

"No, it's not, but thanks for assuming that, asshole." Lydia shoves her chair back and leaves the kitchen. She jogs up the stairs and into her bedroom, slamming the door.

The longer she waits, the worse this'll become. She wants to be angry at Eddie, but this is all her fault. She thought she would never be forced to choose, so she kept lying to him, over and over, and now everything's about to fall apart.

No matter how bad it hurts, if she breaks things off tonight, then Eddie will never see the worst parts of her.

There's a gentle knock on her door.

"Come in."

Her mom walks in, red-eyed and sniffling. "Can we talk?"

10

Lydia turns off the shower, dries herself with a fluffy, white towel, and changes into Kathy's spare clothes. They're baggy and short on her, and in the steamy mirror she looks like a different person, but it's not just because of the clothes. Her eyes are hollow. She's exhausted and needs to eat. She'd rested her head against the tile wall in the shower for a split second, only to jump when her eyes closed and the solar eclipse reappeared, nearly halfway across the sun. She kept her eyes open after that. She doesn't want to see the eclipse reach totality, because how could anything good come from *that*?

She opens the bathroom door to the heavenly smell of coffee and toasted bagels, the summer sunrise streaming through the front windows, and the little demon cat still under the couch, its reptilian eyes never blinking.

The front door stands wide open, and she catches herself staring at it, a twist in her heart. There's no sign of Kathy, but a loud noise is coming from outside.

What if Kathy knows the attacker and brought them here? Lydia would have no warning, no way to defend herself.

It was careless to take so long in the shower.

She sneaks into the kitchen, finding coffee-filled mugs and plain, buttered bagels neatly arranged at the small table in the corner by the window.

Through the thin window curtain, she sees Kathy in the driveway with a handheld vacuum, cleaning the passenger side of her SUV. She's erasing any evidence that Lydia was here.

Before Lydia can assume the worst, Kathy switches off the vacuum and answers her cell phone. Her voice is too distant to hear, and she could be talking to anyone, but Lydia has an immediate fear that it's about *her*.

She takes a seat and starts on a bagel to give herself something to do. Part of her wants to look around the house without Kathy present, but she might not have enough time.

Who is Kathy talking to? Lydia leans away from the window and listens to the clock on the wall tick one agonizing second at a time. In the distance, a dog is barking, and she wonders who the nearest neighbor is.

Kathy finally ends her call, shuts the passenger door, and comes inside.

"Help yourself. I've got creamer in the fridge." Kathy sets the vacuum by the front door and kicks off her boots. "Sorry about that. Your mom called me."

Lydia gasps. "What did you tell her?"

Kathy washes her hands in the sink. "We usually walk on nice days, but I told her I was coming down with something. Problem is, she said nothing about you."

"So she doesn't know?"

Kathy shakes her head. "Whatever happened last night, your parents didn't expect to see you this morning."

Lydia eats the rest of her bagel and tries to make sense of it. Why wouldn't her parents expect her to be home? Eddie lives with her, and there's nowhere else she generally goes to spend the night. Sometimes she stays with Aimee, her one surviving high school friend, but that's only ever on weekends, not... whatever the hell day it is.

Kathy grabs a garbage bag from a cabinet, disappears down the hallway, and returns a minute later. "I tossed your dirty clothes in here, if that's all right. We might need it later, you know, for evidence."

Oh, *now* she's worried about evidence. Lydia feels incredibly ungrateful for all the help she's received, but something's still bothering her. A lot of things, actually. "Did you ask my mom anything?" she says. "Any sort of prompting questions about me, or Eddie?"

Kathy sets the garbage bag on the kitchen floor. "I'm waiting on you. I thought it best to wait until we decided how to handle this."

True. Lydia should've thought of that. She needs to calm her nerves. "Can we get started?"

Kathy places a blank notepad and a pencil on the table and takes a seat. "I'm old school," she says, picking up her coffee and taking a long sip. She sighs and smacks her lips. "I don't want to push you on this. If you don't want to tell me what happened, you don't have to. I'm here for you, for whatever you need."

"Thank you. For the food, and everything."

Kathy touches Lydia's hand, staring deeply into her eyes. "I believe you, Lydia. No matter what. Just tell me the truth and start from the beginning. I'll take notes if I need to because memory is a monster. The longer we wait, the more details might slip away."

Memory is a monster. Isn't that how Lydia's mom used to describe losing Sammy? Like traumatic memories were a tumor, something living and growing and terminal that you carried around.

Lydia finishes the bagel and half her coffee before beginning. It doesn't feel real at first. It's like recalling a bad dream. But she starts with the grave and stumbles through the rest. Kathy takes notes instantly, her fingers rasping against the notepad and leaving slanted, loopy cursive behind.

She wonders why Kathy isn't more shocked by this, but then, surely a veteran 911 dispatcher can compartmentalize and avoid highly emotional responses. Surely, twenty-five years of hearing unspeakable things *does* something to a person.

There's no trace of surprise in Kathy's eyes, just understanding. Like she knows how tough it is to be buried alive. Lydia waits for outrage or disbelief and instead gets a chilly calculation. Lydia can't decide if she's upset or glad to have such a logical friend to lean on. Then, to top it off, Lydia wonders if Kathy's holding back because she doesn't find Lydia's story believable to begin with.

"Hold on." Kathy waves the pencil. "Back up. After the footsteps went away through the woods, you heard two car doors?"

"Yes."

"At the same time, or back-to-back?"

"Back-to-back."

Kathy makes a note. "You said they made the same sound, like a driver-side, passenger-side, closing their doors?"

She can't fully remember. "I think so. It happened fast."

"Too fast for one person to close both doors?"

Lydia starts on the next bagel. "I don't know."

"Okay, undetermined." Kathy waves the pencil again. "Now during that, you heard a voice? A man, woman, or child?"

"I didn't hear the words, so I can't even tell you the gender and age. It could've all been one person. Closing two doors, talking to himself."

"Himself?"

Lydia nods. "It was a man, wasn't it?"

Kathy leans back in her chair and rubs her forehead. "We can't assume anything, because like you said, we don't have enough details. But yes, probably a man. If statistics are anything to go by."

Lydia hates the thought of it: a real, breathing human with enough hatred in his heart to try and end her life.

"I wasn't alone."

Kathy blinks, setting the pencil down. "What do you mean?"

"There was another body in the grave with me. A man."

"Did you know him?"

This strikes Lydia as a strange question, but maybe she's overthinking it. "No, I have no idea who it was."

Kathy's sitting very still now, hardly moving her eyes. "What happened to him?"

"He ran off into the woods, and I never saw him again."

"And you're sure you didn't know who he was?" Kathy's face is blank, almost lifeless.

"I didn't see him. My eyes were messed up from the dirt. By the time I cleaned my face, he was gone."

"Just checking," Kathy says, breaking her trance and taking a bite of her bagel. "We must be thorough. All right, anything else happen after the man ran away? See anyone? Hear anything?"

For some reason, she keeps her encounter with Alex to herself. There might not be anything to it. "Someone drove my car away."

"You saw them do that?"

"From a distance, yes. I couldn't identify anything about them, it was still too dark."

Kathy seems troubled by this. "Okay, we'll circle back to that. Do you remember anything from last night? Before you woke up? Anything that could help us understand, if such a thing is possible, why someone did this to you?"

Lydia's lack of memory isn't helping her case, she knows that. If Kathy has a hint of suspicion inside her, it's kept alive by Lydia's vague notion of how she ended up in that grave.

"I've been trying to remember, and nothing's coming to mind. What day is it?"

"Tuesday."

Lydia tries to think. "Okay, so yesterday... I don't know, when I think about it, I get woozy. I think I had a big breakup with Eddie. But I can't... there's nothing concrete."

Kathy nods. "I know. Your mom called me yesterday and shared the news. It makes sense why your brain is going back to the breakup. It must've been a shock."

Kathy may be the only one trying to understand why Lydia said no to Eddie, but she doesn't know the full story. If everyone knew Lydia's sins, would they still see her as the victim, or would they think she deserved it?

"Last I heard, you broke up with him. And if I had to guess..." Kathy wipes her mouth with a napkin. "Things did not end well."

11

Lydia vaguely remembers breaking up with Eddie last night, but nothing is clear. She searches her brain for answers and gets nothing in return. It's hopeless. Her mind doesn't feel like her own.

"Hey, it's okay." Kathy places her hand on Lydia's arm. "You've been through hell. I can see that. And I want to find who did this. That's why I'm asking so many questions. You've been through something I can't even imagine, and it might've hurt you in ways you can't fathom right now. So let's do this slow, okay? Because you need to rest. You must be exhausted."

Lydia *is* exhausted, but sleep sounds impossible. Plus, she's terrified of closing her eyes. Is the eclipse going to happen whether she looks at it or not?

"I can't sleep. I need to keep going."

"Are you sure? You need it, Lydia."

Why is she stuck on this? "I'm positive," Lydia says curtly.

Kathy takes a bagel and pulls it apart before eating. "Why don't you want to sleep?"

Because I don't feel safe here, Lydia wants to say. "It's stupid. It doesn't make sense."

Kathy smirks, refilling her coffee. "You've managed to avoid death and climb out of a grave, sweetie. I don't think anything's off the table."

She has a point. Why not tell her the truth? So Lydia explains the eclipse she sees in her mind, and somehow this is more of a surprise to Kathy than the rest. She watches Lydia with extreme focus, showing true concern for the first time.

"Any idea what this eclipse thing means?" Lydia says. "Because it's really freaking me out."

Kathy steeples her fingers and gazes out the front window. Her pretty blue eyes sparkle in the morning sun, and the spilling light illuminates the hardened lines on her face.

"Trauma is a supernatural event," she says finally. "It's so unique. I don't care how much we study humans, or the brain, or childhood development. Something *happens* when we're hurt beyond repair, and it's so hard to explain. I wonder if this eclipse and these lost memories, if it all stems from what someone did to you."

Lydia thinks back to when she was little and in this very house, asking her mom why Kathy didn't have kids, in front of Kathy. It's one of those childish moments you can't understand at the time, but you remember the sick feeling of doing something wrong, and only years later do you lie awake in bed and think about it a hundred times and wish you'd never done it.

Lydia won't ask, but she doesn't have to.

"You've thought about Sammy?" Kathy says.

Lydia nods.

"When I lost my daughter, just before you were born, I started seeing things." Kathy's mouth turns at the corners, and her eyes start to shine. "I would hear her door open at night, like when she used to come snuggle in my bed with me. I would hear that door open and these small footsteps in the hallway. Every night. For a year after she passed, I would hear these things. Can you believe that?"

After this morning, Lydia will believe anything.

"Sometimes, I still hear those footsteps. I..." Kathy's holding the table with both hands, like she's afraid something will pull her away. "I recorded them once, on my phone. I'll show you, if you want. *Tap, tap, tap.* Little footsteps. Almost like how Lucy used to walk. But I never looked to see what was walking toward me because it didn't sound like *her*. It sounded like something pretending to be her."

Lydia's never seen this side of Kathy before. It's terrifying. "Have you talked to anyone about this?" Since Kathy goes to Pastor Michael's church, she may have consulted him.

Kathy shakes her head and releases the table. "This is about Sammy, isn't it?"

"I don't know how, but it feels too similar."

Kathy rubs her eyes. "Part of me had to relive Lucy's death through Sammy. But I was there for your mom. I understood what she was going through, and that's something neither of us can ever forget. She..." Kathy pauses again. "She dealt with ghosts of her own. What I'm saying is, we've been through some truly horrible nightmares, Lydia. In those woods, in this town. And whoever did this...needs to be taken care of. You understand?"

She understands. Ironically, Kathy would rather rely on a shot at revenge than the legal system, and Lydia can't fully blame her.

"Speaking of the preserve..." Lydia trails off. *You're very familiar with that area,* she wants to say. She thinks of Kathy on that dirt road, holding her tackle box and fishing rod. Kathy told her she came out of the woods because she saw Lydia. That means Kathy was walking directly toward the grave before getting sidetracked.

"Lydia? You all right?"

She's not all right. She doesn't know Kathy's exact fishing spots, but if there are no coincidences, then how come Kathy was heading for the grave?

"All that time you spend fishing, have you ever seen or heard anything in those woods?"

Kathy's eyebrow twitches, and she looks at her notes. "Like a ghost?"

"Just anything."

Shifting in her chair, Kathy looks out the window. "I have not," she says slowly. "But those woods are cursed, aren't they? You're proof of that." She sighs. "Not to say... I don't mean to say any of this is your fault, Lydia. You did nothing wrong."

I'm not so sure, she thinks. Kathy's lying about something. She can't figure out what, or why, but if Kathy knows something about what happened last night, why is she keeping Lydia in the dark? Whether Kathy's upfront with her or not, Lydia has to start piecing together what happened; time's slipping through her fingers, and with every passing minute, the eclipse nears totality.

"I think I can get a head start on this," Lydia says, "with your help. Whoever did this must have considered a lot of potential outcomes, right? But they never expected me to survive. If we can find him before everyone knows I'm missing, we'll catch him off guard. We might only have hours before that happens, depending on where Eddie and my parents *think* I am."

"I think you're right. So, what's next?"

There's really only one option. "We need to talk to Eddie."

12

Lydia watches Kathy scribble on her notepad.

"You know this looks really bad for Eddie, right?" Kathy says. "Boyfriends, husbands, they're always the first suspect, and usually for a good reason. What you have here is a good reason."

No one knows about Jack. Not yet.

Lydia crosses her arms. "But it's impossible to imagine him doing this."

"I know, but he's close to you, he's capable, and there's a prime motive: you rejected him."

"I thought the same thing. But can you even imagine it?"

"How long you two been together?"

"A year. We've been living together for six months."

Kathy taps the table. "Do you know what your parents have kept from you? The things they've shouldered your entire life, or since Sammy died? The long nights at the bakery, or your dad crying at my desk after a child died in his ambulance."

"That's not the same."

"Listen to me, Lydia. You're young. Not everyone is an open book. There are always things you don't know. Are *you* really telling me people don't keep long-term secrets?"

Ouch, does Kathy know? Lydia shifts in her chair and stares at the kitchen tile. She's right, of course. Lydia's a perfect example of living a lie. But how can Kathy see that? Or is she taking a shot in the dark because she knows Lydia's holding back information?

"Okay," she tells Kathy. "We question everyone. Is that what you're saying?"

Kathy smiles. "Now you're thinking. But your parents don't need vetting. Your boyfriend of one year is another story."

Okay, I get it, Lydia thinks. "So we start with Eddie and work through the rest. If we can piece together where I went last night, we can set up a timeline. If we're assuming whoever attacked me knows me and knows about Sammy, then our list of suspects is going to be short and personal. It also means whoever did this is one off-hand comment away from knowing they failed, right? As in, if anyone knows I'm alive, it could be dangerous?"

"That's why this stays between us for now." Kathy flips her notepad over and picks up the pencil. "We don't know where your phone is, so finding that could tell us a lot. But if your attacker was smart enough to take your phone, they probably got rid of it. Any online accounts we can get into would be the next best thing."

Lydia paces in the kitchen. "What if it was just some random, weird guy I dated in high school? Everyone in Blue Hill knows about Sammy; maybe I'm not thinking big enough, and he's been stalking me for years or whatever."

Kathy shrugs. "Maybe. But then who was buried with you? And why would that matter to someone you haven't talked to in years?"

"What about my car? I heard a vehicle leave. They either left and came back, or a second person drove my car away. Should you ask my mom if my car's in the driveway at home?"

"And if it is?" Kathy asks.

"I don't know. It would confirm they know where I live. That's something."

"Do you keep your insurance card in your glove box?"

Lydia has to think. "It's very expired, but yeah."

"It has your address on it. Right now, your car could be anywhere, and it wouldn't tell us much of anything unless we do a forensics sweep. Let's start with everything online and eliminate the possibility of a digital trail. Then we find your car."

Well, they have to start somewhere, although she wishes Kathy would stop outright rejecting her ideas. "Can I use your phone then?"

"Hold on." Kathy gets up, makes a kissy noise at Tiger, who's still under the couch, and grabs her laptop from the recliner in the living room. She sets it on the kitchen table and removes their mugs and plates.

Lydia opens the laptop and turns it around so Kathy can unlock it, then she tries to log in to her bank, and it sends her a verification code. Luckily, she can send it to her email. She logs into her email and briefly scans it. Nothing out of place here, just the usual promotions, and her six-digit code. Finally, she unlocks her bank account. There are no pending transactions from yesterday.

Banking is a dead end, so Lydia logs into Facebook and Instagram. She doesn't post very often, and when she does, it's usually rock climbing photos. Scrolling through her feeds and Eddie's accounts is also a dead end. He hasn't posted in months.

While Kathy tidies the living room, Lydia waits for her opportunity. She scrolls her social media feed until Kathy goes to the bathroom, and then she switches back to email and starts a draft:

Hey, weird question, did I contact you yesterday?

She thinks about the man in the grave and adds to her email: *Where were you last night?*

As she sends the email, a car door slams, and Lydia jumps in her seat. Her mind is reeling, forcing her back into the grave, face planted in the mud as the would-be killer drives away.

Her body remembers that sound.

She closes the laptop and looks out the window. Her mom is standing in the driveway, holding a basket.

"Shit! Kathy!" Lydia drops to the kitchen floor and crawls into the hallway. Kathy rushes out of her bedroom, one hand on her holster.

"Why is my mom here?"

Kathy steps around Lydia. "Hide in the spare room. I'll find out. Maybe I can ask about you."

But if her mom doesn't know what happened to Lydia last night, why not tell her everything?

Kathy senses her thoughts. "No, Lydia, it's not worth it. If we tell your mom, we have no clue how she'll react. But I promise you it won't be good. Think of Sammy; think of what this could do to her."

It isn't right. Her mom should know about this. Yes, there's an advantage to staying hidden, but it feels like Kathy's intentionally keeping Lydia away from every connection to the outside world.

"Trust me," Kathy whispers, turning away. "Hide!"

Ignoring her gut, Lydia runs in a crouch into the spare bedroom and shuts the door. She presses her ear against it but can't hear anything. Kathy either met her mom out in the driveway, or they're talking by the front door. But why is her mom here, and why bring a basket? Kathy lied about being sick, so maybe that's all it is. A wellness checkup.

Lydia looks around the spare room, realizing with a shudder that it's Lucy's old bedroom, the one with the footsteps.

It doesn't help that the white headboard and small dresser remind Lydia of her own current childhood bedroom. The room is painted a soft yellow, with bright white trim and lace curtains over the windows. There's a small dress hanging on a hook on the wall. It's so pretty, Lydia can't help but wonder what dress they buried Lucy in. It seems like it would be this dress.

How many of Lucy's things are still in here? It's been twenty-something years since she died. How could Kathy live in this house, with the empty room and the midnight footsteps, and still keep her mind? Lydia has visited more times than she can count, and she's never seen this room or heard Kathy talk the way she did at the table. It's like Lydia's seeing her surroundings for the first time as a grownup. Her memories are colorful picture books of playing soccer in the backyard or watching TV on Kathy's couch while her mom baked something in the kitchen. Only now is she starting to wonder what happened behind the scenes all those years ago; all the quiet conversations and subtle looks she missed.

Lydia turns away from the small, tragic dress and moves to the window facing the side yard. She can barely see the driveway and the rear fender of her mom's car. The two women are out of sight.

The room's other window faces the back of the house and the woods extending behind Kathy's property. Not much to look at. Lydia circles the bedroom, trying to listen through the door again, and getting nothing. She goes to the front window, unlocks it, and cracks it open. Voices echo from the driveway. So they never went inside, which is probably smart, because aren't Lydia's muddy shoes by the front door?

Lydia squats beside the window, straining her ears. It's no use. Their voices are too dim.

But that means Kathy's outside the house and preoccupied, and even as the idea comes to her, Lydia knows it's wrong. She shouldn't go snooping but she has to do something. She's going crazy in here, and although she wants to trust Kathy, there's still a nagging in her mind that all of Kathy's responses have been weirdly rehearsed.

Lydia opens the bedroom door and edges into the hallway. Through the front window above the couch, she sees her mom and Kathy talking in the driveway, their faces partially hidden by the overgrown bushes in the front garden.

Rushing across the hallway, she opens the door to Kathy's bedroom, taking another look at the women in the driveway. Her mom isn't showing any signs of leaving; Lydia should have a few minutes to look around, even if she doesn't know what she's looking for.

Tiger's eyes are on her as he moves from his hiding place to the front door. He's poised, his back arching, and Lydia's really done with his attitude. What did she ever do to him? She gives Tiger a sassy little wave and walks inside Kathy's bedroom, leaving the door cracked.

13

How well do you know the Pratt family?

After living in Hope for two years, Michael has managed to build a relationship with almost everyone. He likes to walk through town on nice evenings, and he meets many pleasant people this way.

But he's spent very little time around Lydia Pratt. Unlike others in her life, such as the devout Kathy LeGrand or the flaky Will and Sharon Pratt, Lydia's never attended a Sunday morning service, not even with Eddie. The few times Michael had taken a walk and seen her in the yard of her family home, usually in the company of her parents, she never asked him questions or tried to get to know him. She is... or she was... a closed book.

The Pratts appear to be a normal family. And although appearances are deceiving, Michael has no reason to suspect anything unthinkable goes on inside their house.

So he tells Eddie, "I know Will and Sharon a little. Lydia, not so much."

Eddie stands and paces in front of the small stage and podium. "Did you know they lost a son, Sammy? Like twenty years ago?"

"I did not know that."

"They lost him in the nature preserve. They rented a cabin for a Fourth of July party, and he walked out late at night, and even though they found him some hours later, he had died from a fall, I think. I don't remember."

"That's awful."

"I know." Hands on his hips, Eddie pauses in the center aisle. He looks around the church like he's trying to picture something. "The family doesn't talk about it. Is that normal?"

"Depends. People process trauma in wildly different ways. It's a wonder Will and Sharon are still married, given the stats on families who lose children."

"It's one of Lydia's earliest memories," Eddie says, staring at the floor. "She was five years old at the time. Sammy was two. Is there a chance none of them ever recovered from it?"

"Grief is a cancer, I'm afraid. If they haven't found a way to cope by now, it'll kill them sooner or later." Poor choice of words, but Michael can't take them back. This situation keeps growing stranger. "Does Sammy's passing have something to do with Lydia?"

Eddie grimaces, checks the clock on the wall. "How much do you know about the nature preserve? Have you heard anything? Or hiked in there?"

If Eddie's about to suggest the two of them go tramping through the woods alone, Michael's going to make a run for it. "Eddie. You seem a little scattered right now. You're throwing a lot my way, and none of it is making sense."

In a blur, Eddie rushes to Michael's side. "Haven't you been listening to me?"

"I have, and that's why I'm worried about you. Can you slow down and tell me where Lydia is?"

"You're not listening, Pastor."

Eddie's hot, agitated breath lands on his face. Michael backs away. "How about we go for a walk?"

"Why?"

Because I'd like to be where someone can see me, Michael thinks. "Fresh air might help," he says.

"You're not listening."

Michael walks toward the front door.

"Pastor!"

"Take a walk with me, Eddie, and I promise I'll listen."

"Wait, wait, wait."

Michael pauses in the foyer, hands in his pockets.

"I really do need your help, Pastor." Eddie holds his palms together, as if in prayer. "But I need you to promise me two things: that you'll believe what I'm about to tell you, and you won't go to the police until we both agree it's time."

"Eddie."

"Can you promise that?"

"Am I going to be in danger if I agree?"

"I don't know. I swear I don't know."

If Eddie's having a split from reality, then his words are of little value. What happened to Lydia? The way Eddie's acting, she's either dead or seriously hurt. Did Eddie kill her? Leave her for dead? Michael wonders if time is a factor here, but he can't rush this without pushing Eddie into a spiral, and that's the most dangerous outcome.

He feels a light breeze on his neck and looks up at the empty bell tower above him.

If he's going to put himself in harm's way, it'll be on his terms. And looking at this tower gives him an idea.

"I promise you. I won't go to the police unless it becomes my only choice. Am I clear?"

Eddie slowly nods.

Michael cracks open the front door, a little relieved. "Then come along. I have a job for us while you tell me this story."

He walks down the steps, knowing Eddie will follow.

"You don't lock the doors?" Eddie asks, catching up to him.

"My church is always open for company. Besides, Hope isn't like other towns. Nobody wants to rob a small church in the middle of nowhere."

It's a warm, clear afternoon. Not much traffic, but there never is in Hope. Michael smooths his hair down, squinting at the pale blue sky. *Is today the day I get my miracle?* He asks the God in the sky. *Have you been leading me here all this time?*

They walk around the building to Michael's parked silver Tacoma.

He starts to unbutton the truck bed cover, and Eddie works on the other side, snapping off each button until they've rolled the cover back and secured it against the cab. The truck bed is empty, for now, and things feel much calmer out here.

Michael leans against the truck and smooths his hair down again. "Do you know anything about the history of this church?"

Eddie can't hide a sarcastic smirk, but Michael doesn't mind. He knows how young people think.

"No sir."

Not many people know the story, somehow. "This little church has a short steeple, as you can see. Well, it *used* to have a bell. A certain pastor, some seventy years ago, put this church to good use. He had a loyal congregation."

Did Michael intend to sound jealous? Maybe a little. As if complaining to Eddie here is going to change anything.

"What happened?"

On Main Street, a vehicle drives past. A sheriff's SUV, with Alex at the wheel. Never been to a Sunday morning, but Michael will keep working on him. God knows what horrific confessions are bottled inside that man. He's very well respected in the community, and it helps that his parents, who left Asia and moved to Central Ohio decades ago, own the best Thai restaurant in Blue Hill.

Alex looks at them as he passes, and Eddie nods in his direction. The sheriff turns his eyes back to the road and drives out of sight.

Not much traffic in Hope.

Michael clears his throat. "So, this pastor has everything going for him, or so I was told."

"Who told you this story?"

"Margaret, that old little lady off Wilfred Street."

"And she knows this, how? Because she was alive seventy years ago?"

Michael snaps his fingers. "Bingo. So! Long story short, one Sunday morning, our popular pastor is at his post, opening the church doors, and ringing the *only* church bell in all of Hope."

"You know there's nothing impressive about that."

"But on this particular Sunday morning, he rings the bell, and it snaps loose. It falls on him, poor fellow, and crushes him through the floor. According to Margaret, he *popped* like a balloon."

"What the hell are you talking about, Pastor?"

"I'm telling you what happened."

"But *why*?"

Michael taps the truck with his finger. "We're going to do something I've been dreaming of ever since I moved here."

"Don't tell me."

Michael smiles. "We're going to find that bell. And I have a feeling we're going to need it."

Eddie waits for the explanation, but Michael savors the moment. Whatever's happening in Eddie's head right now is dangerous, yes, but not out of control. If Michael pushes him in the right direction, he might escape this confession unscathed.

"I told you," he says, "I believe in miracles, and evil, and the supernatural. You know why churches have rung bells for thousands of years?"

Eddie sighs. "Why?"

"Because they ward off evil spirits. We might need some of that, don't you think?"

14

After her mom's abrupt exit from breakfast, Lydia didn't expect to see her so soon, especially with tears in her eyes.

She once drove Lydia to soccer practice in Blue Hill and pulled over on Route 4 because of a dead dog in the road. She grabbed an empty grocery bag from the trunk, picked up that dog with both hands, and literally raised it above her head like an offering to the vultures before throwing it into the ravine.

Lydia was ten years old at the time, and she cried for the rest of the drive and all through soccer practice. That night, her mom sat on this same bed, looked Lydia straight in the eye, and said, *He didn't feel a thing. You can't hurt the dead.*

But today her mom comes into Lydia's bedroom looking extra deflated, her dog-throwing days long behind her. She shuts the door and sits wearily on the edge of Lydia's bed. Her right hand absent-mindedly smooths out the bedsheet, and considering what Lydia and Eddie get up to, she wishes her mom would stop touching it.

"What's wrong?" Lydia asks. Is her mom really this upset about her rejecting Eddie?

Her mom looks around the room, eyeing the empty liquor bottle on the dresser, and beside it, the jewelry case. She moves off the bed (thank God) and over to the dresser, picks up the case and opens it, giving the engagement ring all of two seconds before putting it back. She stares at the contents on the dresser like it's a sad picture of Lydia's life.

"Eddie told me you turned him down," she says, lowering her voice. "How'd he take it?"

Lydia doesn't know what to say at first. "He's upset, but I don't blame him."

"There's something I need to tell you," her mom says, sitting on the bed again. "Was Eddie acting normal last night, after you started drinking?"

It's embarrassing to admit, but she won't lie. "I drank a lot. I honestly don't remember."

Her mom keeps watching the door as if expecting Eddie to barge in at any moment. "You have to remember *something*."

"No. I blacked out. It's not even the first time. I accidentally drank too much last New Year's Eve, you remember that? Took me three days to recover."

"I think Eddie spiked your drink."

What the hell is she talking about? "Mom, nothing happened last night, other than me and Eddie trying to forget that I turned him down. It was probably super awkward because we live together, so we drank. What are you even implying? Spiked my drink with what?"

"I saw him last night," her mom whispers. "In the kitchen, taking a long time with the shot glasses. There was something different about him. He didn't see me at first, but once he did, his whole face changed. I know I'm reaching, and maybe it was nothing, but I don't trust him, Lydia." Her voice is strangely flat, like she's rehearsed this. Maybe it's been on her mind all morning.

Lydia wants to understand, but this is Eddie they're talking about. "I don't think Eddie would ever hurt me or get revenge because I turned him down. But it won't matter anymore because I'm going to break up with him tonight."

Something flickers on her mom's face. "When did you decide that?"

"This morning."

"Is there someone else?"

"Why are you guys asking me that? How's that supposed to make me feel?" Lydia refuses to put up with this. Why is everyone targeting her today?

"Lydia." Her mom glances at the closed door. "You can tell me anything."

"I'm not cheating on Eddie! Don't you realize how mean that question is?"

"I just think you need to be careful. I'm not sure Eddie's in a good place right now, and you might think you know him, but there's a side to him that we don't see. Has he ever made you uncomfortable? Did he do anything last night to make you drink so much?"

"Mom, are you serious?"

She raises her hands in defense. "I know, I sound crazy. But you're not acting like yourself. I can't explain it, but I feel like I don't know who you are right now."

Lydia can't believe this. Her mom, of all people, should know who she is. This is the one person she should be able to count on. Lydia suddenly wants to cry. "You know who I am, Mom."

There's no recognition on her mom's face; her eyes are dry.

It's her eyes, Lydia realizes. Her mom's eyes are older than the rest of her. It's the one thing she can't reverse.

Her mom sighs and walks to the door. "I know I love you, I know you're my daughter. But that doesn't mean I know the girl inside your head. No one does."

Lydia leans against the wall, almost hitting her head on a floating shelf of old soccer trophies. She wants to be upset with her mom, but there's a sliver of truth in what she's saying. Maybe more than a sliver.

"I just don't know what I want." Saying this proves nothing, but Lydia needs *something* here. A hug, reassurance, something only a mother can give.

But her mom stays by the door like she can't wait to leave. "I know, Lydia. Maybe the problem is you don't know what's inside your head, either."

Lydia nods. "I think you're right."

"You promise you'll break up with him? Tonight?"

"I have to."

Her mom tilts her head. "If things are over between you two, don't draw it out. Men don't like to feel led on. It makes them angry."

Lydia almost rolls her eyes. "Eddie's never been angry at me."

Her mom half-smiles, twisting the doorknob. "Before now, you never gave him a reason to be." She opens the door and leaves the bedroom.

It's the right thing to do; she won't lead him on.

But no matter what happens, he can't learn the truth. If there's anything Eddie hates, it's being lied to.

15

Lydia's never been inside Kathy's bedroom before, and despite her familiarity with the rest of this house, being in here feels wrong. It smells like dirt and pine. There's a queen bed shoved into the corner and a picture on the dresser of a young Kathy with her arms around the one and only Sharon Pratt. They were young, maybe in their thirties, and it was taken in the living room of this house. Same setup, older furniture. Beside this one, more pictures are displayed in old frames.

There's a large group photo of Mom, Dad, and Kathy at a grill out with the Blue Hill Fire Department. This one's a little newer, maybe fifteen years ago, and there's a slew of faces Lydia only slightly recognizes. She never really got to know her dad's work friends outside of the immediate circle. Alex is hovering behind the group, raising a beer bottle in salute. She's not sure how a sheriff got invited to that function, but maybe since Blue Hill is still a smallish town, you need to expand your circle for the sake of the cornhole tournament. He probably just showed up.

But something's weird about this photo. Alex's holding an alcoholic cider in a glass bottle. Her parents and their friends always had a range of alcohol at these parties, but only her mom drank cider. She distinctly remembers Alex and her dad playing bocce ball in their backyard and lining their beer cans on the back deck's railing, which drove her mom crazy.

In this photo, two large coolers are in the background. Why would Alex drink the cider if there was plenty of beer? She never recalled him drinking from glass bottles at all; he always made a show of crushing his spent beer cans in his fist.

Lydia thinks about how she and Eddie will share a stick of gum, and before she can stop herself, she pictures her mom all those years ago, finishing a half-gone bottle of cider while eyeing Alex from across the lawn.

She forces the thought away; she's making immature assumptions.

Another photo on the dresser shows a child with a missing tooth, a very young Kathy, judging by the grainy picture quality. Next to that is another girl, maybe two or three. She's standing on the edge of a cornfield with one foot inside the rows and a mischievous smile on her face, like she's planning to run away and hide.

Lucy.

Then there are two more photos: one with Kathy at some national park, and the other in a hospital room, with Kathy sitting beside a hospital bed, holding a newborn in her arms. In the bed is Lydia's mom right after giving birth. Her hair is bundled around her young, glowing face, as Kathy looks at the baby with wonder. Lydia feels a swell of pride. How did she ever doubt Kathy? The woman who came to the hospital and held her as a newborn? And the look on Kathy's face is like she'd been crying tears of joy.

There's a date stamped on the edge of the photo, partially obscured by the frame. 5/14/2006. Sammy's birthday. So Lydia isn't on the dresser at all, just everyone else in Kathy's life. Including Sammy.

She doesn't want to think about that right now, and she's forgotten what she came in here for. Lydia turns away from the dresser and surveys the rest of the room. She opens the closet to find clothes, shoes, and storage boxes. Riveting stuff. What is she expecting to find? A picture of her with a big red X on it?

There's nothing here except old, painful memories. If anything, these photos prove Kathy's loyalty to the Pratt family despite their hardship. Most people would've distanced themselves from all that suffering.

She goes to leave the bedroom right as Tiger zips through the opening. He dives under Kathy's bed and spins around, hissing loudly.

"No! Bad cat! Get out of here!"

Was Kathy's door completely shut when Lydia came in? She can't remember. She is the worst detective alive. How can she not remember if the door was shut or cracked open? If it had been shut, then Kathy will know Lydia came in here thanks to this stupid cat.

"Hey buddy, you little shithead." Lydia kneels on the wood floor and stretches out her hand. "Come here kitty, come on."

Tiger flashes his teeth. What's his deal? Is she going to have to drag him out?

"Please come here!" she snaps. "Come here *right now*."

Tiger backs up, hissing again. A car door slams in the driveway. That's peachy. Her mom must be leaving, and now Lydia's out of time. She either has to fight Tiger to the death under Kathy's bed or give up and hope Kathy doesn't notice anything out of place. She has roughly one second to decide. Maybe less. It could be too late already.

She'll leave Tiger under there and hope for the best. Maybe Kathy *did* leave her bedroom door cracked open. But something behind Tiger catches her eye. At first, she sees a small, skinny person stuffed under the bed, in the corner, with their head facing the wall. But her eyes quickly adjust, and she's mistaken, of course. No humans under Kathy's bed. Just a shovel covered in clumpy dirt.

Lydia's stuck in time, staring at it. When the front door opens and closes, she knows it's over.

Kathy's going to find her here.

16

There's nowhere to run.

Lydia drops to her stomach and grabs the shovel from under the bed. Tiger sprints away from her and slips through the bedroom door, swerving to avoid Kathy.

"Lydia?" Kathy pushes the door open but stays in the hallway. "What are you...?"

Lydia stands, gripping the shovel, and points the metal end at Kathy. "Why do you have this?"

Kathy lifts her hands like she did on the dirt road earlier. As if Lydia's the crazy one. Kathy opens her mouth, but nothing comes out. She clearly didn't think Lydia would find the shovel, and now she's stuck.

"Kathy! *Why* do you have this?"

Again, nothing. Kathy breathes through her mouth, very controlled.

Even with those hands raised, Lydia knows Kathy can quickdraw her gun and put a bullet between Lydia's eyes. There's little she can do to stop it, except throw the shovel, but she'll probably hit the doorframe, and Kathy has the hallway she can retreat into before bouncing back and dumping her whole clip into Lydia's body.

"Why is this under your bed!" Lydia tightens her grip on the shovel. Throwing it is her best bet. With a lucky hit, maybe she'll survive this.

"Please, put it down," Kathy finally says, "and let me explain something to you."

"What *else* could you have used this for?"

"I found it." Kathy steps into the doorway, giving Lydia a perfect shot. "I saw it in the woods on my way to the river. Just hiding in the weeds. Then I saw you, and I walked over. But I must've been close to the grave."

"Bullshit, you *found* it?" Lydia's voice cracks. She keeps picturing the shovel flying at Kathy, tearing into her throat, her mouth, anything that'll bleed.

"Yes, I found it, and I know how it sounds, Lydia. I know what you're feeling."

"You don't have a fucking clue what I'm feeling."

Kathy's hands are up again, higher. She's preparing to catch the shovel.

"Lydia, I saw it in the woods, and I thought nothing of it. Just a weird thing in the middle of nowhere. But after I talked to you, and you told me you were attacked, I knew that shovel meant something."

"I don't believe you."

"I went back for it! While you showered, I drove back over and picked it up, with gloves, because it might be important."

Is that why she was vacuuming her SUV? "Then why the hell did you hide it from me?"

"Because of how it looks!" Kathy's eyes are bugging out, and she keeps glancing at the wavering shovel. "I wanted to wait and explain it to you calmly, in a way that made sense, so we could avoid *this*!"

"How stupid does a killer have to be to leave a shovel in the woods? You magically finding it doesn't make sense. Why are you lying to me?"

"I'm not!" Kathy inches forward. "I didn't put you in that grave, Lydia. I'm trying to help you find who did. Can't you see that?"

Lydia *wants* to believe her, but she's not dropping the shovel.

Kathy moves closer, bringing her face dangerously close to the shovel's blade. "Come on, Lydia, you know I'm telling the truth. Why would I bring you here if I was the one who buried you in those woods? What purpose would that serve?"

Lydia has no answer, but that doesn't mean anything right now.

Another step, and Kathy's left eye is aligned with the shovel's point. Only inches away.

"It makes no sense to bring you here if I already tried to kill you once," Kathy says. "Does it? I would've shot you on the access road. Or led you back to the grave, made you get in, and shot you there! We were in the preserve at sunrise, with no one around for miles. If I wanted you dead, why would I bring you here, and give you food and a shower and listen to your story if I knew all the answers? What would be the point?"

Lydia can't refute that either. She's trying to come up with a reason not to believe her.

But before Lydia can answer, Kathy takes the shovel with one hand and jerks it out of her grasp.

Lydia stumbles to her knees, and Kathy tosses the shovel behind her and slips the gun from its holster with smooth, practiced precision. She levels it at Lydia's forehead, breathing heavily.

Then Kathy kneels, places the gun in Lydia's hand, and lets go. Lydia grips the handle, her pointer finger settling on the trigger.

"You hang onto that," Kathy says. "God knows you need it more than I do. And maybe then you'll start trusting me."

Kathy stands up and wipes a bead of sweat from her forehead. She picks up the shovel and turns to Lydia.

"We have a big problem," she says, still out of breath. "It's about what your mom told me."

Lydia swallows, slowly dropping her arm until the gun is pointing at the floor. "What?"

"She says Eddie hasn't been at the house since yesterday. That when you two left for dinner last night, neither of you came back. She thinks you both worked it out, and you're at a hotel, celebrating."

17

While Michael is thankful he's no longer stuck in his church with a potential killer, he still has nothing to defend himself with if Eddie decides to bash his brains in.

He thinks of all the ways this could go wrong, driving on Route 4, with Eddie in the passenger seat. The windows are down, a warm breeze is rushing in, and Eddie's talking about what living with the Pratt family is like.

"Lydia and I stay busy, and I'm not usually around Will and Sharon without her," Eddie says. "But when I talked to them a few weeks ago about my proposal, Sharon was super weird. I said I wanted to ask Lydia to marry me, and she said, 'Good,' just like that. Kinda monotone, a little bitchy, but I couldn't tell if she was annoyed at Lydia or at me, and I wasn't about to ask. The point is, I've never even seen Lydia fight with her parents. Everyone gets along, but maybe I missed something." Eddie takes a breath. "I missed a lot of things, that's clear to me now. Will and Sharon are quiet people, and while I used to think that was a good thing, I don't anymore."

"How do you mean?" Michael's only half-listening. Eddie's been referring to Lydia in the present tense, which would reassure Michael, if not for Eddie's questionable state of mind.

"They don't talk about anything. They're easygoing, you know that, but when it comes down to it, you feel like they're keeping to themselves, like you're never really seeing who they are. Lydia can be like that. Maybe she gets it from them." Eddie smiles sadly. "By the way, where are you taking me?"

"Foley Farms. Burt had the bell last, or so I was told."

Eddie sends a text on his phone. "How long will this take?"

Michael's phone is still at the church, and he can't shake the feeling that Eddie wanted him phoneless for a specific reason beyond privacy. "It won't take long, but it depends on whether we find the bell or not. Don't we need it for your fight against evil?"

Eddie doesn't smile. He gazes at the nature preserve. "Do you know about Moon River?"

Michael feels a twitch in his stomach, a hunger pang. "*Should* I know about it? Me and rivers don't get along."

Eddie cocks his head. "Huh. Before Hope was founded, a small settlement lived where Blue Hill is now. Apparently, when yellow fever hit back in the day, they forced half the town to camp out by the river as a precaution. This was forever ago, before hospitals, before anything. Guess what river had a flash flood during the spring season?"

Michael's stomach grumbles again, hard enough to make his body ache. He knows where this is heading.

"Yep. Half the sick village drowned, and most of the bodies weren't recovered. The river wiped them off the face of the earth."

"That's lovely. Why do they call it Moon River?"

"Native Americans called it that, I think. Of course, they had their own beliefs attached to it. But for the people of Hope and Blue Hill, it's a symbol of death. God knows how many villagers were drowned and buried in that riverbank."

It couldn't be a coincidence that Michael's spiritual journey began in a river, with the old man.

"Is there something about those woods that bothers you, Eddie?" Michael turns down a gravel driveway, under a sign that says: FOLEY FARMS. He drives slowly, surveying the bean fields around them.

Eddie gives a hollow laugh. "Yeah, you could say that. Do you believe places can be haunted?"

"I do." He thinks about Darling and the only unexplainable thing he's ever witnessed.

He parks in the big driveway. In front of them is a sprawling ranch with a wrap-around porch and lavishly pruned gardens. Michael knows it's empty because Burt's truck isn't here. He's probably in Blue Hill, buying supplies, and his wife, Mary, works at the post office. Nobody is home, and that feels lucky.

"Is the nature preserve haunted?" Michael asks. "Did something happen to Lydia there?" Opening the truck door, Michael steps out, nodding at the massive red barn in the distance.

"I think so," Eddie says, getting out of the truck.

"To which part?"

"The haunted part." Eddie looks around. "There's no one here."

"We're just looking." Michael starts walking down the gravel driveway to the barn, kicking up gray dust behind him.

Eddie catches up. "I don't know Burt that well. Or Mary."

"I know them both very well," Michael lies. "They're good people."

Eddie doesn't question him. Why would he? "So you've seen the bell already?"

"No, never seen it. This could be a dead end." He pauses, afraid to ask Eddie more questions. "Now, why do you think the woods are haunted?"

They reach the red barn, which is latched and locked.

Eddie glances through a small window. "I guess we'll have to try again later."

Michael shakes his head, looking the building up and down. "I think the Lord will provide, don't you?"

There's that young, sarcastic smirk on Eddie's face again. "The Lord provides for breaking and entering?"

"I'm not breaking anything, Eddie. Burt doesn't care about this bell. No one does except me. He'll understand."

Eddie stares over the bean fields. "I lived in Blue Hill, growing up, and everyone there hates talking about the preserve. The north end has all these trails and foothills, so it attracts hikers from everywhere. At least one hiker a year goes missing here. You know what the park rangers blame? The river. When it rains, the river can carry something hundreds of miles and bury it in a log jam in the backwoods of southern Ohio. People talk about the woods like they're haunted, but it's more than that."

"How?"

"I remember when Sammy died. It was a big deal in Blue Hill. After that, the stories went wild. Missing hikers is one thing, but a toddler getting lost? The worst part is that people turned his tragedy into ghost stories and speculations. Kids were saying he haunted those woods, which must've been an absolute nightmare for Lydia and her parents. But my friend growing up, he kept saying a toddler doesn't go that far without help. He kept saying something lured him into the woods."

Michael feels a shiver from the thing inside his stomach. "Do you believe that?"

Eddie nods. "You'll feel it if you go in there. Someone like you, attuned to the world we can't see, you'll feel it in your bones."

They're inching closer to the truth, but it's dangerous. What happens if Eddie snaps and remembers murdering his girlfriend?

Michael backs away and examines the barn. "Did something bad happen to Lydia in those woods?"

Eddie stares at him, his eyes glowing. "Yes," he whispers.

Now they're getting somewhere. "Was it evil?"

Eddie can only nod. His chest is starting to heave, and Michael's afraid to ask him more questions. He needs a way to protect himself.

Michael goes around the side, scratching his head. "I bet I can reach that roof." He points at the overhang above the barn's entrance. "And get in through the hayloft doors."

"Oh sure, want me to give you a leg up?" Eddie asks, clearing his throat and pretending to be normal. "Or should we just throw a rock through the window and call it a day?"

"You're lucky I'm a patient man. Help me up."

"This is insane."

Michael looks at the overhang, then back at Eddie. "You're asking me to keep a secret from the police. You think evil has come to our town. Do you want my help or not?"

Without another word, Eddie laces his fingers together, allowing Michael to set one foot inside his palms. When Eddie pushes up, Michael grabs the overhang and drags himself over the gutter. Not bad for an old guy, but he's feeling younger by the minute. He stands on the roof, tiptoes to the hayloft doors, and pries them open.

Eddie turns to the driveway, casting a hand over his eyes to block the sun.

Michael edges around the hayloft doors and jumps to the platform on the left side. Hay bales are stacked around him, and he quickly maneuvers through them to find a ladder on the other side. On the main floor, the barn is full of equipment. He slips past the tractors, plows, and walks the barn perimeter, because where else would you put an old relic if not in a dusty corner somewhere? What a waste.

Michael finds plenty of old machinery, wheelbarrows, tools, and worktables, but nothing that resembles a church bell. He even told Eddie he thought it was here, and now he's irritated that he's wrong. Old Burt must've chucked it.

Circling inside the barn one more time, Michael stops at a worktable, scans the various containers filled with junk, and finds the perfect thing: a six-inch rusty needle file. He taps the point with his finger. Plenty sharp.

He slips the file inside his back pocket.

Hopefully, he won't have to use it.

18

Lydia and her dad drive out to the shooting range before anything else bad can happen. Her dad, of course, seems perfectly at peace in his own world. Unlike Lydia, who practically jogged into her dad's old Jeep and left without saying a word to Eddie.

In the backseat, her dad's shotgun is tucked inside a customized, fleece-lined, black rifle case. They packed a few dozen rounds of birdshot, a few boxes of clay discs, some water, and a small, portable radio.

No one is at the shooting range but them. Lydia isn't surprised, given it's a weekday morning. She can't remember if it's Wednesday or Thursday, and she left her phone at home, another insult to irritate Eddie, because she needs time to think. Her mom's words are stuck firmly in her brain: *Men don't like to feel led on. It makes them angry.*

"You okay, honey?"

Lydia nods quickly. She gets out of the Jeep and grabs a box of clays and the orange plastic thrower her dad has used for years. "Yeah, I'm fine. I'm exhausted."

"You mean hungover?" Her dad slides the gun case over his shoulder and grins. "Kind of an awkward breakfast this morning, or was it just me?"

Lydia shuts the door with her hip and follows him to the range. They place their supplies on a wooden bench, and Lydia opens the box of clays.

"It *was* weird," she finally says, a little thrown off by his perception. Since he retired from the Blue Hill paramedic team, he's been mostly hanging out with his friends at the station. If he's not over there, he's doing crosswords, taking long walks, and going to target practice. He's been so distant and aloof that she doesn't expect him to pay attention to anything.

Her dad unzips the gun case and raises his beloved double-barreled, break-action shotgun. "While you were talking with your mom earlier, Eddie filled me in."

"What did he say?"

He loads two rounds into the shotgun and props it up against the wooden railing in front of them. "He told me you turned him down. I didn't ask him why. I'd already given him my blessing."

She places an orange clay disc inside the thrower. "I guess I didn't give him a reason."

"You guess?"

"It happened fast."

"Ah." He hands her safety glasses and earmuffs. "Do you think? Well. Do you think maybe you're trying to forget the proposal? Like you almost just want to move on and pretend it didn't happen?"

Lydia slides the glasses over her face and the earmuffs on her head. She nods at her dad, and he nods in return. With a small step back, the thrower firmly in her hand, Lydia swings, launching the little clay disc across the field. The air shatters around them, and the disc explodes into a couple of dozen shards. She locks another disc into the thrower and launches it straight ahead, at eye level. The disc is barely clipped, but it still comes apart, crashing into the field in pieces.

Her dad sets his earmuffs to the side. "You almost got me with that second one. You always throw high."

Lydia pulls her own muffs around her neck. "Didn't fool you." She places another disc in the thrower while he reloads the shotgun. "I think you're right," she tells him. "I want to move on, but it can't work like that, can it?"

He shakes his head. "I think Eddie loves you, honey. He might wait, but you've given him a reason to doubt. If you need time, he'll give you time. If that isn't the issue, you might want to figure out what is. I think you surprised him. He didn't believe you'd say no."

"Am I making the wrong choice?"

He laughs. "That's not up to me. You can't marry Eddie for any reason other than love. That's all that matters. Your mom and I want you to be happy, of course, and we like Eddie a lot, but," he raises the shotgun, "in the end, it's up to you."

Lydia winds up and flings the disc away, curving it sharply to the right. Her dad waits for it to start dropping and fires, misses, and fires again, nailing it the second time.

"Oh boy, you're making this tough," he says with a smile. "I shoulda had that the first time."

Lydia grabs another disc while he reloads. "Why'd you wait?"

"Because I wanted to show you something. Throw it again just like last time, hard right. Ready on you."

Lydia cocks her arm back and lets it fly, same spot as before. This time, the disc gets about twenty feet away before it's obliterated into a shower of clay splinters.

Her dad takes his earmuffs off, looking pleased with himself.

"Did I miss the lesson?"

He leans against the wooden railing and clears his throat. "I waited the last time before I shot, and I missed. I got it the second time, but it was a tricky, almost lucky shot. Just now, I didn't give the disc enough time to get away. You see? Once it's sailing and *falling* it's much harder to shoot. You got to shoot before it can run, or you'll miss it."

"So if I shoot Eddie when we get home, it'll solve my problems?"

He laughs. "Eddie put the ball in your court. The longer you wait, the harder it might be to resolve."

"I'll break up with him tonight," she says, leaning against his shoulder. "I don't want to lead him on, and I can't see us getting married. It's not what I want."

He plants a kiss on top of her head. "You'll figure it out, I know you will. Want my help with anything? Need me to throw his stuff on the front lawn?"

"Stop, no, it won't be like that."

"What if we get dinner then? Or do you need a night out with your girlfriends at the bar and old dad here will cramp your style?"

"I can't with you right now, are you serious?"

"Serious as a heart attack."

She hugs him, smelling his aftershave. "Dinner would be nice."

He squeezes her tightly. "I'll call you tonight then, after you've talked to Eddie. You're still my little girl, don't you know? Some things never change."

They break apart, looking away from each other to hide their damp eyes. Lydia glances at the parking lot and sees another car next to her dad's Jeep. It's a sheriff's SUV.

Her dad looks over his shoulder. "Must be Alex. When did he get here?"

It had to have been a few minutes ago, when they were shooting, because they didn't hear him pull up.

Lydia almost waves, but she can't tell if Alex is looking at her or if he's still in the SUV. The windshield is a blurry reflection of trees and clouds.

"I'll see what he wants. Maybe he needs to talk to me." Her dad walks to the SUV's passenger window and leans in. Lydia tries to read their body language, but she can barely see Alex's dark outline.

She picks up the empty shotgun shells and dumps them into a five-gallon bucket stationed beside a nearby post.

She almost wants her dad to be with her tonight, but she knows nothing bad will happen. Just a messy breakup.

When Eddie eventually comes around, she'll fight to be his friend. That's what she wanted originally before they slept together, and she doesn't want to lose him completely. Maybe if she gives him the hope of a friendship, he'll understand she never meant to hurt him. Maybe he won't press her for answers.

God knows, he's better off without them.

19

Lydia stands in the hallway of Kathy's house, the gun still in her hand. She watches Kathy place the shovel by the front door and sit at the kitchen table, calm and collected. Back to business.

Tiger is back under the couch, and contrary to what Kathy said earlier, he is definitely not warming up to Lydia.

"Where were we?" Kathy asks, tapping the table. "Anything from the bank? Social media? Emails?"

Lydia shakes her head. "What did my mom say about Eddie?"

"Just that he never came home. I didn't ask questions." Kathy leans back in her chair. "It's not normal for me to withhold something like this from your mother, even though I know it's the right thing. It doesn't feel right. She deserves to know."

Lydia steps into the living room, pointing the gun at the floor. It's awkward and heavy in her hand, and she doesn't need it. It's true, Kathy has no intention of killing her, but she doesn't buy the bullshit shovel story, and it's making everything Kathy does feel fake. Lydia had this same feeling earlier, and now it's stronger than ever.

For reasons she can't understand, Kathy isn't on her side. And if not, then whose side is she on?

Lydia can't keep doing this. She sets the gun on the table and scoots it over to Kathy. "I'm sorry," she says, trying to appear sincere.

Kathy holsters her weapon and straightens her jacket. "You've gone through something no one should have to go through. I'd be a little surprised, honestly, if you weren't seeing a monster everywhere you looked."

Lydia smiles. She's so rattled and traumatized, isn't she? Seeing monsters? Can't be trusted? Yes, all signs point to Lydia's unspeakable victimhood, and it's making her very paranoid, isn't it? Poor, poor Lydia.

She sits at the table. If she makes it obvious she doesn't trust Kathy, they might end up in another standoff.

"Now, before we continue, do you want to sleep? We keep pushing you like this and it's going to backfire, I know it."

Lydia closes her eyes. The eclipse is down to a half-coin of sunlight left, and already the sound of fire has diminished considerably, which Lydia thought would be nice, but now wonders what will replace it? She's already afraid of what'll happen when the sun is blotted out, let alone the deep silence that may overcome her brain.

"I can't sleep," she says. The eclipse will happen whether she's awake or not. "We need to find Eddie before everything comes out."

"I agree with you, Lydia, but consider the implications of what your mom told me. You *and* Eddie didn't come home last night."

"I know, that's why we need to find him and hear his side of the story."

"What do you suggest?"

Lydia looks outside. "I'll hide in your car while you drive us to Blue Hill. He works today, so we'll start with the rock climbing gym and go from there."

There's a flicker of pride in Kathy's face. "You'll hide in my car?"

"Yes, and you'll have to talk to him. We'll make up a story, or you could swing by the gym looking for me, and then you ask Eddie if he's seen me."

Kathy's smiling now. "You sure you're up for this?"

Why does Kathy insist on treating her with kid gloves? Like everything she's suggesting is simply *cute* and nothing more. "Do you have a better idea?"

"Maybe you should sleep? It might trigger a memory from last night."

Why is Kathy so focused on making her sleep? What does she need to do while Lydia's unconscious? "We're wasting time." Lydia moves to the couch and slips on her dirty shoes. They're still damp and smell like river water. Tiger slinks out from under her and runs to the corner, hissing.

Kathy's still at the table, watching him. "He's being very odd."

Lydia opens the front door. "If he wants me gone, he's about to be a happy cat."

Clearing her throat, Kathy stands and stretches her arms. It feels deliberate, like she's stalling.

Lydia walks outside the house and immediately doubles over. A sharp pain bites her stomach, setting her insides on fire. She falls to her knees, hearing Kathy call her name as a crow lands ten feet from her and hops through the grass, its head twitching.

She throws up, her stomach convulsing. Kathy starts rubbing her back, but Lydia veers away, staggering to her feet. "What did you give me?"

The crow cocks its head, squawking once, like it's asking a question.

"Lydia, I have no idea what you're talking about."

"Let's just go." Lydia stumbles toward the SUV. The crow leaps back, flutters to a nearby tree branch, and caws at them.

Kathy gives the crow a hard stare. "I don't think you're fit for this. Should we wait?"

"For what?" Lydia leans against the SUV, her stomach finally settling. "So they can get away?"

Another crow lands near the driveway, eyeing her. Lydia looks up. The oak tree in the front yard is full of crows, all eerily silent. She moves toward the tree, and the crows erupt into chaos. Cawing, flapping their wings, fighting to get away from her.

There's a look on Kathy's face, like the crows have confirmed her darkest fears. Her cheeks are pale as she searches the empty skies before removing a key fob from her pocket and activating the trunk. "If you want to go, we can go."

"Not in the trunk."

"It's spacious, look." Kathy points to a spotless, empty trunk. "And you can see over the seats. You won't be stuck at all, and the back window is tinted, so you'll be hidden."

This isn't what Lydia had in mind, but she sees the logic in it. Or it's a way for Kathy to control her. Even still, it won't matter soon. Kathy's been enormously helpful, but she's hiding something, and Lydia won't wait around to find out what that is. It'll be too late by then.

Play along, Lydia thinks.

She gingerly climbs into the trunk and sits cross-legged. She might not be trapped, but she's still stuck in the back of a moving vehicle with a woman she doesn't trust.

There is one person Lydia does trust in all this, but she never checked her email again, so she doesn't know where he was last night or if they saw each other. She'll figure that out soon enough, without Kathy's help.

"Ready?" Kathy has one hand on the trunk door and one hand on her belt, not far from her gun.

Lydia nods. Kathy lowers the door until it clicks shut. And in the warm, silent car, Lydia hears the distant fire in her ears. She can't help it. She closes her eyes and looks at the sky inside her mind.

Only a quarter of sunlight is left.

20

Lydia knows Kathy will be eyeing the rearview mirror like a hawk. That's why she kneels inside the trunk and rests her chin on the backseat, as if to merely get her bearings. She then lays her head to the side, where she can see the right half of the SUV.

Kathy watches her in the mirror, her eyes soft and inquisitive.

Trying to keep her head still, Lydia scans the right side for anything out of the ordinary. Kathy swept it out earlier, but maybe she missed something, assuming Kathy has anything to hide at all.

But the SUV is spotless. Kathy doesn't strike her as being overly clean, so why does her car look newly detailed?

Lydia turns her head to the left side, briefly meeting Kathy's eyes in the mirror. She's being too obvious. Kathy can tell something's off.

The left side is equally clean. There's nothing out of place. Nothing to find.

What will she do if they find Eddie at work? If he's not there, she'll know something bad happened to him. Maybe he was buried with her and is lost somewhere in the preserve or was taken in by a stranger.

Or they got him, she thinks. That's the real reason no one is concerned about Lydia yet. The man from the grave never made it to safety.

But if that's true, then the attacker knows Lydia's alive and well and roaming the countryside. They'll be searching for her.

Lydia blinks and stares at the foliage out the window.

What if they find Eddie at work, and he's acting normal?

She'll know he had something to do with the grave. With nearly killing her.

Her heart is a mess either way. Whether his truck is in the parking lot or not, she feels lost.

They reach Moon River Climbing right as Lydia's head starts to feel too heavy. She's so exhausted, it's like there are invisible strings attached to her eyelids, and someone's giving them playful, insistent tugs. If she doesn't sleep soon, she'll hallucinate. She's probably doing that already. How else can she explain the eclipse?

The parking lot is mostly empty, but business will pick up in the afternoon. From a distance, you wouldn't know this is a climbing gym.

The owner, Kevin, bought an old, condemned brick church and carved through the sanctuary and into the basement, making it one big open space. He constructed towering walls and padded the floors but left the tall stained-glass windows intact. When you stand on the floor and look up, sunlight burns through the windows, giving the whole gym a soft overlay of purple light. The balcony from the old church was also kept, and visitors use it to watch friends and family climb.

Kathy points to the corner of the lot. "Bingo."

Lydia glances over the seats, adjusting her stiff legs. Eddie's red truck is right where anyone would expect it, and parked in reverse, because he backs in everywhere he goes, and is obnoxiously proud of it.

"But is Eddie inside?" Kathy asks, turning off the ignition. "Stay low. I'll be back in a jiffy."

Lydia's so distracted by Eddie's truck and what it means that she almost forgets her escape plan.

"Kathy, can you leave it running? It's kinda hot back here, and I'm still feeling sick."

Kathy stares at Lydia in the mirror, weighing the risks, imagining a vomit-soaked trunk. She starts the SUV and cranks the AC. "You'll stay low?"

Lydia knows what Kathy's really asking. "I have no choice, right?"

Kathy accepts this non-answer, but she should know better. She should roll the windows down and take the keys, but she leaves the SUV running and walks inside, throwing a cursory, doubtful look over her shoulder.

Lydia waits for the doors to close on Moon River Climbing. They're made of solid wood and have no windows; Kathy can't see the parking lot from inside.

She counts to twenty, and then she's moving, scrambling over the backseats and swinging her body behind the wheel. She leaves the SUV and jogs over to Eddie's truck.

How long does she have?

She tries the door handle. It's locked. Putting one shoe on the back wheel, she grabs the side and jumps into the truck bed.

Crouching, Lydia watches the gym's entrance through the back tinted window and waits.

Sure enough, the door cracks open and Kathy peers out. She doesn't trust Lydia at all, but she can see her SUV is still in the parking lot, and she must assume Lydia's still in the trunk. Layin' low. Satisfied, Kathy shuts the door and hopefully descends into the pit to find Eddie.

Lydia cups her hands around her face and peers inside Eddie's truck. The backseat is full of random climbing gear and old fast-food bags. There are a few empty bottles of Pepsi, a snow scraper, and a blanket they've shared at drive-ins and camping trips, making love under the stars and keeping each other warm. It has a fierce grizzly bear on it, and Lydia's name is written on the tag in faded Sharpie. It's the only indication of their relationship in his truck, but it's one of the most important things they share. He keeps it neatly folded in its own seat, and seeing it now makes it nearly impossible for Lydia to believe Eddie would ever hurt her.

But until she can confirm his innocence, Eddie's a suspect. Along with almost everyone else at this point.

She'll go home eventually, but not until she's checked on the people closest to her that aren't her parents.

Lydia climbs out of the truck bed and, with an eye on the front door, runs around the left side of the church building. The side door is locked, and the windows are too high for Lydia to see down into the pit. She hops onto the metal railing beside the door and tilts forward until both hands catch the side of the brick wall. Walking her hands to the left, she braces herself against the windowsill, her shoes outstretched on the railing.

She presses her face to the window. It's not very conspicuous, but there are only a few climbers in there, and only one of them is high enough to see Lydia peering in, and it's a kid too distracted to sightsee at the top of a wall.

Lydia looks down. On the edge of the padded floors, near the lockers and bathrooms, Kathy and Eddie are mid-conversation.

She's hoping their body language will tell her something, but they're so far down, the angle isn't perfect, and she's certain it's a waste of time.

A car drives by on the road behind her, but they don't stop, and Lydia doesn't look their way. One more minute and then she'll run.

Eddie's running his hands through his hair, and Kathy's waving her arms somewhat dramatically. Lydia almost wants to rush in there just to see their reactions. Will that tell her something? She can't assume anything, but why is Eddie at work like usual, instead of wondering where she is? Especially if he hasn't gone home today?

Now Eddie's gesturing, pointing, opening his hands as if to show Kathy they're empty. None of this makes sense. Why does it look like they're arguing? Is Kathy openly confronting him?

The stairs to the pit are beneath the window, and Kevin suddenly comes into view as he jogs down them and pauses halfway. Only now does Lydia see her hunched shadow projecting on the stairs, and before Kevin can turn his head to look at the source, she's gone.

Jogging through the parking lot, Lydia slides into the SUV and puts it in drive. "Sorry Kathy," she whispers. "I'll make it up to you."

She turns right out of the parking lot and speeds through Blue Hill, holding her breath at red lights, checking the surrounding lanes for familiar faces. Slouching in her seat does no good; it's like the whole world can see her.

Jack lives in a row of apartments on the east side, and when she pulls in and sees his car in the shared lot, she parks beside it. If *he* is inside and acting normal, then who the hell was in the grave with her?

21

Michael drives into Hope with the needle file poking him uncomfortably through his back pocket. Eddie hasn't said much since they left the farm, but maybe he's thinking about the preserve. When they drove by it, Michael felt the thing in his stomach start to bend out of excitement or fear. He couldn't tell. But the quickness in his heart tells him something bad is about to happen. He hasn't had a feeling like this since that stormy day in Darling.

"You hear what I said, Pastor?"

Michael blinks. "Sorry, one more time."

"I asked you what we need to hang the bell, once we find it."

"Oh." Michael turns onto Clements Street and drives past his little church. "I have a ladder that can go up into the steeple. I checked everything once, so I know where the bell used to be. The mechanism is still there. The bell just needs lifted into place and bolted in, like an old-fashioned church."

"How long will that take?"

"Not long, and we'll need to stop for rope, but we'll find the bell first."

"Why on earth do you know so much about bells?"

Michael smiles. "I used to study Catholicism. They love their bells."

They park outside the tiny post office, and Michael unclips his seatbelt.

Nothing is sitting right with him. So far, Eddie has asked him a series of vague, scary questions, mentioned a crime, and claimed there's something evil happening to both Lydia and the town. This whole bizarre interview is starting to feel like a very sick joke.

"I'm running inside to find out where this bell is," Michael says, sharpening his voice. "When I come back, I need some details. At least an idea of what you need my help with. I'm taking a huge risk, being with you right now, especially if you're involved with a crime, big or small. I'm taking a chance here, you understand? Can you repay the favor and be straight with me?"

Eddie leans forward, seemingly unbothered by that speech. "I know you can keep a secret. Testing you was never the point."

"Okay. Then what's the point?"

"To get you away from your church," Eddie says.

Michael shivers. Well... he didn't expect that.

"We need your church," Eddie whispers. "And I need you to be there, as a friend and a man who's not afraid of evil."

"What are you doing to my church?"

The pause is far too long. Michael imagines wrapping his fingers around Eddie's throat.

"Preparing it," Eddie says. "I can't tell you why. None of it will make sense until you see it for yourself."

"You have no right to do anything to my church without my consent."

Eddie shakes his head. "You're not actually a pastor. So is it really still your church?"

Michael doesn't know what to say. Not a single peaceful response comes to mind. He wants to reach across the car and dig his nails into that smug face.

"I know about Darling," Eddie says. "You wanna talk about honesty? You first."

Michael leaves the truck and slams the door. That little shit. How could he possibly know about Darling?

In that shoddy town two hours south of Hope, Michael used to dress up as a priest and ride up and down the bike trail for hours. It amazed him how many people would see him on his bicycle, flag him down, and dump their life story in his lap. He would ride home every evening to a lonely house and a frozen dinner meal, but rarely did he crave food. Their confessions always satisfied him.

He played dress up every day and mostly met folks from neighboring towns. No one in Darling liked to bike ride except some kids, and they avoided him like the plague.

It was nearly sunset, and the beautiful scarlet sky had been slowly poisoned by dark clouds. The bike trail was deserted, and Michael decided to head home before the rain came. But he found a bike in the ditch and an old man who had crashed and flown fifteen feet into the woods, puncturing his stomach on a tree stump.

Miraculously unlucky.

Michael dropped his bike and ran into the woods, already reaching for his phone when the old man jerked against the stump and screamed.

Don't move, just lie still, Michael had said, patting the man's back, but he knew it was no good. The stump had cut deep, and the old man started begging Michael to pull him off so he could die lying down.

It seemed like a reasonable request, so Michael put his phone away instead of calling for help. It would take a miracle to help this man.

He grabbed the old man's shoulders and eased him off the stump, gently setting him on the forest floor. The poisoned sky had reached Darling, and the woods had grown very dark and quiet. Far away, Michael heard a squeak... squeak... squeak of metal, like a spinning weathervane, even though they were not close to any houses or farms.

Can you baptize me, Father? the old man had asked.

Michael looked through the woods at the Little Miami River. Are you sure?

Please.

Michael helped him stand. With slow, meticulous steps, he led the old man toward the river as thunder echoed across Darling.

The storm had arrived.

The old man was losing blood in six different spots down his chest, stomach, and pelvis. Poor bastard. Michael tried to keep a little space between them, but their bodies kept colliding, and by the time they reached the river, they were both soaked in blood.

Hurry, the old man groaned. Please, Father.

Michael jumped into the muddy riverbank and helped the old man down. They waded into the water, Michael's heart at full throttle. How lucky he was! All that bike-riding and praying over strangers and hearing their countless, cyclical, sinful habits all came down to trailside semantics. Just blabbering. Not now, no, this God-fearing man wanted to be baptized like a true believer. Michael led the old man in deeper until the water lapped at their stomachs. The river smelled like spring. Black clouds spilled across the red sky overhead, and the wind hummed through the woods. It felt too perfect, too real to be a coincidence. Michael would meet his Creator tonight. He knew it. The old man would show him the way.

As he held the old man upright in the river, that faint squeak... squeak... squeak started again, but much louder. He scanned the other side of the river, and though he still doesn't believe what he saw was real, he vividly remembers what it looked like: a lighthouse in the woods, with a burned-out, dark headlamp slowly spinning.

Squeak... squeak... squeak.

Michael couldn't take his eyes off the lighthouse; he'd been looking for a miracle his whole life, and as he watched that headlamp spin behind tangled branches, a lumpy weight settled inside his stomach and started spinning with it.

The lighthouse, previously painted white, had been consumed by a dark, green ivy. Broken windows ran up the side, and even though Michael couldn't see the bottom of the structure, he knew a little door would be there, maybe cracked open, with a warm light inside.

The old man struggled to breathe. Hurry, Father.

As the clouds swirled above them, a great wind came from the depths of the earth and rushed above the river, tearing through the forest like an invisible tornado. Trees snapped in half. Loose branches flew into the river.

Michael held his ground, bending like the trees, and clutched the old man to his chest. He had to do this before it was too late.

The headlamp whirled faster and faster as a tree splintered and fell across the river directly behind them.

Michael tried to say the Baptismal words, but the wind drowned them out, and when the old man's eyes flickered open, he smiled at Michael and said he'd see him in Heaven one day.

Michael said, Yes, you will and held the old man under the water.

A sound like a freight train ripped through the woods. Broken limbs and trash floated by them while the old man kicked his feeble arms and legs. Michael was doing him a favor. No one wants to die slowly.

If there was ever a night for a miracle, it was this. The storm, the lighthouse, the old man on the side of the road like an offering, it all led to one thing: proof.

Show me your power, Michael said when the old man went limp in his arms. I'm waiting on you to give me a sign.

He pulled the man from the river, freshly baptized! And carried him to the bank and stretched him out in the mud like a thing to be evaluated.

Come on! Michael screamed. Why do you hide from me?

The wind swallowed his words. The old man stayed in the mud.

Bring him back, raise him up, show me your power, Michael chanted, lifting his hands to the sky. SHOW ME WHO YOU ARE.

The old man never moved. When the water had risen to their level, Michael climbed out of the bank and ran through the woods, sobbing. He looked over his shoulder once and didn't see a lighthouse or hear the headlamp spinning. Maybe the storm drowned it out. Maybe it was never there.

He fled Darling that night. Ever since, he's wondered if someone will come for him; if the old man's murder will be solved, or if authorities have long chalked it up as another casualty of the storm.

Michael enters the post office and smooths his hair back. Eddie doesn't know what he's talking about, and Michael wants to throw him out of his truck and drive off. Forget Lydia; forget the miracle. He's not going to let Eddie threaten him.

No. He can't run from this. Regardless of how pissed off he is, if there's a miracle waiting for him, then he must endure it. He can't go his whole life praying for a sign, just to bail at the last second. That's not how miracles work.

They require faith and action. And when the time comes for Michael to act, he will see it through to the end.

22

Lydia sits on her bed and checks her phone. After they returned home from the shooting range, her dad disappeared into the garage to clean and oil his gun, while she hid inside her room for a long time.

She has four missed calls from Eddie, along with a text: **Come see me at work, please?**

Does he sense what's coming? The background on her phone is a picture of them on their first date, a picnic at Hollow Hill. They're standing at the summit of the small cliff, their faces touching, their happiness evident. Before they climbed, Lydia remembers brushing Eddie's hand and saying *Don't drop me.* She felt his eyes on her body as she stretched and reached for every hold, the harness pulled tightly around her thighs. She caught him staring, and maybe that was when she knew she could have him. All of him. No questions asked.

It was the moment she betrayed them both and pretended to need something she didn't truly want.

Feeling guilty, Lydia puts her phone away and finds her dad in the garage. "You seen Mom?"

He looks up from his shotgun and stained cleaning rag. "Yes ma'am. She asked me all about our trip, and now she's in the garden, I think."

"I'm going to see Eddie at work and hopefully figure out what to say at dinner tonight."

"You sure you don't need help?"

"I think I can handle it, don't you?"

He chuckles. "Oh Lydia, I've been telling you that your whole life. Just be safe. Eddie's a good guy. I think he'll do the right thing."

It's not Eddie you need to worry about, she thinks sadly.

She imagines what he would say if he knew her secrets, and out of everyone in her life, his disappointment would hurt the worst. Because no matter how strongly he disagrees with her life choices, he'll still hug her at the end of every argument and promise to always be her shoulder to cry on.

He's aged a lot recently, and Lydia hates to admit it. Even when she gives her mom a hard time about looking younger, she's secretly pleased. She wants them to always be as they are now, and not a day older.

Her car keys are missing from the ceramic bowl on top of the little bookshelf in the living room, where everyone tosses their keys; she can't recall moving them.

Lydia cuts through the dining room and out the sliding back door, where a small deck opens to a spacious backyard. How many parties have her parents hosted out here? How many cornhole tournaments, drinking games, and bocce ball can one family play? For the Pratts, the answer is never enough. But now that her parents are leaving old careers in search of new lifestyles, she wonders if the parties will continue and feels a strange longing for the way things used to be.

A long garden bed lines the back of the house, where her mom is weeding and dropping the little green stalks into a wheelbarrow. For a decade or more, from Lydia's birth to her teen years, her mom added to the soil bed behind the house until it became a garden. Lydia spent year after year following her mom through Home Depot's flower department, trailing at local flower shops and playing follow the leader, holding the new plant in her lap on the car ride home; holding the little white label while her mom cut the earth and planted the flower and kneaded the soil with a forceful tenderness Lydia both envied and despised. Her job was to throw away the labels and empty plastic pots after it was done, and she only did that because she wasn't allowed to touch the garden. It was, like baking, a rare thing her mom loved.

Lydia knows every plant in this garden, even though she's never picked one out, planted them herself, or even watered their brown leaves on rainless summer days. "Hey Mom, have you seen my keys?"

"They aren't in the bowl?"

"Nope."

Her mom stands with a grunt and stretches her legs. "Check behind the bookshelf. *Some* people like to rifle through the bowl and knock the keys down."

Lydia smiles. "That was one time."

"We looked for hours."

"And I found them!"

"It doesn't count if *you're* the one who lost them." As Lydia turns away, her mom calls out. "Hey, you think about what I said earlier?"

"About what?"

"About not making Eddie wait."

Lydia's had this feeling running through her head since she woke up, and only after seeing her dad in the garage did she start to understand it. Everything's changing, and she's powerless to stop it.

"I don't want to lose him," she says, struggling to find the right words. "But I don't want to marry him, either."

"Then *what* do you want?"

"I want things to stay the same."

"You know that's pointless. Why are you pretending nothing ever changes?"

"I'm not pretending."

"Yes you are." Her mom's voice finds an edge but doesn't go over it. "Wake up, Lydia, and accept that you can't have *everything*."

Lydia throws her arms up. "I know I can't have everything."

"Then why are you acting this way?"

"I told you, I don't want to lose him!"

The backyard grows desperately quiet.

Her mom kneels in the grass, pressing her gloved hands to the earth, as if it can help her understand her emotional, complicated daughter. "Lydia, enough."

No, Lydia's tired of this. She doesn't blame anyone but herself for ending up in this situation, but can't her mom see the broken parts in her? Doesn't she care how they came to be? "But you know why, Mom. You've always known why. When Cassie moved away, I was what, thirteen? I lost my best friend and I cried for weeks, and you never once asked me why it hurt so, so much because you already knew."

"Your dad and I talked about it. We thought it was normal, teenage behavior."

This is impossible and unproductive. But before Lydia storms off, she'll at least tell the truth, for once. "I've spent my life terrified of losing you, and Dad, and anyone close to me, okay? Terrified. And I know we don't talk about Sammy nearly as much as we should, but growing up, and being unable to tell you guys how deeply scared I was of losing you, made everything so much harder. I wanted to talk about him. I wanted to hear more stories. I wanted to feel okay moving on and growing up, and you were never open to discussing it. You always changed the subject. On his birthday, you hide away and avoid me and distract yourself and make up excuses, and after a lifetime of that, I can't talk about him without feeling like I want to die."

Her mom curls her fingers, digging into the soil. "You look like him."

"*But I'm not him.*"

"I know, dear, but you look like him, especially when you cry." She positions herself over the garden and resumes weeding. "It's a miracle our family has survived this long, Lydia. You're too young to understand what trauma does to people. If you want to go on blaming me and everyone else for your choices, that's up to you, but stop pretending like you didn't *choose* the situation you're in. I know I made mistakes when I was younger, and I realize that more than ever, but at least I can admit my faults."

Lydia feels a small switch inside her, a filter turning off. "Where were you when Sammy walked out the front door?"

"*Lydia*, don't."

"Was everyone watching the fireworks, or were you somewhere else?"

Her mom suddenly clutches a handful of violas and yanks them out by the roots. Dirt sprays across the yard as she throws the ruined flowers behind her. Then she's crawling, reaching for more, and soon her daylilies and peonies are shredded and tossed aside. She doesn't stop. The trillium and hellebore go next, and soon a third of the garden is destroyed, and her mom is wildly beating the Siberian bugloss with her fists and quietly sobbing.

Lydia rushes inside the house and slams the sliding door behind her. She runs into the living room and pushes the small bookshelf to the side, snatching her keys from the floor.

She has to get out of this house.

Her dad's calling her name from the garage, but she doesn't respond.

In her car, she speeds down the little street and runs the four-way stop at the intersection.

Tears blur her vision. One day, she'll put down the shovel and fix all the things in her life that have eroded around her like sandcastles in high tide.

But for now, she'll just keep digging.

23

The apartment complex is quiet. No one's in the parking lot except for Lydia, and the balconies and sidewalks are empty. The only sound comes from a pair of squirrels racing atop a nearby dumpster.

There's a strong chance no one would recognize her anyway, but she still doesn't want to be spotted if she can help it. Waking up in a grave really changes how you view the world.

She leaves the SUV and jogs to apartment ten on the first floor. The spare key is taped underneath the mailbox, so she peels it loose and unlocks the door, slipping inside and locking the deadbolt behind her.

The apartment is dead silent. There's usually a fan, or Jack's on the phone, or he's typing emails and humming. It's never this quiet.

"Jack?"

The living room has a single couch with a TV on the floor, surrounded by disconnected cords and piles of DVDs from the 2000s. Jack has lived here for eight months, and he refuses to buy furniture or hang anything on the walls. He claims to be a minimalist, but Lydia isn't convinced. If he planned to stay here long-term, he would decorate.

There's a grease-stained pizza box on the counter with two stale pepperoni pieces inside. Jack uses paper plates, red Solo cups, and plastic silverware, so the sink is always clean. He orders carry-out and drinks plastic water bottles. The fridge is stocked with fruit, milk, and yogurt to supply his smoothie addiction.

That's how they met. At Moon River Climbing, over a year ago, Jack came in for a rock climbing lesson. He'd packed two fruit smoothies, a granola bar, and said things like *show me the ropes*, which made Lydia laugh and also want to smack him. She gave him a belay class, and when he asked if she could be his climbing partner after her shift ended, she agreed. This was right when Eddie and Lydia were constantly flirting and nothing more. As it turned out, Jack went to school with Eddie. They played football together. As Lydia and Jack climbed later that day, Eddie came over and talked to Jack for half an hour, earning a lot of side-eye from Kevin, who should have the phrase, "If you got time to lean, you got time to clean," tattooed on his body. The old football buddies were reunited, but their only connection in the present day was, of course, Lydia.

"Jack?" Lydia swallows, her throat dry. Why is it so painfully quiet in here?

The bathroom is empty and clean, mostly because there's nothing in there to make a mess of. The toilet paper isn't even on the holder; it's on the floor by the toilet, like that's any more convenient. Lydia puts the roll in the holder and goes into the spare bedroom, but it's completely empty, as usual. At the end of the hall, Jack's bedroom door is cracked open, and there's no sound coming from it.

At the gym, they tell people to remove their jewelry before climbing. Jack hadn't shown up with any, but he did have a tan line on his ring finger, and even that didn't stop him from watching Lydia's ass when she climbed the wall. But after that day, Jack never came back to the gym, and he never crossed paths with Eddie again, as far as Lydia knows. Jack texted Lydia the next day after smoothly acquiring her number 'in case they met up and climbed again.' Despite the fun she had teasing Eddie and their childish, competitive climbing adventures, Lydia started texting Jack every day, and after a week had passed, they went on a date. Not wanting to hurt Eddie's feelings, Lydia never told him. It was, after all, only a date. And Eddie had yet to ask her out.

Lydia gently opens the bedroom door, her heart thumping, but the room is empty. The standing fan in the corner is turned off. The computer is also off, his headset resting on the charger. His dresser looks like it's been ransacked, but that's how it is every day. All the drawers are at different degrees of hanging open, and his clothes are half pulled out, half on the floor like a cascading waterfall.

They first had sex a year ago, in Jack's car, in a lonely, unkept parking lot deep inside the nature preserve. Earlier that day, at the gym, Eddie had asked her out, and she said yes. She didn't want to let him down, and she had done her fair share of flirting and felt she owed it to him. There was also the issue of Jack and his wedding ring tan. Despite her feelings for him, she didn't want to get involved in someone's marriage. But when Jack texted her hours after she agreed to go out with Eddie the next day, Lydia saw this as her only chance with him because she knew, deep down, that dating Eddie was the right choice. The safe bet. Jack was the opposite of that, and she could feel the butterflies dancing when they met up that night and crossed a line they could never come back from.

In the cool, air-conditioned car, Lydia had asked Jack if he was married, and he said yes. She told him sorry, but she didn't date married men. Jack seemed to understand, even as he pouted.

The next day, Lydia went out with Eddie, and in some ways, they acted like they were best friends just hanging out, and some of those feelings never went away. She started dating Eddie with pure intentions. Even if she had sex with Jack after planning a date with Eddie, when she became Eddie's girlfriend, Jack was nowhere in the picture.

Lydia checks the patio, but it's also empty. Jack likes to sit out here and smoke and talk about philosophy. There's a half-used cigarette on the round glass table between two lawn chairs. Lydia steps outside and taps the cigarette with her finger. Stone cold.

She goes back inside. How long should she wait for him? He's probably jogging through the nature preserve since his car is here. And he's not working from home today because there's no coffee mug at his desk. Maybe he used a vacation day, but nothing explains where he is.

"Jack!" She runs back through every room, checking different places, as if he's hiding from her. Something's wrong. If his car is here, then where did he go?

The apartment is too quiet and empty, like it was eight months ago, when Jack invited Lydia over to see his new place. He knew she was dating Eddie, yet she came anyway. What did that tell him? They both stood in the living room with the single couch and TV, and Jack, with a beer in one hand, told her how he was separating from his wife, and how he'd acquired this apartment while they sorted through their divorce. They have two kids. A whole life to dissect and throw away.

Lydia was never unhappy with Eddie, but no matter how hard she'd tried to convince herself otherwise, he was still her second choice. And now Jack was single, living alone, and working from a home office in his bedroom. She told him she was happy with Eddie, and Jack said he didn't want to change that. Lydia's commitment to Eddie didn't bother Jack, and when he kissed her that night in this empty apartment, Lydia kissed him back. He was a fantasy, a chaotic gravitational pull. She loved them for different reasons, and part of her believed she could have them both.

While she had sex with Jack in his near-empty new bedroom, she imagined decorating the walls with art, filling the apartment with plants and furniture, and maybe a dog. Living the life couples do. But Jack didn't want to rush things, and neither was he in a hurry for Lydia to break things off with Eddie. He couldn't commit to anything while in the middle of a divorce, and she told him she'd wait.

A few months later, Eddie moved in with her. His lease was up, and it felt too natural and smooth to deny, even if it made Lydia feel more guilty for keeping this secret from him. She told herself she'd make it right one day; part ways with Eddie, keep their friendship, and move in here with Jack once he was ready for her.

But eight months have gone and there's still no art on the walls.

She checks the bedroom again, but there's nothing to suggest where he is. He has to be running. His running shoes aren't by the front door, and you can't miss them because they're lime green and ugly as hell, and Lydia teases him about it whenever he puts them on.

The bed's unmade, but Jack's probably never made a bed in his life. He's always rushing around, speeding through traffic, never on time for anything.

She needs to stay alert and search for answers, but her brain feels like it's shutting down. Jack should be here. Is he dead? Did Eddie find out about their relationship and scare him off? Did Jack leave her? Did he put her in the grave?

Her eyes are starting to burn, and she takes a long blink, immediately finding the eclipse in her mind, the moon rolling over the sun like an eyelid drooping down to sleep.

It's almost time.

She's alone again, stuck inside an apartment she should be buying furniture for. There should be pictures on the walls and a small dining table with two chairs. Instead, she's in *his* apartment, and he's not here. She's out of time because full totality is happening, and she feels the need to brace herself even though she doesn't understand what it means.

Another blink, a single flash of sunlight left.

"No," she whispers. "I can't do this." Even going back to Kathy sounds appealing. Why can't someone be here with her? Is she going to die alone? Is she going to crawl out of another grave alone? Face the Reaper alone? See flashes of Sammy's ghost in her mind, all alone and lost, and... shit, what's happening? Why does the final sliver of sunlight look like a smile?

She sits on Jack's bed, thinking of all the times she came here after work, after telling Eddie she was stopping to clean her car, or pick up a library book, or walk the preserve. How many times has she crawled into this bed and removed her clothes while Jack worked at his desk? It's pure torture, and it's what he likes; his woman in his bed, waiting impatiently for him.

The bed sinks beneath her like quicksand, and she sees Jack standing over her with his dumb smirk. He wants her. He always wants her. In the drifting, weightless ocean of her hallucination, Jack slips into bed, and her worst, unspeakable fears are confirmed: he's not breathing, and he's covered in soil.

A twinkle of sunlight left. What happens when it's gone?

In the corner of her eye, Lydia sees his computer monitor. She untangles from his cold, stiff arms and swims to the edge of the bed, spills across the floor, and pulls herself into his chair. The world ripples around her, almost to a boiling point. The eclipse is nearly complete; she can hear the sun even with her eyes open. She knows his PIN because it's the same as his phone. An idea forms—the only solid thought firing in the soupy synapses of her brain.

Lydia logs into her Apple account and clicks on the page with her cell phone. Since Find My iPhone is turned on, it takes her directly to where her phone currently is. She zooms in on the map and the glowing blue dot hovering over Hope. She already knows the location, even as she scrolls up close on Fourth Street, at the end of the road. She's not surprised that her phone is at her house, where it belongs.

Exactly where she should be.

If the attacker didn't politely leave her phone on her nightstand, then which member of the household has it, and why?

The sound in her ears stops. Shaking, clutching the desk with both hands, Lydia closes her eyes.

The sun has gone, and she's alone in a black void, standing on clouds. As the moon tilts across the sky, it begins to shrink. The eclipse is running away from her, taking the sun as well, and she wants to chase after it, but a small hand grabs her wrist.

Sammy is by her side, flashing his signature mischievous grin, something she'd forgotten about. Seeing it now makes her feel so empty inside because what's to stop her from forgetting it again?

"Can I stay?" she says.

The moon is a coin in the sky, nearly gone.

Sammy squeezes her hand, and in a voice that's more mature than his own, he says, "You're not ready."

Before the moon disappears on the horizon, the eclipse ends. Sammy leans his head against her leg as the sun splits the dark sky, and light spills through her eyes, and—

24

Behind the sun, the moon is oval and lumpy and doesn't look like a moon anymore.

It looks like a grave.

"Lydia!"

"It's not a moon," she says.

"Lydia!"

Hands are on her body, dragging her away from the moon and the sun, and... Sammy.

Lydia finds herself in Jack's apartment, falling from his desk chair and landing roughly on the carpet, twisting her arm and leg awkwardly. She blinks, tears streaming down her face. Why is she crying?

Voices drift over her, strangely calm. She looks at the black cords under Jack's desk and wonders how they could all be necessary. Someone's talking to her, and who else but Jack? Did she faint? Is she having a stroke?

"Lydia?" a woman's voice, very timid and unsure. Older and motherly. Followed by a man's voice, also subdued. But not Jack. If he's in the bedroom, he's silent.

Lydia's on her back, staring at a pair of familiar faces. Normally, she'd be fine with their company, but not in this apartment.

Not in this room.

Kathy LeGrand and Alex Lee tower above her. Alex is wearing his sheriff's uniform and gear, his hands folded across his stomach. Kathy is on one knee, extending her hand. "Lydia? Can you stand?"

Sure she can stand. She's not sure how she ended up on the floor anyway.

With Kathy's help, Lydia gets to her feet and sinks back into Jack's chair. His computer is on, showing a map with a blue dot in the center. It's her cell phone. Why was she tracking it?

"What's going on?" Lydia turns to the two of them, feeling so lost as to what's happening, she can't even guess. "Is Jack okay?"

Kathy and Alex look at each other. "We think so," Alex says. "We're actually here for you."

She rubs her eyes. Afternoon naps make her feel like the sole survivor of a cryosleep spaceship mission. Holy shit, is she on drugs? Why does her stomach feel empty? When did she last eat?

Lydia stares at the intruders again, who are now looking as lost as she is. "Well? Did I commit a crime? Or is this an intervention because you found out about me and Jack?" She *should* be having a panic attack right now, but her mind is too far behind reality.

"Um. Well." Kathy scratches her nose. "What exactly are you doing here?"

"I come here after work sometimes, to see Jack. He must be on a run." Lydia closes her eyes and wishes they would leave. "You gonna tell Eddie?"

Alex clears his throat. "It's not about Jack or Eddie. Lydia, it's about you."

"What about me? I got off work, came here, and passed out. I don't even know how you guys got in here. What *are* you doing?"

Their eyes grow large and blank. Why are they looking at her like this?

"Can you please just tell me what's going on?"

"You're wearing my clothes, Lydia." Kathy's voice is so hesitant and quiet, Lydia almost didn't hear what she said.

She glances at her clothes and jumps to her feet, shoving the chair backward. "What the hell?"

"Lydia, slow down."

"What am I wearing?"

"I told you," Kathy whispers again in disbelief. "I gave you a change of clothes. Do you remember anything?"

Lydia looks around, half-expecting to find her normal clothes in a pile somewhere. Did someone drug her? "Remember what?"

Alex makes a face. A cross between surprise and horror. "Someone tried to kill you, Lydia."

Kathy inhales sharply, covering her face.

"Hold on. What?"

"The grave," Kathy says, "Going to my house, riding in the trunk, Moon River Climbing, *stealing my car*, does any of that ring a bell?"

"Someone tried to *kill* me?" If this happened today, well, Lydia's the last to know. And here she is all worried about Eddie finding out about Jack. Still, that might be worse.

"She doesn't remember," Alex says to Kathy. "Are you listening to me?"

"Please shut up," Kathy says. "Just shut up. We don't know *anything*. That's the fucking problem."

Lydia is more alert now, and what seemed to be a very strange, highly improbable event between her and a pair of old family friends has turned into something else entirely. She's clearly in the dark here, but they've only now realized that. Somehow, that matters to them. Their faces are struggling to reconstruct into readiness, but it's obvious they were unprepared for this response from her, and that brings up many deeply troubling questions.

Then, Kathy dips into the hallway and practically drags Alex with her. Intense whispering ensues.

Lydia glances back at the computer monitor. Why is she tracking her cell phone? How did she end up at Jack's apartment without her phone? Didn't she come here from work?

There's an email notification in the corner of his monitor. Lydia clicks on it. The email is unread, and it's from her Gmail account. The stamp says she sent this email today, several hours ago, and yet she doesn't remember doing that.

It reads: *Hey, weird question, did I contact you yesterday? Where were you last night?*

Not the most coherent email she's ever sent, but two things bother her immediately, excluding her lost memory. One, her message implies she hasn't seen or talked to Jack since before yesterday, and yet something occurred last night that she doesn't remember, but thinks Jack is somehow involved in. Two, Jack works from home and suffers from severe email addiction. There's no way he'd avoid checking it all afternoon.

There's a creak in the hallway and Lydia closes both tabs. Whatever this email and her lost phone mean is surely about to be explained. Kathy and Alex are wedged in the doorway, giving her a look of pure astonishment.

"Can we make coffee?" Lydia says. "I'm a tad overwhelmed by this, to be honest."

Kathy and Alex glance at each other like they're afraid coffee is code for something.

Lydia doesn't wait for their approval. She walks past them and into the kitchen. It takes a minute to start the coffee maker, and the smell of it brewing makes her feel more normal. There's a single plain black mug on the drying rack, the only mug in the apartment. Lydia never spends the night, so there's no point in keeping one here for herself. Maybe there was an issue at the office, and they told Jack to go in, and that's why he's not here.

"Is Jack's car here?"

Kathy and Alex do their little glance. It's getting old.

"Yes," Kathy says very slowly.

"Why can't I remember anything?"

Kathy fake smiles. "Let's move to the living room. There's a lot to go over."

"Coffee's almost done." Lydia takes the mug from the drying rack and waits for the coffee maker to beep at her. No one is saying anything, which is good. It buys her time to think.

Alex is standing by the front door, his boots still on, his radio silent. Maybe turned off. He's not wearing a body camera. Unless Kathy's explanation starts making sense immediately, Lydia will jump from intense worry to extreme panic. These two shouldn't be here. The door should've been locked. Jack should be here. And out of everyone from the old friend group, Kathy and Alex were not close. They never hang out just the two of them, as far as Lydia knows, and she can't think of a single good reason as to why they are the ones here with her, and not anyone else.

She pours her coffee and sits in the living room. Alex hovers in the hallway, staring at Lydia like she's got something on her face. What got into these two? And why does she feel unsafe around them?

"There's no easy way to say this." Kathy sits on the couch beside Lydia. "But this morning, I found you in the nature preserve, on that dirt access road close to the Reaper, you know?"

Lydia *should* remember something like that. She has no choice but to take Kathy's word for it.

"You told me someone had attacked you and buried you alive. Do you remember any of this?"

Lydia shakes her head. It's the truth. Her memory of today is blank, but she *does* remember breaking up with Eddie last night, and that feels relevant. Do these two know about that?

"Holy shit," Alex says.

"Do you know who did it?" Lydia asks. "Have you been investigating this?" It's the only explanation for Alex's presence.

Kathy and Alex shake their heads in unison, and Lydia's gut turns again. She wants to trust them, but why was she searching for her cell phone earlier and sending emails to Jack? Why have they completely ignored Jack's absence and Lydia's hidden relationship with him?

"Where's Jack?" she says again. They have to answer this if she's going to believe anything they say.

"We don't know." Kathy looks at Alex. "We're working on that."

"Is he missing?"

"Lydia," Kathy's voice is strained but still motherly. "We think we know why you can't remember anything about the grave." Kathy glances at Alex again, and he gives a slight nod.

Lydia has to endure this whether they tell the truth or not, because she genuinely *doesn't* remember this morning, and she'd like to know the reason. "Why?"

There's a twitch in Kathy's eyes. "Because you made it up."

25

Michael is clutching the steering wheel so tightly that his fingers are bone white. How did this all get away from him? Eddie came prepared; he had manipulated Michael out of his own church for some nefarious reason and needed his help for something Michael knew was wrong and dangerous. It's only a five-minute drive to the antique farm, where the bell, according to Mary Foley, was supposedly last seen, but Michael's back is already slick with sweat. What's to stop Eddie from telling everyone that Michael's a fake pastor? What'll prevent him from killing Michael when it's all said and done?

"Before this morning, I didn't know anything about you," Eddie says, reading his thoughts. "And I never meant for it to be personal, okay, Pastor? I'm having the worst day of my life. I have no reason to spill your secret or discredit you. In fact, the more I found out, the more I knew it was worth coming to you with this."

"Thanks Eddie, I feel reassured now."

Eddie ignores him. "I made some calls this morning, including a certain Catholic seminary in Pennsylvania. I found your class photo online, from a cookout or something."

Michael never thought a harmless picture years ago would come back to haunt him, but that was before Darling and the old man.

"The other call was to a recovery center in Darling, and they told me you worked there two years ago."

Yes, Michael remembers the recovery center. He's so pleased to hear that they remember him.

Eddie continues. "But according to Brian..."

Fuck you, Brian, Michael thinks.

"You disappeared from the recovery center, and from Darling completely, the same time as those serial killer murders."

Michael had followed the news closely after his departure. It wasn't a miracle, but maybe divine *luck* that his encounter with the old man coincided with a generational storm and a psychopathic rampage on Darling's streets that very night.

"Maybe what Brian failed to mention, Eddie, is that Darling got absolutely rocked by a string of killings. None of which had anything to do with me, but I had to get away from all that death. I knew one of the victims because his father came to the center."

Eddie nods. "But before you lived in Darling, you were expelled from the Catholic seminary. Why?"

"You know you should get into investigative research or something. They'd love you. You're wasted as a rock climber."

Eddie ignores him again, making him feel foolish. He needs to get back under control.

"Why'd they expel you?"

"You tell me. You got the answers."

Eddie briefly closes his eyes. "Look, Pastor. I'm tired, okay? I'm not out to get you. I wasn't looking for dirt; I just found it by accident. That's not my fault. Besides, I'm bringing this to you *because* of your past, you know what I mean?"

Michael's starting to get it, but it doesn't instill confidence. If anything, he's getting a terrifying sense of where this is headed. He slows down and turns onto a private drive. He's never actually been here before, but he's driven past the sign numerous times. They park in a small, gravel lot outside of an old brick antique store. Relics of the past are scattered around them, surrounding the gravel lot and even into the woods, where rusted plows and garden statues watch from behind honeysuckle bushes, and windchimes dangle from tree branches.

Michael takes his seatbelt off and lets the truck idle for a moment. "I was asking a lot of questions about demonic possession. It made the Fathers uncomfortable. Father Mason, especially. He could tell I was more than curious. I wanted to know everything about the spiritual realm, and he didn't like that."

There's a long pause. "Do you still want to know?" Eddie narrows his eyes. "Are you still more than curious?"

The thing in Michael's stomach starts to jitter, and it sends a cold shiver through him. "You told me earlier that there's evil in this town. I haven't run away yet, have I?"

Eddie slightly shakes his head. "Not this time."

Ouch. Fair enough. "Are you saying this is a purely spiritual matter? Because you've already mentioned a crime, and I've already told you I won't call the police, *yet*, so when are you going to tell me what happened?"

"We had a fight," Eddie says. "I proposed to her. She turned me down and lied about the reason why."

"Why'd she lie?"

Eddie sighs, and there's a tremor in his voice. "Because she was cheating on me."

"Howdy!"

Michael flinches, looking at the bald middle-aged man standing outside his truck, ducking slightly to see through the open window.

"Sorry boys, didn't mean to scare."

Michael shakes the man's hand through the window. "Are you Horace?"

"Yes sir."

"I'm Pastor Michael, from Hope. This is Eddie West, rock climbing extraordinaire."

"Oh really? What brings y'all to the farm?"

Michael gestures to the relics. "Do you believe in miracles, Horace?"

"No sir, unless rain counts. I know what the science says, but rain don't feel natural, does it?"

"It's funny you say that." Michael chuckles. "I happen to agree with you. We're on the hunt for a particular church bell."

Horace hooks his thumbs through his belt loops. "The one Burt Foley dropped off?"

"That's the one."

"Burt drove to the back of the field and tossed it. I don't think I ever even laid eyes on it, but you're more than welcome to walk back and check. I told him to put it far away. I don't refuse stuff, but that thing feels unlucky. I'd rather it be gone, honestly. It's yours if you want it."

"Thank you, sir."

"I'll be in the shop. Holler if you need me." Horace disappears inside the old antique store.

They leave the truck and walk to the edge of the lot, guarded by a gnome statue with a moss-covered nose. Behind the store, the trees open to a long, flat field, like a runway, with hundreds of antiques lining both sides of the aisle, as far as they can see.

"Near the back, huh?" Eddie mutters. "I guess we have time."

Is that why Eddie keeps checking the clock? Is he meeting someone after this?

"Miracles require action, Eddie." Michael strides into the field. "So, when did you find out Lydia's been cheating on you?"

"After our fight. She took off and wouldn't tell me where she was going, and I started drinking."

Michael almost feels bad for Eddie. A confession of this magnitude requires guts, something Michael apparently doesn't have, because he will never in his life tell a soul about the old man in the river. The thought of it paralyzes him.

"How do you know if…" Eddie trails off, sighing. "Can you be possessed and not know it?"

"It's possible, maybe. That's the kind of question Father Mason would've found suspicious."

Eddie exhales through clenched teeth. "How would I know?"

Oh Eddie. Michael feels an ache in his heart and stomach. A rustling. The poor kid. He really did kill Lydia, didn't he? As Michael suspected, Eddie must've fractured his brain. Reality has no hold over him. He believes the Devil did his dirty work, when in all likelihood,, Eddie snapped after Lydia's rejection, and these are the pieces of him barely holding together.

"Where there is demonic influence, the work, the outpouring, is evil. You shall know a tree by its fruit, yes? Look to the fruit."

Eddie, hands in his pockets, is struggling to keep his eyes dry. "I'm scared, Pastor. There are things I don't remember about that night."

He blocked it out, Michael thinks. *I have to be careful.* One word can bring everything back and trigger a very bad response. But it may be too late. Eddie's starting to shake.

"Eddie, what's wrong?"

"I went after her," he whispers. "After I was already wasted, I got behind the wheel, and I *drove* after her."

Eddie's so close to confessing, Michael wants to reach inside and rip the truth out of him.

"If I had stayed home," Eddie says, "she would still be alive."

26

Lydia wishes she'd never spoken to her mom and witnessed the destruction of her beloved garden. In a way, it's her fault, isn't it? For saying those things? For hurting her.

The only time Sharon's ever lost control in front of her daughter was two decades ago, when they lost Sammy. Lydia distinctly remembers her mom collapsing on the front lawn. That's not something you ever forget. Growing up, her parents were the pillars of her childhood and witnessing one of them fall and sob into the grass felt like a literal foundation crumbling beneath her. Maybe the cracks in their relationship began there, and not the night of July Fourth.

More and more, Lydia doesn't understand the two people who raised her, and she's not sure she wants to.

The drive to the gym is always beautiful. Route 4 goes on for some time, looping around the nature preserve before branching off into northern roads. Through the trees, Lydia can make out the Reaper's dark hood. A few climbers are at its base, surely pointing at its complexities and challenges, and not its heavy gaze, its open mouth, and razor-sharp teeth.

She drives through Blue Hill and parks at Moon River Climbing. Eddie's red truck is in the corner of the lot, *not* parked in reverse, for some reason. He must've been rushing.

A shiver of déjà vu runs through her. She used to love the sight of his truck and his reassuring grin through the windshield. She loves the memories they made on road trips, like the time his battery died at Cuyahoga Valley National Park, and they had to startle some sketchy RV campers for a jump; or when they drove down to Red River Gorge and spent more time debating and searching for the right trail than they did hiking.

Now, the truck fills her with dread; maybe because it's all coming to an end.

She walks inside. Kevin's at the counter, helping a newbie rent the right shoes for bouldering. Behind him, a wood-paneled wall is covered in framed photographs. Kevin used to get around in the climbing community. He has pictures with Jon Krakauer, Alex Honnold, Sasha DiGiulian, and more Lydia doesn't recognize.

"Lydia, what are you doing here?" Kevin asks once the customer jogs downstairs. "Eddie covered you today."

"I know, I'm here to see him."

"He's got a belay class in ten. He's down there somewhere."

"Thanks, Kev." Lydia moves to the balcony and looks over the gym. Eddie's sweeping the hallway by the lockers and bathrooms. A handful of climbers are on the walls, all regulars. The dreamy stained-glass light fills the gym, and Lydia briefly forgets why she came.

"You all right?" Kevin is spritzing returned shoes with a spray bottle before wiping them down. "You look a little uh, under the weather."

"You mean I look like shit?"

"Whoa, I didn't say that. I would *never*."

Lydia rounds the counter and heads down the stairs. "Just a rough day, Kev."

Eddie watches her advance, holding the broom close to his body.

"You got my texts," he says casually. "Thanks for coming."

"Kevin says there's a class soon, so I won't stay long. What's up?"

Eddie leans against the broom, staring at the high windows. "Things were kinda weird earlier. You took off with your dad, and we didn't get a chance to talk."

I know, Lydia thinks. *That was intentional.*

"Have you thought anymore about it?"

She thinks about how they felt knocking on that RV door in the national park, hoping they wouldn't get murdered. Then she thinks of her mom's garden and all those torn-up flowers. That's not who she wants to become. But is that what happens when you let secrets fester? Do they turn into parasites? "I've been thinking a lot today, about us, and the future, and I want to talk to you about it, about everything, over dinner tonight. Now's not the right time or place."

On cue, one of the regulars on the floor waves to her, and she waves back. They can probably all tell there's a fight happening, because even Kevin is still spritzing shoes instead of making fun of her.

Eddie looks away. "What did I do wrong?"

"Nothing."

"How can you say that?"

She sits on a nearby bench. "Eddie, I'm sorry." Should she do it now? Just end it and walk away?

"What are you sorry for? Is it because you can't tell me why you don't want to get married?"

"It wasn't my plan," she says. "I never even thought about it."

"What plan? You knew I wanted to! I mentioned it how many times?"

Did he bring up marriage a lot? Lydia can't recall a single instance, but then again, it's the sort of thing she would neatly brush aside and ignore, which makes her feel even worse, if that's possible.

He looks so pale and earnest. Lydia would regret breaking up with him here, in this place they both love, around people they both know. It should be at a neutral spot. Nothing too fancy. Eddie deserves to hear her side, even if she'll only tell him lies.

"Can we start over? Let's get dinner, and I'll tell you everything on my mind," Lydia says because it sounds believable. "At that salad place downtown. We haven't been there in a while."

His face turns to stone. "Roxy's?"

Lydia nods, thinking it's a quaint, simple, non-alcoholic spot to break things off. She doesn't love their salads anyway, so tainting that restaurant with soon-to-be bad memories seems like the best choice. Eddie, on the other hand, is giving her a hard stare.

He knows it's coming, she thinks. *He knows, and it's killing him.*

Eddie puts the broom away, running a hand over his face. "What time?"

"Six-thirty?" Early enough to pick at her food, break up, and still catch a late meal with her dad. Something greasy and delicious.

He looks up at the counter, at Kevin, who's pretending he isn't watching them.

"What's wrong, Eddie?"

He shakes his head and steps onto the padded floor. "I feel like I don't know you anymore." He walks away with the last word, and Lydia lets him. She knows this is her fault. She should've never let him move in; never let things get this far. But his words still hurt, and he's the second person to tell her that today.

Maybe she deserves to suffer like this.

Going back up the stairs, she tells Kevin goodbye and leaves the gym. The sunlight is blinding, and she shuts her eyes to steady herself. Blurry images rotate in her vision, and she feels the sunlight scraping the inside of her skull like a gold blade carving a jack o' lantern. She opens her eyes and stares at her shoes until the dizziness fades. She might throw up, but she's okay for now. A vehicle passes by in a blur, and Lydia catches the back of a sheriff's SUV. It can't be Alex again, right? There are plenty of sheriffs in Blue Hill.

She slides into her car and sends Jack a quick text: **Can I come by?**

When he doesn't respond, she puts the car in drive and heads for his apartment. She can let herself in with the key under his mailbox. She'll surprise him and tell him her plan to break things off with Eddie, and maybe he'll change his mind and commit to being with her.

In the rearview mirror, an SUV is far behind her, and there's no mistaking the light rack on the roof or the guard on the grille.

A sheriff is following her.

27

Lydia's mind is spinning. Not only does she not remember anything before waking up in Jack's apartment, but according to Kathy and Alex, she *fabricated* a story about someone attacking her. Kathy finishes retelling her side of what happened this morning, and it's so wildly bizarre, Lydia struggles to believe what she's hearing.

"But why would I lie to you?" she asks them.

Kathy keeps pausing and pursing her lips, making her nostrils flare. She ruminates over every word. "I called Alex while you were at my house earlier. I had him check the woods, and he didn't find anything. There is no grave, Lydia. I don't know what happened to you. I'm not saying you're lying, exactly, but no one tried to kill you, at least not in the way you explained it to me. There's no grave, no tracks, no tools. Alex found *nothing* out there."

Lydia stares at her hands, hoping to understand why she would pretend someone tried to kill her. "You checked the woods off the dirt road, where you found me?"

Kathy and Alex nod their heads in sync. "I spent an hour out there," Alex says. "Found nothing. We're not trying to screw you over, Lydia, you know that. We just can't understand why you'd lie, or what the hell's going on with your memory." Alex says this last part like it personally pisses him off.

"You found nothing at all?"

"No ma'am." Alex meets her eyes, but only for a second.

Why does it feel like he's lying? Why are these the only two people concerned about her right now? She turns to Kathy. "Why didn't you ask me to show you the grave?"

Kathy goes pale. "Do you remember something?"

Lydia shakes her head. "You said you found me on the dirt road. I was upset and told you I was attacked, but you took me home without asking any more questions. Nothing about the grave, or where my things went, or why my car wasn't there? Did I walk to the preserve and pretend to be attacked and hope someone came along to find me?"

"Lydia, sweetie, I know it's hard to get your mind around. Imagine how we feel!" Kathy smiles thinly. "We are on your side, but Alex found nothing indicating a crime happened in those woods. No sign of your things, your car, or other people. That doesn't mean you made it all up, I get that, but that's how it looks right now."

Her head hurts. How can she even start to sort through this mess? "How did you find me *here*?"

Kathy removes a cell phone from her pocket. "Sorry. I didn't know what you were going to do. I left this under my seat, and when I saw the car was gone, I called Alex. He picked me up, and we tracked my phone here."

"I'm sorry I took your car. I don't remember why I did it."

"I know." Kathy smiles again. "You're not in trouble, okay? It's more important to me that we figure out what's going on with you, so forget about the car."

"Where's Jack?"

Alex taps his belt, his mouth moving like he's chewing gum. "We don't know. We were hoping he'd show up."

"I could call him if I had my phone." Why was Lydia searching for her phone on Jack's computer? It appears to be at home, which is the next logical place outside of herself. But how'd she end up in the woods this morning without it?

"Until we know what happened to you last night," Kathy says, "there's really not much we can do. We want to believe you, but we can't find the grave, so what does that leave us with?"

Lydia inspects her hands. Her palms and fingers aren't as soft as they used to be, not since she started climbing. She can't have nice nails. The Reaper abhors such things. Her only hope of ever summiting that cliff is if she free climbs, and she knows it. The rope is a weakness. It's a way out. A free pass. Take that away and what's left? She'll either beat the Reaper or die.

"I'm sorry for everything," she says, still looking at her hands. "Sorry I put you through this."

Kathy pats Lydia's knee. "I know."

"Can you take me home?"

Kathy and Alex exchange glances. "We can," Kathy says. "But think this through. You're here, at Jack's. With no memory of today or last night. How can you explain any of this to Eddie, or your family?"

"Aren't they worried about me?"

Kathy sighs. "I have an idea. Why don't we take you back to the woods where I found you and see if you remember something that'll help us find the grave. If we find it, then Alex can move forward with an investigation, and we can take you home and tell your family that someone attacked you."

The woods. Just the three of them. Why does that image fill Lydia with dread?

"If we find the grave, then we'll know you were telling the truth."

"You need me to prove myself?"

Alex comes into the living room, staring down at Lydia like a child. "What else can we do?"

"I don't know. Just believe me?"

"That's not how courts work, Lydia, you know that. We need evidence, and your testimony is clearly compromised."

They don't want to take her home. They want her back in those woods. If there's no grave there now, there will be soon, because these two are lying through their teeth, and Lydia can't figure out why. If they truly cared about her, she'd be at a police station or a hospital getting her head examined.

She has no memory of today. She can't talk to her parents, Eddie, or Jack. She's alone with two people who aren't very involved in her current life, and yet suddenly seem to know what's best for her. She's being told about all the strange things she did and said earlier in the day, including stealing a car, and she's forced to believe it because she has no other choice. She's being gently led, and she can feel it. They want her in those woods so they can discredit or kill her. Normally, believing an old family friend wants to murder you *is* unstable thinking, and although her mind has forgotten the last twenty-four hours, her body hasn't. There's a tension thrumming inside her bones.

What if her body remembers what happened, and it's trying to warn her?

But even if they're lying about something, they would never *kill* her. She's being too paranoid, which is exactly how Kathy described her behavior earlier.

Kathy takes Lydia's hand. "Are you okay with this? Maybe your memory will come back, and we'll find the grave. I would take you home, but we have to consider the cost. If, bear with me here, if you've lied about something, then there's time to rectify it before you face your family and Eddie."

Is that what this is about? Lydia cheating on Eddie?

"I'm sure you're telling the truth," Kathy says, everything in her voice screaming the opposite. "You wouldn't lie about *this*, right?"

They know she's a liar because of whose apartment they're in. No wonder they don't trust her.

Lydia looks at her fingers, and she finally realizes what's been bothering her. She jerks her hand away before Kathy can see it. Lydia knows they're lying about the grave and maybe everything else. She knows because of her hands. Her not-so-nice nails, all of which have dirt under them. As if she'd been digging through the mud. Or crawling out of a grave.

Lydia stands, tucking her fingers inside her palms. "Let's go then, and I'll prove it to you."

Kathy and Alex do one of their obvious glances.

"Just, don't tell my family or Eddie about Jack, okay? I'll tell them myself. I owe it to them."

Kathy nods and stands with her, adjusting her jacket. "Then let's go."

28

The grassy path is barely wide enough for a pickup truck, and far too narrow for Michael's comfort.

Eddie has confirmed Michael's suspicions: Lydia is dead, and Eddie is likely the killer. According to him, if he had stayed home, Lydia would still be alive.

Although he barely knew her, Michael's trying to comprehend her absence and what it'll mean for Eddie, her family, and this community. How awful for her parents, losing two children to the same cursed woods. Is Eddie right about them? Should Michael fear whatever's lurking in that forest?

"Did you kill her?" He crosses his arms to appear relaxed, but his fists are clenched. Eddie's only five feet away.

"How do I know if I'm possessed?"

"That's not important right now, Eddie. What happened to Lydia?"

"You're missing the point."

"Yeah, I agree! What happened? It's a simple question!"

"No, it's not." Eddie scratches his head and squints at the sky. "I can't stop thinking about it. How do I know if something's influencing me? Do you know what that looks like?"

Michael resumes his walk, keeping an eye on the antiques littered down the path and into the woods. "You may be overthinking this, Eddie. A gap in your memory could be from the alcohol. Possession is extremely rare." *Like miracles,* Michael thinks. But he'll keep that to himself. Already, Eddie's former promise of a miracle is looking bleaker by the minute. The needle file is still in his back pocket, and although Eddie appears to be unarmed, now is not the time for lax judgment. Michael's come too far for that.

"Possession, it must be stated, is not a one-size-fits-all conversation. There's possession, there's influence, there's simply the existence of things we don't understand and can't make sense of or reason with. It would, I think, benefit us both if you tell me what happened after you went looking for Lydia. I know you're set on telling me later, but if you think there's a spiritual influence of any kind. I might figure it out as you talk."

This could backfire, but Michael's ready for anything. There is, of course, a slight chance Eddie's telling the truth, and he simply doesn't recall murdering his girlfriend because *something* did influence him. But Michael will resort to that belief when there's no other choice.

"Well, after I drank and drove around, I found Lydia's car parked out by the Reaper." Eddie continues to look for the bell, even though he's too distracted to be useful. "But there was another car I didn't recognize. So I parked my truck and walked into the woods to look for them."

Eddie, what have you done? Michael thinks, resisting the urge to tap the needle file for good measure.

"I couldn't see them at first, because it was dark out, and they were sitting on a blanket on the other side of the river."

"They didn't hear or see you coming?"

"Well... I was quiet."

Michael swallows. He can feel his fingers twitching like a gunslinger. Soon, everything will click like a landmine inside Eddie's head.

"I hid in the woods and tried to listen to them. Lydia kept laughing, and at first, I thought she was with a friend, like Aimee. But that wasn't Aimee's car, and Lydia has other friends, but no one she'd go on a late-night walk in the woods with." Eddie squats beside an old anvil and touches the rusted edge with his finger. "But the other person was a guy. Someone I know."

"I'm really sorry, Eddie."

"I could've walked away and accepted defeat. I could've been a man about it, but instead I sat in the dirt and listened to their conversation echo off the Reaper." Eddie stands again and wipes his hands on his shorts. "I couldn't hear exact words, but I knew the guy's voice. His name is Jack. He and I used to play football for the Blue Hill Tigers. We were best friends in high school, but we don't talk anymore. I mean, he's married, he has kids, how did he and Lydia even start talking? When did it start? Eventually, they came back toward the parking lot and walked over the bridge, but they weren't saying anything. Just walking and holding hands."

"I can't imagine. That must've been awful."

Eddie picks his way down the path, his mind far away. They're sinking deeper into the antique farm, near the end. Michael clears his throat. "Did Lydia and Jack drive off then?"

"No. They kept walking. I left my hiding spot and followed the path back to the parking lot, but they weren't there."

Eddie's breathing quicker now. He stops at a small farmhouse bell. "I suppose this isn't it."

"No, too small."

The antique store is out of sight, and it's still only the two of them out here. Michael reminds himself of this every two seconds.

He shifts to the other side of the path. "I don't know why you're telling me this, Eddie, if you didn't kill them."

"I don't know what happened."

"Don't lie to me."

"I didn't *want* them to die."

"That's not an answer. Who killed them?"

"What if something *influenced* me?" Eddie squats down, exhaling in jagged, rushed breaths. "How would I know?"

"Eddie, the Devil didn't make you hurt them. I believe in that, yes, but you wanted to hurt them, didn't you? Anyone can see you were upset. You had a good reason to be, and maybe you made a mistake. Mistakes happen, even serious ones, and it has nothing to do with the supernatural."

"No, I don't know what happened. I would never do that. I would never hurt her!"

"What if they saw you, and maybe they said something so heartbreaking, you couldn't get past it. It's okay, Eddie. I'm telling you, I understand more than you realize!"

"How do you know something didn't make me do it? You! Of all people! I could've been pushed, right? My mind wasn't all there. Between the vodka and the woods, everything was dark and blurry. What if? No, listen, what if something told me to do it, yeah, because I saw something in my truck that night. While they were still alive, I went back in my truck, and I saw a mask."

Michael trips over a gnome; he'd been backing up without realizing. "Eddie, what mask? And why did you get back in the truck? You need to walk me through this if you expect me to believe you're innocent!"

"The mask," Eddie whispers, breathing harder. He's on the verge of a panic attack. "The horrible mask. It whispered to me."

"What did it say?"

Eddie, in tears, sits in the grass and hugs his knees to his chest. "It told me to drive." He bows his head, and his shoulders tremble. Nothing is held back; the grief takes over, and he lets it bend and twist his body into something soft and breakable.

"Eddie, I could be wrong. I don't know everything, but I don't see the signs in you. What I see is betrayal and pain. I see humanity, not evil. You're hurting, you're upset, and maybe you made a mistake, but that has nothing to do with true evil. I know you. I know you're not a bad guy, I know you love Lydia. You wanted to marry her! You envisioned the two of you joining together and becoming one flesh. Where is that version of you right now? You are not fully yourself, true, because whatever you did is actively damaging your mind and soul, but the real Eddie is still here. You are not possessed; you are *human*."

Eddie sniffs and tries to breathe deeply. "Are you sure?"

"Yes."

"You know what evil looks like?"

"Yes."

Eddie weaves his fingers through his hair and grips it. "Can you help me?"

"Whatever you need, I'm your guy." Michael expects Eddie to give it up and call the police. Maybe he wants Michael to stay with him if the police allow it. He's so unstable, Michael hates to think of him going through that alone. But then his mind flips back to when Eddie said they needed his church for something, and he knows the story is far from over, and Eddie's confession is only a piece of a larger puzzle.

Rolling to his feet, Eddie wipes his eyes and steps forward. "We'll need to be careful."

Michael jerks back, flipping the file from his pocket and pointing it at Eddie's throat.

"Pastor?"

"Stay back." Michael presses the file against Eddie's throat. "Other side, now."

Eddie backs away, raising his hands.

"I know you killed them, and I'm so, so sorry. Truly. But we need to call the police. We've wasted enough time. If their bodies are out there, they need to be found. Her parents need to know. I stand by what I said. You are not evil. You are fully human, the good and the bad. Just a human." Does he sound bitter? A little. He was so looking forward to a true miracle. He's had enough simple-minded, hot-headed humans to last a lifetime. Eddie, sadly, is no different.

Eddie walks down the path and crouches beside a lopsided brick chimney. "You said bells ward off demons?"

The thing in Michael's stomach starts wiggling happily.

"Because I think I found it."

Michael moves closer, keeping the needle file firmly in his hand. Sure enough, the mid-size bell in front of them is in great shape, having sat in an enclosed barn for so many years. There's a dark stain across the front, a deep maroon against the black metal.

"Is that his blood?"

"I'd like to think so."

"Can we hang it up? Will it drive demons away?"

"What does it matter if you're not possessed?"

Hands on his hips, Eddie blinks the last of his tears away. "Do you know what the point of this was?"

"I really don't."

"I haven't slept. I've been convinced that every time I look in the mirror, I'm going to see something evil standing behind me, like in a horror movie."

"That's not how it works, Eddie."

"I know. But that's why I keep asking you about the signs, because I need someone to tell me that it'll be okay, that I'm not too broken or too far gone to come back."

Michael has some opinions on that subject, and he'll keep them to himself. "Everyone can find forgiveness."

"I know." Eddie rubs his eyes. "I need someone to know my side of the story, so I told you. Just in case."

"In case of what?"

"No matter what happens tonight, Pastor, you know me, right? You know my heart. And you know I never meant to hurt anyone."

"Eddie, who else knows about this?"

Eddie checks his phone. "It's almost time. I'm going to make a call, and we'll get started. This is bigger than us. It's bigger than the town. What happens tonight could change the world."

The thing is surging against Michael's stomach like it's trying to see through his muscle and skin. "Will I see this miracle you've mentioned?"

"If you promise me something."

"What?"

Eddie runs his palm over the bell. "If there is evil in Hope, and if you see it tonight, can you help me kill it?"

29

After that painful conversation with Eddie, Lydia wishes she could stop at Jack's apartment, but she's too nervous. The sheriff's SUV has been following her since she left the gym, and if it's Alex, he could recognize her car. She's been too careful all this time to let it slip now. Of course, the sheriff isn't *actually* following her, but she won't risk it.

She turns right on Fifth Street and continues past the Blue Hill movie theater and the used car lots. The sheriff also turns down Fifth Street.

It must be a weird coincidence. How many times has she been followed by a cop, convinced she's about to get pulled over, only for them to eventually go somewhere else? There's no reason to be scared. She hasn't done anything wrong.

But her body's trying to convince her otherwise.

When she turns onto Route 4 and heads toward home, she gets a text from Jack: **On a run, call you later?**

There's so much she wants to say to him. He has never encouraged her to break up with Eddie. He says, more times than she can count, that he's not ready to commit to anything so soon after his divorce. Whether to stay with Eddie or not has always been solely her decision. Now, if they break up, will Jack change his mind?

She sends a text in response: **I need to see you later tonight, maybe we can walk somewhere?** Dropping her phone in the passenger seat, she watches the rearview mirror.

Up ahead, two cars are parked on Wiggins Street, on the edge of the dirt access road: her mom's gray Toyota and Kathy's black SUV. The women are standing near the vehicles, having just started their walk, and they both glance in Lydia's direction.

She doesn't know if being around her mom is a good idea right now, but part of her is afraid to be alone.

Turning onto Wiggins, she parks beside them and holds her breath. Sure enough, the sheriff flies down past the preserve and disappears around the bend. Is it Alex? Why does he keep showing up today? She can't pinpoint why, but there's a funny feeling worming inside her stomach.

Lydia leaves her car and approaches the women. She's positive her mom will pretend the garden incident didn't happen, and she's okay with that. "What are you two doing out here?"

Kathy pauses to let her to catch up. "Taking advantage of the nice day. What are you up to?"

"You can keep walking. I'll tell you." Lydia falls in between them, and they stroll down the dirt road. "I just came from the gym. I talked to Eddie."

"Your mom filled me in," Kathy says. "Sorry to hear about you two."

"It's okay. I guess things need to change." She looks at her mom, who's busy staring off into the woods. "We made dinner plans, so I'll break up with him tonight." How much has her mom told Kathy? Did she mention Lydia's unforgivable comment? Or the destroyed garden? If Lydia has to pick the strongest trait she shares with her mother, it's the ability to move on from a horrible thing like it never happened.

"Are you nervous?" Kathy asks.

Lydia's never broken up with someone before, and she imagines it will be extremely difficult. "Yeah I'm kinda dreading it. We're going to the salad bar downtown. Things might get weird at home. He'll probably grab his stuff tonight."

"Does he have family nearby?" Kathy asks.

"His dad lives down closer to Dayton. I imagine he'll go there."

"Do you need more time to think this through?" Her mom glances into the woods again, like she's hearing something.

Lydia sighs. "I can't give Eddie what he wants. Isn't that what you said, Mom? *Don't make him wait.*"

Kathy and her mom make eye contact and shift their feet. "I know," her mom says. "Think he'll take it okay?"

"Honestly, I don't know."

"Do you love him?" Kathy asks, rather pointedly.

"Yes, just not in that way." She knows it's dumb. This is the guy she's shared a bed with for the last six months. What does that say about her? Even if her mom and Kathy are old school, she has a feeling they'd forgive and forget everything if she said yes to Eddie's proposal. She could've stopped waiting for Jack, won the approval of her parents and friends, and gained a caring, easygoing husband. Is that why Kathy and her mom are looking at her like she's nuts?

"We were just talking," Kathy says, nodding toward her mom. "I've never seen you climb. Can you believe that? All these years."

"I'm always at the gym," Lydia starts, "if—"

"Why not now?" Her mom stands on the edge of the forest. "Show her how you climb the Reaper."

"I *can't* climb it. I always fall at the top. And I don't have my rope, or harness, or shoes. I need shoes."

But her mom and Kathy are already slinking into the woods, lifting their hands against the branches and spiderwebs.

Lydia points to her right. "There's a road and a nice path here! We can take the bridge across the river! Hello?"

"Come on," one of them says. Lydia's already lost them in the dense woods. But in she goes, pushing through the forest, where everything is muffled and directionless.

"Mom?"

"Over here!"

She follows a narrow trail, nearly running into the two women.

"Why are we going this way?"

"Shortcut," Kathy says, waving a fly away from her face. "Straight shot to the river." She slips between the trees and she's gone again, but Lydia's mom hasn't moved. Her hands are on her hips, her sleeves rolled up. She's looking around again like she's still hearing something.

"You okay, Mom?"

She frowns. "I'm thinking about tonight. I don't know how it'll go."

They start walking, picking through thorn bushes and stepping over roots. Kathy's jacket is barely visible ahead, but it's all they need to stay on course.

"I'm not worried about Eddie," Lydia says. "There's no way around this. I don't want to marry him. I didn't... I never thought I'd have to turn him down, you know?"

"I know."

Her mom sniffs and looks behind them. "It also doesn't help, being in these woods."

"I told you we should've taken the path!"

"It's not that." Her mom steadies herself against a tree. "We searched these woods." She keeps walking, one resolute step at a time, but her eyes are misting over as she inspects the ground for roots. "I think about Sammy every single day. I think about how I could've prevented what happened, the things I could've changed, and of course it means nothing, does it? It happened and we can't go back."

Her mom rarely talks about Sammy like this, and she understands why. There is no true diagnosis for grief. It's too deep, too personal to the individual. Someone can wear a scar on their soul and you'd never know it. Not without coming to these woods and seeing these signs.

Despite the remnants of anger toward her mom, days like today remind Lydia, somewhat brutally, that nothing lasts forever. No matter how hard she clings to what she has, it will always slip away.

Her mom is swaying like a reed in the wind, bone-tired and defeated. Lydia tries to hold her hand but her mom flinches and pulls away.

"Sorry," her mom sniffs. "Coming here was a bad idea. I can't do this with you right now."

Lydia understands. Or she tries to. She doesn't carry the blame they all shoulder. She doesn't know what it's like. Part of her wants to be enough for her mom, but she can't compete with Sammy, nor does she want to. He takes up most of her mom's heart, and that's okay. He deserves every piece of it.

"Do you remember a lot about Sammy?" her mom asks. Kathy stops up ahead, staring at the forest floor. She turns around and watches them advance with blank, empty eyes.

Kathy has spent more time in these woods than anyone. After her daughter died, she grieved by hiking and fishing. Right now, the memories are hounding both women, and Lydia wants to help them by changing the subject. There's a time and a place for therapy, and this is not the time, and these woods are not the place. She wonders how they can live so close to so many painful memories without going insane.

"I remember the cute stuff," Lydia says. "The little things he did and said that make me cry if I think about them."

Her mom licks her lips, holding one hand to her eyes and squeezing them shut. "Shit, Lydia."

Kathy backtracks toward them and points at something. "Sharon, how's your balance?"

Twenty yards ahead, a tree had fallen perfectly across Moon River. They follow Kathy over to it.

Lydia shrugs. "We're only a minute from the Reaper. Who wants to go first?"

Her mom and Kathy point at her, their faces grim. Why are they both taking this hike so seriously? She can understand where her mom is coming from, but why is Kathy treating this like an expedition?

"I'll show you how it's done," Lydia says lightly, though neither of them cracks a smile.

She steps onto the tree, lifting her arms for balance, and tries not to worry about the cracking sounds coming from inside the trunk. She catches her reflection in the smooth water, along with a pair of hands reaching for her neck.

Her mom is right behind her, pulling a stray leaf from Lydia's hair. Then her fingers poke and prod Lydia's skull like she's searching for something.

"Mom! What are you doing?"

"Checking for ticks," her mom laughs, gripping Lydia for balance, lightly squeezing the base of her neck. "Sorry, I thought we were all going at once."

"Let go. You're going to knock me in." Lydia shuffles forward and smooths her hair out, her stomach turning.

"You all right?" her mom says with amusement. "You used to have better balance."

Lydia tiptoes along the tree, her mom close behind her, their shadows overlapping. She tries to hurry so her mom won't crash into her. She loses her footing and—

30

Lydia trips on the final stretch and lands on the opposite bank, rolling to her side. Her mom hops off the tree and towers over her, smiling. She offers a hand, and Lydia takes it.

"Why'd you rush me?"

Her mom shrugs. "I thought you'd be faster."

"I'm too old for that," Kathy says from across the river, fixing her bucket hat firmly on her head. "I'll take the bridge and meet you at the Reaper."

Her mom motions for Kathy. "Come on now. If I pulled it off, you can at least make it halfway."

Kathy raises her hands in surrender and steps onto the tree. Same as them, she slow-walks across, her arms outstretched. Her jacket sways as she walks, revealing a small gun holstered on her right hip. Lydia had forgotten about Kathy's concealed carry.

Kathy jumps down and straightens her jacket, giving Lydia a brief glance before smirking and adjusting her hat.

"What are you so pleased about?" her mom asks.

Kathy starts down the trail. "The tree didn't make a sound for me."

"Oh, shut up," her mom says. "Lydia and I broke it in, that's all."

Lydia doesn't remember the last time the three of them did something together, but she likes the spontaneity of it. Her mom and Kathy take the lead while Lydia hangs back, thinking of all the times she brought Eddie here. All the climbs, picnics, sex, and river jumping. They even camped out here once, under the Reaper's dark gaze. She had nightmares about Sammy that night, and they never did it again. Sometimes she'll meet Jack here after one of his long runs. Aside from his apartment, it's the only place they feel safe to meet, especially if his car isn't in the parking lot.

The Reaper is patiently waiting for them. A dark shadow lies at his feet. Kathy and her mom stare at the cliff, then back at Lydia.

"You can climb it, right?" Kathy asks.

"With my equipment, I can get to the overhang. But that's where I fall."

"Can you boulder for us?" her mom asks.

"I already told you. I don't have shoes."

"For me," Kathy says. "So I can see you climb."

Lydia shakes her head and approaches the wall. She's inside his shadow now, where the air is noticeably cooler. Wiping her hands on her pants, she finds a hold, plants one foot, and climbs. She doesn't boulder often, and when she does, it's at the gym. This is a whole different feeling. No gear, no chalk, just a human versus a small cliff.

She goes higher, slipping her right hand inside a crack in the wall while raising her left foot to catch the next ledge. In the distance, she hears a car door slam, but she doesn't stop to look.

"You're doing amazing," Kathy says, almost in a whisper. Lydia feels their eyes on her body, watching her legs and arms work in unison.

Heavy footsteps rattle the wooden bridge. Lydia pauses, her cheek to the rock, and rotates her head to look back.

Alex stands on the bridge, his hands and neck stained with blood; his uniform covered in dark, wet patches. "Lydia?"

Kathy makes a humming sound. "Hey, Alex, uh, are you okay?"

"Oh, yeah, I'm fine." He looks at his uniform and tries to wipe his sticky hands on his shirt. "Can I please talk to you for a second? It's important."

Lydia's already climbing down, one careful hold at a time. "Of course. What's wrong?"

He gestures behind them, at the parking lot, where his SUV is parked. "Alone, please."

Kathy and her mom look at each other. "Alex?"

"I'll explain everything, I promise. But Lydia first."

Lydia jumps to the ground and brushes the dirt from her hands. Why is he here now? If he was following her earlier, why didn't he stop when she did?

"Lead the way," she says, shrugging at her mom and Kathy. But inside her chest, her heart is spiraling.

Alex doesn't say anything. He turns his back on her and scans the woods like it might be full of enemies. They head for his SUV, but Lydia can't fathom why. She's just glad she isn't here alone with him.

The passenger window is cracked open; someone's inside, hunched over.

"He asked for you," Alex says, opening the door.

Sitting there in handcuffs, covered in blood, is Jack.

31

Lydia looks back at her mom and Kathy, watching from the Reaper's shadow. They can't see the passenger side. They have no clue what's going on.

Jack's arms are bent behind his back, and his wrists are bright red from struggling with the handcuffs. There's a gash on his forehead that's still bleeding, dribbling down into his mustache. He's wearing his running clothes: a bright red tank top and gray shorts, along with a headband and an arm strap for his phone, which is missing.

"Lydia," he says, struggling to sit up straight. "Talk to him, tell him what happened."

"Baby, shh." She puts her hands on either side of his head and wipes the blood away with her thumb. "What happened?"

Alex sits in the driver's seat.

"Why the hell is he in handcuffs?"

"Because he was hitting me," Alex says flatly. "He's confused. I know how to do my job, Lydia, and I'm trying to do you a favor by keeping this between us, so don't make me regret it."

"Is he under arrest? Why isn't he in the backseat?"

"Because opening the back door triggers a camera, and that footage gets reviewed. Like I said, a favor. If you're willing to sit back there, we can take him to the hospital, and I'll fill you in."

"What about the camera?"

"I'll say your car broke down and I gave you a ride. No one will care. Not like they would with this guy. Look at him."

Lydia glances at her mom and Kathy again before sliding into the back seat. How will she explain this later?

"He asked for you," Alex says. "Over and over again, he wouldn't stop. I found him a few miles from here on the side of the road. Someone hit him."

Lydia looks Jack over as best she can through the partition cage, half-expecting to see a bone sticking out somewhere. "Why isn't he in the hospital!"

"We can take him now! You were on the way, and he wouldn't shut up." Alex clicks his seatbelt and puts the SUV in reverse.

"What about my car?"

"Lydia," Jack says, "don't leave me."

"Someone can pick you up. We gotta go." Alex turns on the overhead lights and siren and peels out of the parking lot.

"What happened, baby?" Lydia presses her forehead against the cage. She feels Alex's eyes in the rearview mirror, but she doesn't look at him.

"I don't know," Jack says, his head rolling to the side. "I didn't see them coming. I don't know what's going on. Where the hell am I?"

"After I picked him up, I asked him if he saw anything," Alex says. "He said he saw a red truck. Anything you wanna tell me?"

"What? You think Eddie did this?"

"I don't know, Lydia. You'd be surprised what people are capable of," he snaps. "*Does* Eddie have a reason to do this?"

"He asked me to marry him, and I said no, is that a reason?"

Alex huffs and shakes his head. "Did you tell Eddie about our friend here?"

"No."

"Welp, I think he found out."

"Lydia," Jack whispers.

"What is it, baby?"

But he can't continue. He grits his teeth and groans.

Alex snorts. "Jack's not in the best state of mind right now to be giving testimony, but if he said he saw a red truck, I have to consider it, right? Now, are you going to tell me you also think it was Eddie, or do I gotta keep guessing here? How did Eddie find out?"

"Maybe he didn't."

"This guy saw a red truck, Lydia. When was the last time you and Jack talked? Could Eddie have overheard something?"

"I don't know. It's been a week, at least. Eddie wasn't around."

"Are you sure you haven't seen him since?"

"Yes, I'm sure!"

Alex doesn't believe her. But then, she doesn't blame him. He's giving her the same look as her mom and Kathy, as if no one's ever made a bad decision in this town before she came along.

"Call," Jack says. "Call please."

Lydia wishes she could hold him. "Call who?"

"Lydia," Alex says.

"What?"

"Hit and runs are almost impossible to track down out in the country." Alex drives past the hospital and turns down a back road behind the main building, stopping at an empty overflow lot. "Make sure Eddie has nothing to do with this, okay? If you don't check, I will. And Eddie might want to know why. You get me?"

"Alex, come on."

"What happened last night, Lydia?" He parks and turns in his seat to face her. "What the hell happened with you and Eddie?"

"What does that have to do with this?"

"Everything!" Alex hits the steering wheel with his palm. "Are you really *this* blind? Or are you hiding something?"

"Lydia." Jack's eyes flutter open.

She ignores Alex, anger burning in her chest. What right does he have to talk to her like that?

"Just talk to me, baby. What is it?"

Alex gets out and opens her door. "Let's go. Say your goodbyes."

"Why aren't we at the ER drop off? We're nowhere near the entrance!"

Alex shakes his head. "Unless you want to be seen with him, let me do it. I promise you, he's fine. Maybe concussed, and he'll need stitches, but I bet that's it. Take the sidewalk to the hospital grounds and sit tight, I'll find you. But it's way more discreet this way." He opens the passenger door and uncuffs Jack. "Don't make me regret this, dude."

Jack's eyes widen. He reaches for Lydia, and she hugs him. His eyes are red and puffy. "Lydia."

"What, baby?"

"Call my wife." He swallows. It looks painful. "Tell her to come. Tell her I'm so sorry."

Alex looks at her and waits.

She squeezes Jack's hand. "You're divorced, remember? How hard did you hit your head?"

But Jack doesn't fade again; his eyes are focused. "We never got divorced. She doesn't know about my apartment. I told her I was working in the office."

Alex scratches his head. "Oh, shit."

Lydia slowly releases his hand. "You never left her?"

Jack shakes his head. "Call her, please. Tell her to come find me here. I need her." He starts to weep.

Alex's talking and helping Jack back into the passenger seat. He says something about coming to get her. About Lydia sitting tight, as if she has another option. Then Alex and Jack drive off toward the hospital and disappear.

Jack was married the whole time. Lydia had been so blinded by him, so caught up in her own lie, that she never stopped to consider if he led a double life. It worked out perfectly for him. She never went over to his place in the evenings because she spent that time with Eddie. She would only go over during the day, when Jack worked remotely in a secret apartment, where he could have her in his own fantasy land, nowhere near his home. Every night, she went to Eddie, and Jack went to his family. The apartment had only been his office space. His fake life. And to think Lydia had dreamed of putting art up on the walls...

She wants to hate him, but after what she's done to Eddie, how can she pretend life is so cruel and unfair?

Did Eddie find out about Jack? Did he hit him with his truck?

Shaking, she pulls out her phone and calls the gym.

"Moon River Climbing, this is Kevin speaking."

"Hey Kev, it's Lydia. Is Eddie there?"

"Oh, hey Lydia. Uh, no. He said something came up and he left basically right after you did. Some replacement, huh? He didn't even set the route! This is why you're still my favorite."

"Thanks Kev. I'll be in tomorrow. See ya."

Lydia hangs up the phone and checks the time. It's late afternoon. Why would Eddie leave work so early? What's he been doing?

Jack saw a red truck, Lydia thinks. *But in a place like this, there could be a dozen red trucks, so it doesn't mean anything.*

Right?

32

Lydia rides in Kathy's trunk while Alex follows them to the nature preserve. Apparently, they did this earlier. Kathy recommended they do it again, in case there is a would-be murderer on the loose, which is ironic, since Kathy can't seem to make up her mind on whether she believes Lydia's story or not. She's acting as if both options are true: there's a killer, and Lydia lied. How can both be happening at the same time? And what if they don't find the grave? What if they find nothing at all?

Lydia examines the dirt beneath her nails and wonders if going on a hike will actually help her memory because she doubts it. Yes, common sense might suggest she retrace her steps to find her lost keys, but this is a whole damn day; it's a different animal. Lydia knows that. Kathy and Alex *should* know it too unless they're deliberately keeping something from her.

Even if they mean well, this is her life they're playing with, and no one's going to keep her in the dark.

She should never have agreed to ride in the trunk. What will she do if they drag her into the woods? They're both armed. If Kathy has her gun, they can easily overpower her.

Lydia looks around for something to use. Most trunks have a tire iron tucked away. She finds a little door in the trunk lining and unscrews the cap, but the small compartment is empty. No tools. No tire iron.

Kathy must've cleaned it out. Whether it was on purpose or not, Lydia can only guess.

The SUV stops. Both Alex and Kathy slam their doors one after the other, and that combination of sounds spirals through her mind. Earlier, when Kathy rehashed the day's events, she said Lydia remembered nothing about the grave. So why does a slamming door make her heart accelerate?

The trunk opens, and Kathy and Alex stare down at her. The image reminds Lydia of kidnappers in movies because that's what this is, right?

They help her out, their hands lingering on her arms. She pulls away from them, hoping they don't notice her flinch. They're standing on the dirt road, near the empty parking lot. "So, where did I say it was?"

Kathy gestures into the woods. "Somewhere in there."

The sun is setting, and there's no one here but them.

"We're losing light," Alex mumbles. He walks into the woods first, and it doesn't take long for his uniform to blend and disappear into the thicket.

"Lydia?" Kathy takes her arm, and Lydia flinches again. She hears the car doors in her mind, one after the other.

Lydia hugs herself, shrugging Kathy's hand away. "I don't really know what we're supposed to do. These woods are hundreds of acres."

"We're seeing if you remember," Kathy says softly. "Anything coming to mind?"

Lydia won't mention the car doors. She's not sure she'll mention anything. "Nothing yet."

Kathy nods absent-mindedly. "Come on, let's catch up."

Together, they wade into the forest, taking a formation Lydia can't help but notice: Alex in the front, Kathy in the back. Like how you'd lead a class of students. Or a prisoner.

It's far darker in the woods. Strings of red and purple light cut through the trees, but the sun is quickly dropping. They waited too long. Or is this exactly what they want? A perfect cover of darkness. Maybe a tragic *accident*.

They march deeper in until there's nothing but woods. The dirt road is gone, and they haven't reached the river yet. If Lydia were to bury a body, this area would suffice.

She looks for signs: footprints, trash, broken honeysuckle branches, and the grave itself. She's trying to find it, but she can't stop noticing Kathy and Alex's strange behavior. It's obvious they're more worried about keeping an eye on her than finding this grave. Can they guess her intentions? Have they been reading *her* as much as she's tried to read them?

She's not smart enough to hide her body language, and neither are they. The trees are too narrow and compact; there's no wind, no air for them to breathe. No one's fooling anyone.

"Anything?" Kathy asks.

Lydia shakes her head. "I'm sorry. I don't remember, so I don't know what to look for."

Alex grunts. "It's a grave, Lydia, it *looks* like a grave."

She wishes she'd found something—anything in the trunk to defend herself. "I'm sorry, I've never had to find my own fucking grave before."

Alex checks his phone. "Time's up. Come on, Lydia, nothing's ringing a bell?"

He's annoyed, and rightfully so, if he believes this whole thing was fabricated, and no one can prove otherwise.

She wonders if giving them a little something will buy her credibility. Why won't they believe her?

"Lydia," Kathy says, a shiver in her voice. "Do you remember something?"

Lydia stares at them. "I told you, I don't remember what happened before waking up in Jack's apartment! I'm sorry I don't know where the grave is! I don't even remember telling you about it, let alone where it is exactly in these entire woods."

Kathy rolls her eyes. "We know it's not your fault. Don't blame us for trying. We've done nothing but try to help you."

"Are you serious? All you've done is accuse me of lying! You're not telling me everything, are you?" She needs to shut up, but it's too late. There's no going back now.

"We're just trying to help," Kathy says again.

"Then look." Lydia shows them her fingernails. "Look at the dirt! How do you think that got there?"

Kathy stumbles back, her chest heaving. She tucks one hand inside her jacket and extends the other, palm out, as if to ward off Lydia from attacking her.

Lydia should've kept her mouth shut, but she feels a convoluted sense of satisfaction when the calm veneer slips from Kathy's face.

"She remembers," Kathy says, looking at Alex. "We have to deal with this."

33

The trees are closing in around her, making it hard to breathe.

Alex has one hand on his gun. "We don't know what she remembers," he tells Kathy.

"Did you *hear* what she said?"

They're having this conversation without her, which only means one thing. Lydia wants to go easy on herself, considering she woke up from a late nap and is experiencing *the* most disorienting day of her life, but she really fucked up here.

"She's going to remember the rest." Kathy's voice is rising; she looks scared. "I'm so sorry, honey."

Alex takes a small step, raising his hands. "Kathy, wait, just wait."

"She knows, Alex."

Lydia's not included in this because there's nothing to talk about. She's not leaving these woods. End of story. But Kathy and Alex aren't on the same page for once, and that might be all she needs. A split second.

Lydia shifts her feet, trying to play dumb even though she looks like a cornered animal.

Alex keeps his hands out, tapping Kathy's shoulder. "Just take a breath. You can't undo this."

Kathy clenches her jaw. "She remembers, Alex. I am not going to prison because of *her*."

Time's up. Lydia ducks behind a tree and sprints deeper into the woods, jerking left and right to keep the largest trees behind her.

The forest erupts with rapid explosions. Lydia can hardly see in the dark, but she pushes forward, staying low as the woods echo with splitting wood. A bullet zips overhead and she veers away from it. Each pop makes her jump. It's like she's five again, clutching her dad's hand as they run through the woods at night, calling Sammy's name, the fireworks shrieking overhead.

Her foot collapses under her, and she trips and sprawls on the forest floor. She's fallen into a pit of sunken dirt, and when she gets on her feet, she doesn't waste time looking back. She already knows what it is. Her body remembers.

The shooting has stopped. Kathy either ran out of ammunition or realized her mistake: a dozen bullets scattered across a wooded area. Not very smart if you're trying to get away with murder. Kathy should know that, and Alex too. Maybe that's why he didn't fire his weapon.

Lydia inwardly sighs with relief, because now she knows they really were lying the whole time. Maybe about everything. Someone in Hope will have heard the gunfire, but outside the town limits, shooting targets in your backyard is a standard way to spend your evening. No one would think twice.

In the low light, she nearly falls down the steep embankment and into Moon River. She takes off her left shoe, launches it into the water, and runs along the embankment in a low crouch. She then cuts across the woods diagonally, toward the parking lot. If they see the shoe in the river, they'll assume she swam across and is hiding on the other side. There's no good way to escape from the other side of the river, thanks to the ridgeline and the Reaper. They know this. They'll think she's pinned herself against a cliff she can't climb, and maybe they'll pursue.

If they're smart, they'll split up. She's going to pretend they're smart and prepare for the worst. She slows down to a fast walk and tries to make as little noise as possible. If they can't locate her, they'll struggle to keep up. And if she gets across Route 4, she'll be gone in the dark.

Twenty yards from the parking lot, she sees the Porta-Potty, lime-green against the dark trees. Not far now. Branches snap under her weight, and briars catch her clothes. There's a rustling somewhere behind her. Maybe the shoe in the river didn't work, or maybe they missed it.

Ten yards. She's down to baby steps, no noise. Her oversized shirt is painfully white, and she quickly pulls it off and shrugs it over a mid-sized honeysuckle bush. Not quite a scarecrow, but enough to make them pause. In her bra and sweatpants, she gets on her hands and feet and tiptoes out of the woods. The rustling is gone, but her lungs are fighting for every breath, and she can't fully hear past it.

She kneels on the dirt road like a runner about to race. The parking lot is empty, and so is the dirt road, until a shadowed figure steps out of the woods thirty feet to her right. They can see her. They're standing with their head cocked, arms at their sides. Lydia waits for them to jump, but they're forcing her to make the first move. Fine. They shouldn't have hesitated, because now there's a car coming down Route 4.

The figure realizes their mistake and bolts for Lydia. From this distance, in this light, it doesn't look like Alex or Kathy, but who else would be lurking in these woods, trying to kill her?

The headlights casually bend through the woods because the driver is slow and probably on the lookout for deer.

She could flag them down and scream for help, but if Kathy and Alex are desperate enough to murder her in the woods, then they're capable of a lot. Like unloading their clips into a car with a random citizen at the wheel. She doesn't want to get anyone killed, but there's no time to weigh the options. She sprints toward Route 4 as the figure reaches the parking lot. With a burst of speed, she races across the road, directly in front of the car. The driver slams on the brakes. She leaps into the ravine on the other side and barrels into the woods.

The car comes to a complete stop, and a voice calls out. Lydia's far away now, and she's positive Kathy and Alex can't follow her. They probably hid when the car stopped and are lying flat on their stomachs somewhere with their noses to the ground.

As the voice continues to call out, she slows down. The driver is buying her so much time, she doesn't need to run. And when the car finally leaves, she hears its engine but can't see the headlights through the trees.

Her throat is painfully dry, and her feet hurt, especially the left one. It's hard to see, but she knows these woods in the dark. After Sammy died, she would sometimes walk the trails they both loved, as if they held the answer to why bad things happen.

Sammy used to bonk his head against hers. He had the deranged fearlessness of a toddler, and his head was his greatest weapon. Lydia would run while he chased her in his shirt and diaper, swinging his head like a hammer. Sometimes he'd get her with a good one and leave a bruise.

The body remembers.

Lydia walks toward Hope, toward the only place left for her to go. The only place she knows is safe.

34

Michael parks on the street beside his little church. From the outside, everything looks the same. "What did you do to my church, Eddie?"

"I told them you were coming with me," Eddie says, opening his door. "They suggested we use a church, a place of God, you know. It was their idea."

Whose idea? And here he thought Eddie had been calling the shots, but maybe that's far from the truth.

"Who's they?" he calls as Eddie walks up the church steps and slips inside the front door.

That little bastard. Michael gets out and follows him inside. He pauses in the entrance.

There's a man in the sanctuary, hastily removing things from a cardboard box. The windows have all been covered with blackout curtains, and the man is trying to make a pile of tall wax candles, but they keep rolling away on the wood floor. He spins around when he hears them. It's the sheriff, Alex. In plain clothes: a black T-shirt and cargo pants. He's wearing a gun on his hip.

Michael nods. "Hey Alex. Doing some remodeling?"

Alex returns to his task. "Hey Mike."

"So uh, what exactly are you doing in my church?"

"Whaddya tell him?" Alex says, picking up the now-empty cardboard box and moving it against the wall. "Come on, Eddie, what the hell did you tell him?"

"We need him."

"Nobody agreed to this!" Alex yelled.

There's a loud thump in the back room. The door is shut, and a shadow moves beneath it.

"Who else is here?" Michael says.

Alex tugs on the blackout curtains, testing their strength. They've been crudely nailed to the walls. "Don't worry about it, Mike. Holy shit, Eddie, what were you thinking? Do you even know what you've done?"

"My name is Michael, and this is my church, I have a right—"

"We have to be sure," Eddie says. "We have to be one hundred percent positive! How can we do that if we don't know what to look for?"

"Alex!" Michael shouts. "Who else is here?"

"Can everyone shut up?" Alex points at Michael. "Especially you. You're not a part of this. I don't care what Eddie says."

No, Michael won't be bullied in his own church. He marches to the back room and turns the doorknob. At the same time, a hand grips the back of his head, ramming his skull against the door frame.

Michael collapses to the floor, rolling in the dust bunnies like the tall wax candles. He must've blacked out. His head feels like it's trying to float off his body.

Eddie's yelling something.

"Don't you dare," Alex growls. "You chose to bring him here. He's your responsibility."

"I know!"

"Then fucking act like it."

A pair of hands turn Michael over to his back, and a cold gun barrel presses against his cheek. Alex smiles at him. There's a red smear on his upper cheek, close to his ear. It looks like blood. "Listen up, Mike. I don't want you going back there, and since Eddie's leaving us in a minute, I suggest you say please and thank you, and we'll be all right. He wants you here, but I don't. So don't give me a reason to pull this trigger, okay?"

Michael nods slowly, wheezing. From his new vantage point on the floor, he sees something attached to Alex's ankle, underneath his pants. A second gun.

Alex yanks him to his feet, and Eddie steadies his shoulders. Michael taps the file in his pocket. Good thing Eddie's forgotten about it or simply doesn't care. But having it makes Michael feel better, even if it's useless against a Glock. Michael's never seen this side of Alex before. He's never been called Mike and never been assaulted. It's a new day in Hope, and maybe a miracle is lurking nearby after all. In the back room, perhaps?

Alex is pacing by the stage, shoulders back, all macho and tough. But Michael smells fear on him. Eddie, too. What are they so afraid of? Why do the candles and curtains look like the start of a ritual?

There's another thump in the back room, and all three of them look at the closed door.

"I have a few minutes," Eddie says. "Let's pull the truck around."

Michael had almost forgotten, or rather, the thought had been viciously punched out of his brain. "You mean the bell? You still want to hang it?"

"Evil spirits, remember?" Eddie says, nodding at the back room. "We might need it after all."

They step outside the church, and Michael can feel Alex's glaring eyes from the dark sanctuary. There's no escaping this, is there? Alex will gun him down in the street if he tries to run.

Eddie looks back at Alex. "Can you help us hang this?"

"You're joking, right?"

"We might need it. We need to try everything."

"I thought the whole point was to keep this quiet and not draw attention to ourselves. Two things you've already fucked up today."

"This is my church," Michael says. "We'll hang it up."

He climbs into the truck bed with Eddie. They shuffle the bell to the edge of the tailgate and heave it to the front steps. Michael then grabs his ladder from the shed behind the church and brings it into the building. He can't help but notice there's no sheriff's SUV, or even a regular car around his church. Even Eddie's red truck is nowhere in sight; when he came to this church earlier this afternoon, he had parked somewhere else and walked. Alex did the same. Or he dropped someone off in the back room and then left his car a few streets down. Alex doesn't want to be seen here, and that's a sign of what's to come. Michael knows a bad omen when he sees one. But he's come too far to walk away now. They won't let him.

They maneuver the ladder up into the tower.

"You got rope?" Alex asks.

"In the back of my truck. We picked it up before coming here. I'll grab it."

"I got it." Alex walks outside, eyeing the empty streets.

Will this be their last private chat? Michael leans closer to Eddie. "Are we safe with him? Because you promised me a miracle, not a séance or a murder or whatever you're planning here."

"Nothing's safe. But for now, no one's going to throw you out."

"I've been endlessly patient with you today. Can you at least tell me what the intent is here? What's with the candles and curtains?"

Eddie nods, looking away. "We'll tell you everything, I promise."

Michael doubts that, but he lets it go.

Back inside, Alex sets the rope down, crossing his arms.

Michael unravels the rope and ties one end through the two holes on the top of the bell. "The bracket is still intact. I'll climb up, sling this rope around, and we'll hoist the bell up. It should lock into place."

"That easy, huh?" Alex asks.

"Well... this is no cathedral," Michael says. He carries the rope up the ladder and into the narrow tower. Everything is still in good condition. A lot of dust and cobwebs, but no rot. Sliding the rope around the crossbar and frame above his head, Michael lowers it down to the floor, then descends the ladder.

"Will it hold?" Eddie asks, looking up.

Michael doesn't know. "Yeah, it'll hold." He hands his keys to Eddie. "Go slow."

Alex is already tying the end of the rope to the truck's tow hitch. "We should be ready." He jogs back inside, glancing at the streets around him.

"I hope it's everything you dreamed of," Eddie says earnestly, slipping into the driver's seat.

Alex squats beside the bell. "Might wanna move, Pastor," he laughs, glancing at the tower. "I guess you know what happened to the last guy who stood under this bell."

"This is meant to be, Alex. Don't ruin it for me."

"Suit yourself."

Eddie pulls the truck forward, and the rope tightens. A little nudge and the bell lifts off the ground. The frame groans above them, and Alex takes a step back. The truck inches down the street, and despite the creaking frame and strained rope, the bell rises into the tower. Michael watches it from below, at a loss for words. He should've done this months ago. Why did it take Eddie's confession to bring this out of him?

I've been stuck, Michael thinks. *I've been waiting for a miracle and yet doing nothing.*

He feels like he's accomplished more in one afternoon than in his two years in Hope. Seek, and you shall find.

And look at what they found. The bell is suspended against the frame, and Alex is waving to Eddie to stop the truck. Michael climbs the ladder, never taking his eyes from his bell. At the top, he runs his hand along its blood-stained surface.

He pushes the bell into the bracket and secures the bolt with his hand. He'll need to tighten it later, if he survives the night.

He signals Alex, who waves once more to Eddie. The rope is dropped from the truck, and Michael unties it from the bell and instead loops it around the lever. He smooths the rope out, letting it hang freely. As he climbs down, Alex cuts the rope a few inches from the ground and ties the end into a knot.

Michael holds the rope in both hands. He gently tugs on it, watching as the bell tilts to the side, and the frame rotates. When he goes to let go, Alex clutches his wrist.

"It'll draw people," he says, shutting the front door. "Save it for Sunday, Pastor."

Michael releases the rope. *This* is the church he's always dreamt of, minus the candles, blackout curtains, and cultists.

Alex checks his phone. "You need to go, Eddie."

"I know," he says. "I'll be back in a little bit. Is everyone ready?" His voice gives out; he's terrified of what they're about to do.

Alex shrugs. "Ready or not."

Michael taps Eddie's shoulder as he's walking out. "What do you need from me right now?"

There's so much turmoil inside Eddie; his eyes are cloudy. "I need you to wait with Alex and pray we do the right thing."

Doing the right thing would never have led them to this moment, but Michael keeps that thought to himself. "Anything else?"

Eddie leans in so Alex, who's lighting the candles, doesn't hear him. "Remember what we talked about." Eddie shuts the front door and leaves Michael in the narrow entrance, the rope brushing against his shoulder.

He remembers their conversations vividly and recalls what Eddie told him not long ago: that he never meant to hurt anyone; that he needs Michael's help, and he wants someone to know his story. *Just in case.*

What happens when the mysterious others find out Eddie's not on their side?

The thing in Michael's stomach is awake but very still. It's listening to the only sound in the entire church: the continuous thumping in the back room.

35

Alex and Jack are still in the hospital, and Lydia's been sitting near the smoke shack for a long time, getting second-hand smoke from employees who like to bitch about their bosses over a pack of Luckies and a shared lighter.

Eddie called her twice already, and on the third try, she finally picked up and told him where she was. She shouldn't trust him after what happened to Jack, but she knows he's not a bad guy. Even when every sign is pointing to the same conclusion, here she is believing in the best of him, like she did with Jack, and look how that turned out.

Maybe this is what she deserves: losing the two men she loves in a single day. Her worst fears coming to life.

Her mom sent a text about Lydia's car and how she drove it home and Kathy picked her up to get her own car from the preserve. Her mom didn't mention Alex showing up bloodied and whisking Lydia away, nor did she offer to give Lydia a ride. Sharon can be all business in the most ridiculous circumstances, but even this is a stretch. Somehow, her mom already knew about Jack.

Finally, as the light of day fades, a red truck pulls into the hospital parking lot. Eddie parks where she can't see him, and then her phone vibrates in her pocket.

She stands up, stretches, and heads his direction. Despite how things have ended with Jack, she can't tell Eddie the truth. She can't look him in the eye and tell him she's been in love with another man since the day they started dating. She's already breaking his heart, why do more damage than necessary?

Unless he deserves it, of course. If he actually hit Jack, would there be a dent in his truck?

Lydia weaves through the parking lot, and it's apparent Eddie hasn't seen her yet.

She takes a moment to watch him from a distance. He's nervously scanning the parking lot for her. If he's innocent, why is he afraid?

How will he respond when he sees her? Lydia walks toward the front of his truck. They lock eyes; she doesn't smile. She wants to know what he'll do.

Skipping the passenger door, she stands beside the right headlight. The truck's grille is intact, but there's a dent on the right side of his hood. Lydia doesn't remember it being there.

Through the windshield, Eddie watches her with horror.

She yanks open the passenger door. "What did you do?"

He says nothing. He can't pretend he doesn't know.

She slams the door and walks away. She'll find her own way home.

At the end of the parking lot, the red truck pulls up alongside her, and Eddie leans out of the open window. "Lydia, please stop."

No chance. Everyone's acting like she's changed, like they don't know who she is anymore. But what about them? What about Jack, Eddie, and her mom? She's lost faith in all of them today, and who does that leave her with? How dare they pretend she's a broken mess when they're no different.

"Lydia!"

She stops on the sidewalk and rubs her eyes. She won't cry in front of Eddie, but it's hard to resist when he's got tears of his own.

"I'll take you home," he says. "One last time."

Nothing in her wants to get in his truck.

"Come on, Lydia. You know me."

"Then why is there a dent in your hood?"

His face is blank. He can't even drum up a lie.

"I thought we were getting dinner tonight," she says.

"Why do you think I have a dent?"

He wants her to say it. Even if he already knows she's cheating on him, he's making her admit it. And what's worse? Telling him the truth, or pretending she has no idea?

They both know, so what's the point in playing dumb?

When she says nothing, Eddie leans back in his seat and exhales, staring at the road. "Can I take you home?"

"I'll walk."

"It's the last thing I'll ever ask you," he says with a hitch in his voice. "And then we're done."

The two of them were never meant to work out, and still, she hates that thought of losing him. She feels like everyone's slipping away from her, including herself.

"I love you," he says. "Nothing will ever change that."

He's telling the truth. What does she have to be afraid of? It'll be their last trip together.

She gets in the truck and buckles up, wiping her eyes.

They drive in strangely comfortable silence until they reach Route 4. No one's behind them, but Eddie waits at the stop sign, looking both ways. No cars are coming on either side.

"Eddie?"

He closes his eyes. "There's no going back, right? It's too late for that?"

She knows what he means. Like her, he wishes he'd never proposed. "I'm really sorry, Eddie."

Something shifts inside him. Maybe he's found a way to let her go.

He turns right and drives toward Hope. "Listen, Lydia, there's… so much I need to say. You have no idea."

Lydia has an idea. She's got a whole book for Eddie if she can ever tell him the truth.

"My point is, I don't know if I'll get to say everything I want to. There might not be time."

"Eddie, what are you talking about?"

They drive for another few minutes, skipping the road they live on and entering Hope's non-existent downtown. He parks on a random street by an empty, outdated playground.

"Let's walk." He steps out and follows the broken sidewalk deeper into town, even though it's getting dark.

Lydia leaves the truck and tries to keep up. She can't tell where this is going, but she doesn't like it. She's never seen him like this before.

They walk three blocks until they reach the corner of Main, where the little community church sits. Eddie walks up the front steps and opens the door.

She stays outside. "Why are we here?"

Behind him, the sanctuary is dark. Candles glow beneath the cross on the back wall, making the statue of Jesus flicker in the shadows. Inside the door, a long rope hangs down to the floorboards. For an absurd moment, she thinks of some gallows, and imagines Eddie hanging her by the neck from a church steeple.

"I helped put this together." Eddie tugs on the rope, and a slight ring echoes from the bell tower. "Pretty neat, huh?"

"You did this?"

"Well, Pastor Michael and myself. Earlier."

"That's what you spent your afternoon doing after I left the gym? Hanging a church bell?"

Eddie walks inside, letting the rope sway behind him. "It was more than that."

Lydia steps inside the foyer and brushes the rope aside. Above her, the bell is perched in the tower like a mouth with its tongue hanging out. She hasn't been here in a long time, and it's changed significantly. Dark curtains cover the windows. The pews are oiled and gleaming in the candlelight. There's a lonely chair at the end of the center aisle, in front of the stage and podium. In the far-left corner, a shadowed, motionless figure is slumped over on the stage.

"Eddie." Lydia's voice carries in the dark, quiet sanctuary. "Eddie, what is this?"

There's someone standing in the corner behind her, also draped in shadows. They tilt their head to the side.

Eddie stops at that lonely chair in the center aisle and turns around. "Do you remember what happened last night? What actually happened?"

Lydia tries to think. An image of his proposal comes to mind, but the rest is foggy because they drank too much. She doesn't fully remember, and it's starting to scare her.

"It's okay," Eddie says. "I know you don't."

"Yes, I do! You proposed."

"No, baby, that was two nights ago."

No, no, no, Lydia thinks. *That isn't right.* "If that was two nights ago, then what happened last night?"

Eddie takes her hand and brushes his finger across her clean, chipped nails. "You came home."

36

Lydia stares at her parents' house from the tree line. She's been lying flat on her stomach for an hour, swatting away mosquitos and the occasional ant crawling on her arm. A root keeps poking her ribs, but she doesn't want to move. She's counting on Kathy and Alex quickly giving up their chase, and even if they try to find her at this point, she'll hear or see them coming.

Four cars are currently parked at the Pratt residence, belonging to Mom, Dad, Eddie, and Lydia herself. Everyone's home but her, and where do they think she is, exactly? Her phone is also here, according to Find My iPhone. Surely, if they knew her phone was here, they'd be concerned. But if they weren't the ones who moved her phone, then who else had access to this house?

It's unthinkable that Eddie or her parents have anything to do with what happened to her. Someone could've tossed her phone in the flower beds. There's really no way to know anything without going inside and finding her family and her phone.

She trusts them completely, including Eddie, because one thing has convinced her of his innocence: Kathy and Alex's shared secret. Neither of them put her in the grave, but they know who did, and they're willing to cover it up, to the point of committing murder. That level of loyalty would never extend to someone like Eddie.

But what about Mom and Dad?

Lydia shoves the thought away. No. She's missing something. A lot of things. Maybe if her memory came back, she could get farther, but until then, her surveillance will inevitably lead her inside. There's no other way forward.

She gives it another hour, expecting Alex or Kathy to show up at the house and ask for Lydia, but their street remains quiet. It's ten, maybe eleven o'clock at night. Crickets are chirping, there's an owl somewhere and a woodpecker nearby, working overtime.

When the lights go out and the house is dark, Lydia stands and stretches her sore limbs. Ideally, she can get inside with no one knowing. If she's going to reveal herself to anyone, it'll be Eddie. She needs to start somewhere, and he would have a better notion of her whereabouts compared to her parents, who don't pay much attention to what she does.

Lydia walks through the backyard first. There's no outdoor light on their patio, but the back door is surely locked. She tries anyway, and the doorknob turns. The back door swings open, but Lydia stays outside and shuts it.

No. That's too easy. Are they waiting for her? Could Alex and Kathy have already been here?

No, no, no, she's overthinking. Someone left it unlocked by accident, that's all. Only her parents and Eddie are inside, and none of them are connected to that grave. They think she's somewhere else. They aren't worried or leaving the door unlocked to lure her in.

Lydia shivers, steps away from the door. She can trust them and still remain cautious.

Circling the house, she pushes the trashcan against the garage and climbs on top of it. She peels the gutter guard back, wedges her right foot between the garage and the downspout, and hops onto the roof. She then spins around, crawls across slanted shingles, and shimmies over to her bedroom window. It's always unlocked and usually propped open in the summer because her parents despise using the air conditioning unit.

She pushes the screen up to the top half of the window and then opens the lower half. The curtains spin in the night breeze, offering broken glimpses of her dark room. She lies flat on the roof and leans inside the window to help her eyes adjust. The bed is unmade, but she can't tell if the lump in the center is Eddie or not.

She goes head-first, planting her palms on the carpet and slowly bringing her legs through the window. It's scary how easy it is for *anyone* to get inside her room. Standing, she closes the window behind her, cutting off the nighttime sounds. In the swirling shadows, she can't tell if the lump is breathing. She closes the distance, hovering over her own bed like an apparition, an intruder. Yanking the blanket reveals only a pillow, partially folded.

Eddie's truck is in the driveway, so where is he?

Two shot glasses are on the nightstand. No phone, no charger, not even the box of tissues she normally keeps there. Her bedroom is weirdly messy. Neither of them are super clean, but they at least pick up every day.

There are clothes strewn across the floor, carry out bags crumbled in the corner, and a full bottle of Fireball on her dresser. Unopened. They haven't taken shots together in months.

There's something else. A small black box on the dresser, with the top open. A jewelry case. Lydia holds it close in the faint light; it looks like an engagement ring.

Leaving the ring on the dresser, Lydia slowly opens her bedroom door. The light is off in her parents' room down the hall, but in the bathroom to her right, the shower is running. Eddie's the only one who showers at night, and her parents have their own master bath. She tiptoes to the bathroom door, gently turns the handle, and cracks it open.

The overhead light is off, leaving the small nightlight above the sink shrouded in steam. The shower curtain doesn't move, almost like no one's behind it, or they're standing very still.

"Eddie?"

37

Lydia holds her breath as fingers grasp the edge of the curtain and create a small opening. In the swirling mist, the right side of Eddie's face comes into view.

"Lydia?"

How many times have they showered together late at night while her parents were asleep? All the stifled laughter and mixed drinks, the long showers ending in sex, and the way she'd hug his body to stay warm under a single showerhead, it all comes back. Just breathing in the steam and scent of Eddie's soap makes her want to forget everything. Shower, sleep, and reset. It sounds so peaceful.

Eddie's boyish face is the first normal thing Lydia's seen today, and it makes her heart ache to think of him as dangerous.

He closes the curtain. "I was wondering if you'd come back."

He seems unaware about her day from hell. If he knows, why would he keep it a secret right now?

Still, nothing is certain. She can't blindly trust him. "My car's here," she says. "Do you know where I've been?"

"I thought Aimee picked you up or something. I thought you needed space."

Lydia takes off her clothes; the ones Kathy gave her. Did Eddie notice that she's wearing only a strange bra and sweatpants? But if he believes she's been at Aimee's apartment, he might not have second guessed it.

She sees Eddie's water bottle on the toilet tank lid, where they'd normally set their drinks while they shower, and she picks it up. Considering it's made of metal and has a handle; she could use it to hit him. It's not ideal, and the shower's too small for a full windup, but it makes her feel more protected.

Water bottle in hand, she steps into the shower.

Eddie's washing his hair, his eyes open and questioning. He doesn't move at first, and that's when she sees his chest.

Long, red scratches arch from his collarbone to his lower stomach. At least two dozen streaks, some deeper and darker than others, crisscrossing his torso like a convoluted road map.

"What happened to you?" Lydia's imagination is running wild. They look like the marks you'd get crawling shirtless over a sharp and rigid surface, or they were made by a human during primal, violent sex.

Lydia clutches the water bottle and wonders if she can swing upward hard enough to hurt him. It'll work if she hits him in the balls.

He inspects her body up and down like he's looking for something. "Kathy called me."

Lydia knew this was a possibility, even if she told herself Kathy wouldn't spill to Eddie. Clearly, Lydia was wrong to assume anything. "Did she tell you about the part where she shot at me?"

Eddie frowns. "Why the hell would she shoot at you?"

Lydia's throat is so dry, she uncaps the water bottle and takes a long, heavenly drink. "What *did* she tell you?"

Eddie watches her lips when she drinks, the way he sometimes does when he's turned on, but this is different. It's like he's seeing her in a new light. "She told me about you and Jack."

He steps out of the shower and closes the curtain. Seconds later, the door opens and closes and she's left in the bathroom alone, taking sips of whatever electrolyte packet Eddie added to his water to make it too salty.

Eddie knows her secret now. But that doesn't explain how he ended up with the scratches on his chest. She rinses off, leaves the shower, and dries herself with a towel.

She takes one more look at her parents' closed door and slips inside her bedroom.

The lamp in the corner is on, and Eddie's dressing himself in pajama pants and a white T-shirt. He removes a pajama set, shorts and a tank top, from her dresser drawer, and tosses them on the bed for her. He won't look her in the eye.

"I know you're upset," she says.

"I'm not upset, Lydia. I'm way past that."

There's no way to mend this right now, and unfortunately, Lydia does somehow have bigger problems. She changes into her pajamas. "Did you hear what I said? Kathy *shot* at me. With her gun. *She tried to kill me.*"

"How am I supposed to believe you?" He opens the bottle of Fireball and takes a sip. "How long have you been lying to me?"

Lydia can't do this right now. "Eddie, I know this is a lot, but something's going on. I'll tell you everything you want to know, but someone tried to kill me last night."

"Do you remember it?"

He knows.

Lydia isn't holding his water bottle anymore. It's on the counter in the bathroom, where she set it down to grab her towel. He's four feet away, facing her. His hands are free. She knows better than anyone how fast and strong he is. Beating him hand-to-hand won't end well. She needs *something* to hurt him with.

"Do you remember anything?" he asks softly.

She shakes her head. "What did you do?"

To her surprise, his eyes are misting over. "I laced my water with sleeping pills. Not too much. You'll be okay. But you're a few minutes away from passing out, and I don't want you to hurt yourself."

She can't run or do anything to stop him. "I'll scream if you touch me."

Eddie sits on the edge of the bed. "I love you, Lydia, even if you never loved me. But no one's coming if you scream."

Oh God, what did he do? Are her parents dead?

"Why are you drugging me? If you love me, why would you *ever* do that?"

"You're not going to remember this in the morning, if the memory reset happens again, and we think it will."

He said we, Lydia thinks. *So he's working with Kathy and Alex after all.*

Eddie brushes his damp hair back, glances at the closet, and scoots next to her. Somehow, she doesn't hit him or jump backward. Maybe she's too afraid. The way he looked at the closet makes her sick to her stomach.

Someone else is in here with them.

Eddie whispers in her ear. "I'm going to save you, I promise."

She tries to run, but he grabs her wrist and yanks her onto the bed. He rolls on top of her, pinning her arms to the mattress.

"Eddie—" He covers her mouth with his hand.

She bites his palm, and he jerks his hand back. *"Get off me."*

But he's not stopping. He's not even doing this out of anger. This is something else.

Behind her, she hears the closet door open.

"Help me," Eddie says.

Someone hands him the sash to his robe, which is normally hanging in the bathroom, but Lydia didn't notice it missing.

Eddie forces her hands together behind her back and loops the sash around her wrists.

"I'm not going to hurt you," he says, his voice low and sad. "I'm sorry they shot at you. They weren't supposed to."

She pauses to catch her breath. She's trying to see him in her peripheral, but he's too far away. His voices comes from behind her. She can't see the other person, either. Do they want to stay hidden? Is it someone she knows?

"I'm sorry we had to do it like this. We couldn't think of another way."

She tries to say his name, but her lips aren't moving. Her brain is malfunctioning.

"Shh, you'll be asleep soon. That's all that matters. We need you to forget again, Lydia. Just like earlier, when Kathy found you. We think it's connected to sleep. Something about a solar eclipse. In the morning, you hopefully won't remember any of this. And if you don't, we'll move on to the next phase."

What phase? Her mind is a blurred mess of words and mismatched patterns. Hot tears stream from her eyes, wetting the mattress. She's seeing doubles of everything and getting a woozy, seasick sensation.

"Almost time, baby." Eddie inspects her fingers. "I'll clean your nails after this. We don't want to trigger a memory, if that's even possible with you."

Colors and lights swirl around her, and Eddie's soft, parental voice is distorted and drowned out. He's going on and on, and Lydia faintly hears another voice far behind her. A voice she knows and loves. She flips to her side and almost knocks Eddie off. Then she looks behind her.

Her mom is standing at the foot of the bed, watching Eddie struggle with her. He manages to roll her back to her stomach and keep her there, but the image is burned into her mind.

Her mom is holding Eddie's robe in one hand and a nail file in the other. Her eyes are dry, her lips a flat line. She doesn't offer to help him. She won't even hold her own daughter down.

Eddie promised he'd save her, but that's hard to believe right now. Shadows edge into her vision, growing stronger. As the darkness consumes her mind, a cloudy sky opens to a distant moon crossing over the sun, and she hears Eddie's voice one more time. Two final words.

"Goodnight, Lydia."

38

Behind Lydia, Alex steps out of the shadows, closes the church's front door, and locks it. He's not in uniform anymore, and he's certainly not still at the hospital. She has a sick feeling that helping Jack was never his intention.

"I'm sorry, Lydia," he says, and he really means it.

In the back corner, Pastor Michael leans against the wall, his gaze fixed on her. He doesn't look like a participant in this ambush, but more of a voyeur. It's his church, but why is he here?

She spins around. On the left side of the stage, Jack is slumped over. Even now, after learning the truth, her heart breaks for him.

"Oh my God." Lydia runs to the stage and throws her arms around him. "Jack? Are you okay?" His hands are tied behind his back, and his eyes are mostly shut. He's in the same bloodied condition as earlier. Maybe worse. Sure enough, Alex lied about taking him to the hospital. He might've lied about everything.

"What's wrong with him?" she yells at Alex. "What did you do?"

Eddie's still by the chair in the center aisle. "He's been drugged."

"A little too much," Alex says, walking toward them. "My fault."

"He needs to wake up," Eddie says.

"Got it, didn't know that, thanks." Alex takes his gun and levels it at Lydia. "Sit next to Jack, hands behind your back. Right now."

Jack's feverish forehead is resting against her leg. Is he going to live? What's happening is so far outside her reality, it feels like a joke. "Alex, what are you doing? I haven't done anything wrong. Neither has Jack!"

Alex's face briefly softens. "You're mostly right. None of this is really your fault." He motions with the gun. "Sit. Now. Please."

Lydia sits, dumbfounded. Is this all happening because she was cheating on Eddie?

"Hands back."

She holds her hands behind her, searching Eddie's eyes for answers. "What is this?" she whispers.

Jack groans beside her as Alex ties a thin rope around her wrists.

Michael continues to watch, the candles reflecting in his dark eyes.

"Eddie, what is this?"

Alex picks her up and carries her to the center aisle. He stinks of sweat. Is he more afraid than he's pretending to be?

"I could've walked!"

"Don't trust you," Alex says, slamming her into the wooden chair. Eddie holds her knees down while Alex ropes her feet to the chair's two front legs.

Her body's starting to panic. The feeling of restraint—forming in her hands and feet, slowly rolls across her chest like a heavy stone. "Eddie. Hello? You gonna talk to me at some point?"

He releases her knees and backs away. "I'm really sorry, baby."

His voice makes her pause. "Why are you sorry? Why can't you help me?"

But he turns around. He can't bear to look at her.

Alex takes her phone from her back pocket, drops it on the ground, and crushes it with his boot. He kicks it underneath the pews. What are they planning here? They aren't just trying to scare her, they're acting like—

The door to the back room opens and Kathy walks out, followed by Lydia's mother.

Is she hallucinating? Is this some sadistic intervention?

"Mom, what are they doing?" she says, her voice slipping.

Her mom shakes her head and follows Kathy to the second pew.

"It's getting dark," Kathy says. "We have to do this right now."

No one responds.

Alex sits near the middle right of the room, and Michael stays in his little corner.

"*Can someone please say something!?*" Lydia screams.

Their faces are blank, but it's an act. They're scared and struggling to not show it.

Eddie brings the podium down to their level and places it off to Lydia's right. He sets a piece of paper on the podium and clears his throat.

Did he prepare notes for this? "Eddie, please, this isn't funny. I know you're angry about Jack, but whatever you're doing is royally fucked up. Okay? Is everyone seriously okay with this? Mom! How are YOU okay with this?"

"She has to stop," Kathy says. "Eddie, hurry up."

Eddie looks at his paper. "I know. Lydia, can you wait for me to explain?"

"EXPLAIN WHAT!?"

Alex gets up and walks down the center aisle.

Lydia's trying not to cry. "Look at me, Eddie."

He doesn't, and Alex grabs a fistful of her hair and jerks her head back. He forces a rolled-up bandana between her teeth and ties it behind her head, far too tight. She cries now. What does she have left?

Eddie shoves Alex back. "Don't touch her like that."

Alex chuckles, knocking Eddie's hand away. "Someone has to do this, Eddie, and I know it's not gonna be you."

There's a crash on the other side of the room. Jack's thrashing on the floor, but his feet are tied together, and all he can do is kick the wall. Alex rushes over, grabs Jack by the shirt, and drags him close to Lydia.

Jack tries to scream, but Alex is ready with another bandana. Once he ties it around Jack's head, he leaves him to wiggle and kick on the floor.

Kathy stays deadpan, like she's ignoring some embarrassing event. But Lydia's mom is watching the scene with her hands partly covering her face.

Coward.

Where's her dad? Did they...

No, she won't think about that. Whatever this is has nothing to do with him, and they knew that going in. They knew he'd never let this happen.

"Lydia," Eddie finally looks at her, sweat lining his forehead. "Two nights ago, I proposed to you when we were out to eat. I wasn't planning to do it then, but... I felt like you'd been distant for a while." He pauses, licking his dry lips. "I was scared you didn't love me, and I thought, if you said yes, I wouldn't have to worry anymore."

Lydia strains her muscles, trying to loosen the ropes. From the back corner, Michael slowly shakes his head at her. Is he telling her to stop fighting? How can she sit here and do nothing?

Eddie continues. "You said no, and you wouldn't tell me why. We had a fight back at the house, and I said some hurtful things and you drove off." He pauses again, swallowing. "I wish to God I'd just gone to bed. You don't know how much I regret what happened."

Lydia can't slow down enough to believe him. If she thinks it through, she'll notice he's been giving her the same haunted look all day. Ever since she woke up this morning, struggling to remember last night, he had this look. At the breakfast table, at the gym... even her mom, tearing into her garden and watching her climb the Reaper like an interesting insect. They've been looking at her like she's not human, and now they don't have to hide it.

Eddie's going to tell his story, and judging by the tremor in his voice and the nervousness of his hands, he's telling the truth.

Every word.

Two nights ago, something horrific happened to her.

39

Eddie didn't mean to kill Lydia. It was his fault, but because he struggles to remember how it happened, his mind has been gradually splitting in half from trying to make sense of it.

Since Lydia's death, he's lived as two people. *I am myself,* he's thought all day. *But I am also a killer.*

He has two stories from that night, but one of them he'll never tell another soul. Not to a Pastor, nor out loud to himself. Those words can never be spoken. Tonight, for Lydia's trial, he'll tell the story Michael and Lydia need to hear. The second story, the one that took place after the grave, he'll bury so far down inside himself that he won't find it again. He almost envies Lydia right now. How blissful it must be to wake up and forget everything. He wishes it could be just the two of them here, although he had his chance to tell her earlier and he couldn't stomach it. If his plan works, everyone will calm down once the group hears what Pastor Michael has to say about evil and signs of possession. Even Kathy will be won over.

"I knew Lydia was upset, and I wanted to try one last time to make things right," Eddie tells the group. The church is deathly quiet. Even Jack has stopped to listen.

He was deep into his third or fourth vodka, crying on the back deck of his now former girlfriend's house, when Sharon came outside and sat in the chair beside him. She raised his cup to her nose and sniffed it, took a long sip, and set it back down.

"I guess she said no?"

He wiped his eyes, embarrassed that Sharon was seeing him like this.

"I think she's making a mistake," she said, "if that makes you feel better."

"Not really, but thanks."

She stood up and walked back inside, and despite her endorsement, he felt worse now. But the sliding door opened, and Sharon returned with the bottle of vodka.

"This stuff is nasty." She refilled Eddie's cup before taking a long swig from the bottle. "How do you drink it like this?"

He managed to grab his cup and bring it to his lips. "Because I don't care."

"Fair enough. Where'd Lydia run off to?"

"I don't know."

"Hmm." Sharon checked her phone. "She's not saying shit to me about it, so that's promising. I don't understand that girl."

He'd never heard Sharon talk about Lydia like that before. But at the rate things were going, he wouldn't be living with them come tomorrow. Maybe Sharon knew that and wanted to finally speak her mind.

"What do you mean?" he asked. "You think she messed up?"

Sharon tilted the bottle in her lap, watching the liquid turn inside. "Doesn't it make you mad that she won't tell you why?"

"How do you know she didn't give me a reason?"

"Because I know my daughter better than she knows herself. She has a reason for what she does, but she can't say it out loud. It's all stuck in her head, and she won't let it out."

"You just described her perfectly."

"I know. I thought maybe you were the one who'd open her up a little, get her to relax, and talk about the nonsense in her head. I guess we were both wrong."

They stared at the backyard. At the tree with the weathered tire swing, the beautiful garden, and the female cardinal pecking at the bird feeder. The sun had set, and the clouds were tinted blood-red and shaped into thin rows like a ribcage.

"Did you get your say, at least?" she asked. "Or did she shut you down?"

Eddie didn't want to talk about this with Sharon, of all people, but who else would listen to his sob story? "I mean, we argued, but it went nowhere. She kinda freaked out about it. Like she never saw it coming."

"Makes you wonder why she responded like that."

"I know, but what can I do?" He closed his eyes and drank.

"Find her and tell her your side of things. She invited you into this home, into her room, remember?"

Was there an accusation in her voice, or did Eddie imagine it?

"Seems to me," Sharon said, sipping from the bottle, "that she used you. I know, I love her, she's still my daughter, but even I can see the writing on the wall here. She used you, Eddie. And when you proposed, it made her realize how much she didn't actually love you."

"Ouch." He started laughing. "Geez, Sharon, don't kick a guy when he's down."

"Oh Eddie, this is Lydia's problem, not yours. You did nothing wrong." She patted the top of his hand, her fingers weirdly smooth and cold.

He looked at her. "You mean that?"

She nodded, pulling her hand away. "Lydia owes you an answer. If there's more to her rejection, I think you ought to know."

"More to what?"

"You know, if she's been keeping secrets." She took a long drink.

"You think she was cheating on me?"

Sharon watched the darkening sky. "I think it's worth asking, is all. You might find out a lot of things Lydia's been keeping to herself. She lives in her head, remember?"

Maybe she lives in someone else's head too, Eddie thought. Is that why she rejected him? He pursued her from the beginning. He tried everything to get *her attention and claim a spot in her heart. She was so closed off at first, but he liked that. It felt like a challenge. As if he could win her love like an old-fashioned champion; the knight who jousted for the lady's honor.*

Sharon's hand settled over his again, but he didn't mind. He'd never spent this much one-on-one time with her.

"I deserve to know," he said. "She owes me that much."

Sharon softly rubbed his hand. "Yes she does."

He stood up, brushing her hand aside. "I'm looking for her."

"You can't drive."

"I don't care."

Sharon stood with him. "Let me. You shouldn't be behind the wheel."

"Whatever." He carried the bottle inside the house, slipped his shoes on, and grabbed his keys. The more he thought about it, the more it drove him batshit crazy. Sharon was right. Lydia owed him an answer.

"Selfish bitch," he muttered, starting his truck and moving to the passenger seat, placing the half-empty bottle in his lap.

Sharon came jogging from the house, zipping up a light jacket. She slid behind the wheel, turned the truck around, and started down the road. "We'll go around town first, although I doubt she's in Hope."

He agreed. Not much to do in Hope.

They drove past the community church, but the lights were off. The streets were void of people and cars. Hope residents went to bed early. No reason to stay up when there's nothing happening.

He kept saying, "We have to find her."

The drive was a blurry memory, like looking through a car window in the middle of a downpour. Eddie remembered driving past the Reaper and going for two or three miles before turning around. Sharon shut off the headlights on Route 4 and let the moon guide her until she slowed down near the parking lot and stopped on the shoulder, out of sight. He remembered the moonlight reflecting off Lydia's car, parked beside a car he didn't recognize.

He remembered walking into the woods. He remembered the light touch of Sharon's hand on his back, guiding him forward.

He kept saying, "She could be anywhere. How will we find her?"

Sharon's nails dug into the back of his shirt. She stayed very close to him, their bodies frequently colliding.

"She could be anywhere."

Her grip tightened the way his first girlfriend clung to his back inside haunted houses. Hot breath tickled the back of his neck, making him shiver.

"It's these woods," she said. "I'll never leave these woods." She seemed to regret those words and sharply inhaled with a grunt of pain.

When they heard Lydia's voice by the Reaper, Sharon pulled him under the bridge, where they hid like a couple of cowardly trolls. She then rubbed his back while he cried into his folded arms. He must've run through a spiderweb at some point, because she kept picking sticky strands out of his hair and flicking them to the forest floor. Her hands never left him alone.

Lydia was with a man, in the dark woods, in the same spot Eddie and her had made countless memories. How did she justify this to herself? How does anyone?

When Lydia and the man walked over the bridge and back into the parking lot, Sharon helped him to his feet and led him through the woods. The tide of alcohol had risen over his head, and he felt like he was drowning under a clear summer night sky. What a perfect mess his life had become.

He was suddenly behind the wheel of his truck and shifting it into drive. Sharon was fast-talking and still halfway in the vehicle when he pushed the gas pedal.

Lydia's car was still in the lot, same as the man's. They had walked somewhere close.

He pulled into the parking lot and turned down the dirt road, despite Sharon's continual warnings. His vision didn't work properly, and his headlights flashed different colors until everything became a kaleidoscope. He was going to confront Lydia. She deserved to feel the pain roiling inside of him.

He hurtled down the dirt road, the trees bending into a foliage tunnel. Up ahead, two figures were walking, holding hands. Two people in love, except one of them was a selfish bitch who would break your heart and not tell you why.

Sharon was yelling at him, but he didn't slow down, and he wouldn't look at her. Her features were drooping around the edges like a rubber mask, her voice distorted and gleeful, and she kept saying things about the woods, and Sammy, and how the trees were DANCING.

The two walkers were right in front of him, stepping into the woods to get away, raising their hands to block the high beams.

Eddie recognized the man now: Captain Jack, as they called him; his old football buddy.

Jack and Lydia had their hands up, but they couldn't see anything, and neither could Eddie. When the truck jumped and rocked, Eddie thought he'd crashed through the woods and hit some fallen logs. Only after he slammed on the breaks did he look back and realize the lovers were gone.

40

Lydia replays the story in her head. The vodka, her mom in the passenger seat, Eddie swerving to hit them at the last second. She apparently doesn't remember any of it because of her head trauma. Because a fucking truck ran over her. But if Eddie actually hit them, wouldn't she have obvious wounds? Her legs are always bruised from climbing, so that tells her nothing new; the rest of her feels normal.

The only explanation is that Eddie never actually hit her with his truck. And if so, then how did he get that dent in the hood? How did she lose her memories?

"They were dead," her mom says, hunched over in defeat, like she's the victim! Like there was nothing she could've done to prevent what happened! "We buried their bodies in the woods. I swear they were dead."

Lydia's heart is dying inside her chest. How could her mom do this to her? How could she bury her own daughter in the woods? It's suffocating to even imagine, to try and *rationalize*. Lydia doesn't know where to begin. Clearly, they made a mistake. A series of disasters because no one had truly died.

She can't look at her mom anymore. She can't listen to this.

The bandana makes her jaw ache. Her throat is so dry, every time she swallows, she feels like throwing up. Her wrists are bent awkwardly behind the chair, and her feet are losing circulation. She can't quietly wiggle out of the rope if they're all in the same room. She either needs their focus to shift somewhere else, or someone has to untie her.

Michael's presence makes no sense. Why involve him? If anyone would take her side, it's him. Surely, he knows everyone here is suffering from hysteria and groupthink.

She raises her eyes to him, and he lingers on her, raising his eyebrows in return. He knows she has questions. Is he going to ask them? She widens her eyes, projecting HELP ME as best she can.

Michael dips his head very slightly and smooths his hair back. No one looks at her. They're all concerned with Eddie and her mom, the *real* victims here. Eddie's full-on crying, something Lydia's never seen. It makes her hate him less, to see his guilt, but it doesn't change what he did.

Michael glances at Lydia again. "So why didn't you own up to it, Eddie?"

"I don't know," he says in a daze. "I mean, I was scared out of my fucking mind. I panicked."

"And you?" Michael asks Sharon.

Lydia catches her mom's expression, a flash of disgust that only she can see.

"Eddie and I were scared," her mom says. "We knew there was no coming back from this. But we also knew it was just an accident."

Lydia strains against the rope, screaming into the gag. Her mom's treating her like that dog on the side of the road.

You can't hurt the dead, right Mom?

"Just a stupid accident," her mom says. "We called Kathy and told her what happened. The three of us agreed it was a horrible tragedy, but that no one else should suffer because of it. Enough suffering has happened already; why make it worse? So Kathy swung by our house, picked up two of our shovels, and brought one of her own. We dragged them into the woods and buried them."

Lydia needs this to stop. It's killing her. She's so close to giving up, fighting is starting to feel pointless. What does she possibly have left if her family is willing to bury her alive just to sidestep the consequences of their actions?

There's no happy ending here. If they were willing to bury her to hide their mistake, then imagine the headache her return has been? If this is their solution, where does it end? She has trouble picturing them all shaking hands and agreeing to move on. But then, why not? Isn't her memory slipping through the cracks? What's to stop her from forgetting this night altogether?

Michael taps his finger against his nose, and in his own twisted way, seems to be enjoying this. Maybe he knows something she doesn't. Somehow, he might be her best chance of getting out of here alive.

41

Michael can't take his eyes off Lydia.

There's nothing interesting about her. She's a young, pretty woman. A little aloof. Reserved, untrusting. And somehow, she was raised from the dead? Why?

The thing in his stomach convulses. It can smell the miracle in the room, radiating off the girl tied to the wooden chair. He almost wants to draw closer to her, but he's afraid of what'll happen. He's never felt it wiggle like this.

Why her? What makes her so *special*? Does she even realize the significance of what they're saying?

And apparently, she's only half the miracle. The other half is the man tied up on the floor! Michael doesn't know him. When Alex finally brought him out from the back room a few minutes before Eddie returned with Lydia, Michael asked who he was, and Alex wouldn't share his name or explain why he was being kept there.

Although Michael wants to believe this miracle, he won't accept it without proof. He wasn't there. He didn't *see* it happen.

Lydia makes eye contact with him again. She feels alive and well, doesn't she? This whole thing is entirely nonsensical to her because she doesn't remember dying or waking up.

"We need to clear up one tiny issue though," Michael addresses the group. "How do you know they were dead? Couldn't this have been a freak accident? People have been buried alive before. They wouldn't be the first."

"They were dead," Eddie says.

How many times has Eddie replayed this event in his mind? Especially after the "dead" couple woke up, Eddie must've been circling these questions endlessly. It explains some of his behavior earlier. Eddie's so torn between grief, betrayal, shock, and fear, it's a wonder he can function at all.

Michael gestures to Eddie. "How can I trust your word? You were upset and drunk."

"Because I was with him," Sharon says. She doesn't even look at Lydia's distorted, tear-stained face. "I buried my daughter in the woods, Pastor. You think I wouldn't know if she was dead?"

"Okay, let's assume they died. How did they come back?"

No one wants to answer him. Finally, Eddie speaks up, looking at Michael knowingly. "It's a miracle."

"Not in those woods," Kathy says. "We know the stories. Those woods are a playground for the Devil. Remember what happened to Sammy?"

The room goes quiet again. "We don't know that," Eddie says, glancing at Michael. "That's why we have a *pastor* here."

Alex snorts.

"Before we decide anything," Michael says, "we should hear the rest of the story. We know what happened. We know it was a tragic accident. But the real issue comes with the cover up, doesn't it? Because, miracle aside, a cover up is dangerous and stupid."

No one objects to that. Their fear is palpable.

"But when the cover up literally came back to life and started walking around, that was when you really lost control, wasn't it?"

"I hate myself for what I did," Eddie says. "I knew hiding it was wrong." His back is straight, his shoulders set. He's trying to be a different man.

"But for some divine reason we can't understand, they've been given a second chance, and maybe so have I." He focuses on Michael now, pleading. "If there's a chance I can be forgiven, I'll do whatever I have to. I'll make this right."

Oh, Eddie—he's not clear-headed enough to read his audience. Because Michael sees Alex cupping his hands together and opening them back up, over and over, until Kathy shoots him a look and shakes her head so slightly, Michael almost misses it.

Sadly, Eddie isn't the only fool in this room. Michael should've known better than to follow him here. These good citizens, some of them members of his congregation, are first and foremost, *police*. They know how to manipulate the system. Alex is still employed and has connections and resources none of them can match. They're smart people. They wouldn't have let Michael participate in this meeting if they didn't have a contingency plan for what to do with him afterward.

If he doesn't play their game, he'll never leave this sanctuary.

<h1 style="text-align:center">42</h1>

Eddie will finish his story from that night without the second half. But in his retelling, he'll be forced to confront what happened.

Sharon kept saying, "We have to bury them, we have to be quick." Over and over, even while he sank to the forest floor beside Lydia's body and bawled his eyes out.

She tugged on his clothes. "Get up, Eddie, we have to bury them."

Then Sharon called Kathy and the two of them talked. Eddie couldn't form words or hold thoughts, let alone concoct a plan to get away with double manslaughter. They agreed Kathy should come help and bring their shovels.

"Eddie, get up!"

He held Lydia's hand, brushing strands of hair from her face. She didn't deserve this.

"We need to move them!" Sharon's hands fell on him again, yanking his shirt. "Before someone sees!"

A lonely car came rolling down Route 4, going extra slow. Headlights briefly lit the woods, a sliver of yellow flame glowing on Lydia's cheek before the car turned and disappeared. Sharon had dropped to a crouch, and when the car was gone, she leaned in front of Eddie and held his face in her hands.

"There's nothing we can do, Eddie, except make this go away. Do you understand?"

Lydia's hand was growing cold.

Sharon slapped his face, rocking his head to the side. He barely felt it, but he finally saw the ugly light in her eyes and knew he had to act. He bent down, picked Lydia up off the forest floor, and cradled her in his arms. He pushed into the woods, whispering, "Sorry," in her ear every time a branch raked across her head or pulled on her hair.

Sharon was right behind him, looking over her shoulder.

He eventually stopped. He didn't know where he was exactly, but he caught the sound of water trickling nearby. Through the last row of trees, he found the river. The water glowed white in the moonlight, and beneath the surface, shadows squirmed in the cold depths.

"This is the place."

Sharon came to his side. "Why here?"

"We'll move away from the water a little more," he said, walking back through the trees. "Where the villagers were camped when the floods came."

"You actually think these woods are haunted?" Sharon asked. "Oh Eddie."

He stopped in a small clearing and set Lydia gently on the ground. "Maybe it'll help, somehow. This place. It's history."

"What help? You think the ghosts will keep her company? Where was the help when my baby boy was lost in here?"

It scared Eddie, the way her voice broke and jittered like a puppet learning to talk.

"Where was the help when he died? Where was the help when I came to these woods for weeks, looking for his stuffed bear?" She screamed that last word. It made him flinch.

"There's nothing out here, Eddie. My kids are both gone now because of these woods, so what the fuck do you think that means?"

He didn't know. He couldn't see past his dying heart.

She shook her head at the moon. "There's nothing out here but death and loneliness."

Eddie smoothed Lydia's tussled hair and stood up. "Let's get Jack."

They picked their way back through the woods. An SUV was parked beside his truck, and Kathy stood off to the side, a shovel in each hand, staring at Jack's twisted, lifeless body.

Eddie picked Jack up and carried him through the woods, as he had done with Lydia. He apologized every time a branch nicked his sleeping face.

"How did it feel?" Eddie asked Jack as he set him beside Lydia. "Did she give you everything?"

He wasn't angry. How could he be? He was the monster. Not them. A better man would turn himself in, despite what Sharon said. A better man would do the right thing.

Sharon handed him a shovel. She and Kathy wore gardening gloves.

"One grave," Kathy said. "It'll be quicker."

Eddie knew Kathy and Sharon were whispering things about him, but he did his best to shovel dirt and ignore their words. He wasn't sobering up enough, so he took a break after a while and walked back to the truck and found the bottle of vodka sitting cockeyed in the cup holder. He drank as much as his stomach allowed, but he was getting low. His vision was shot already, how else did he hit them with his truck? But soon the rest of him would drift away as well, and Kathy and Sharon could add him to the mass grave if they wanted. He wouldn't care, and he wouldn't be able to stop them.

After a long time, they packed Jack down and Lydia after. Buried them like seeds. A little water, a little moonlight, and watch 'em grow. Eddie's hands were tired, his thoughts muddled verses of prose. No, not thoughts, but impressions. Yes, an impression of Kathy and Sharon's sweaty bodies reeking of fear and exhaustion. An impression of the mooooon, and it's big, goofy smile.

Eddie was back in his truck, in the driver seat, with an empty bottle in his hand. Where'd his shovel go? Kathy stood beside her SUV, and Sharon had walked back into the woods with a shovel still in her hands. Kathy called to Sharon, and nothing happened. Sharon reemerged from the woods, said she thought she heard something, and they whispered so Eddie couldn't hear them, and then Kathy and Eddie left.

He drove slowly, watching Sharon stand on the dirt road with a shovel in one hand and Lydia's car keys in the other. He stopped on Route 4 long enough to see Sharon dip back inside the tree line, but he couldn't fathom what she was doing. He waited a few minutes, until he saw her in his mirror, walking through the parking lot and using the shovel like a hiking stick—the sharp blade scraping against the asphalt. Then he drove home.

In the little community church, Eddie ends his story here. But his brain keeps spinning even though he doesn't say a word.

He made it home somehow, not that he had far to go, but his brain was so fried, he couldn't remember the drive. He sat in his truck as minutes passed. Sharon pulled into the driveway in Lydia's car and parked beside him.

Only the front porch light was on. Will must've gone to bed. Maybe Sharon texted him a reason for staying out, but maybe not. Their marriage never made sense to Eddie.

"We're disgusting," Sharon said. "We need to clean up and throw these clothes away. Shoes, underwear, everything."

She could tell he was nearly zombified from the vodka, and even through his haze, he felt her disappointment. He did kill her daughter, after all. Why would she do him any favors now? Why keep this a secret at all? Was it because SHE was in the passenger seat, helping him drink and drive and hunt her daughter down?

He found himself in the backyard. Sharon had pressed her finger to his lips and pointed at the house. "Will's asleep. We use the hose, we get inside, and we burn our clothes, okay?"

He briefly felt Sharon pulling his clothes off and leaving him naked in the night air. She rinsed him off, the hose water ice cold on his skin, and left him dripping and shivering until she returned with clothes from his dresser. She helped him change, then she undressed and washed herself while Eddie sat against the house, his head resting against the AC unit.

Not once did he avert his eyes. As she scrubbed the dirt and sweat from her pale, glowing body, the runoff formed a small stream. It snaked toward the house and pooled in the grass beside him. He dipped his fingers into the water and thought she looked younger in the moonlight.

She changed into spare clothes and threw their dirty outfits into the firepit. She helped Eddie to his feet and led him inside, telling him for the hundredth time to be silent.

Eddie woke up in the bed he shared with Lydia, but his new clothes were gone. For a moment he thought this was a dream, and Lydia was still alive and on top of him in the sweetest way. He closed his eyes and pretended it was her, and he tried to drift away again into this black pool in his mind.

He barely felt Sharon's nails carving into his chest, leaving deep gouges from his collarbone to his stomach. It seemed like forever until she was done, but she finally climbed off him and left the room, or he thought she did. He couldn't remember anything except his stomach in turmoil and his chest burning like salt on a wound. He wanted to check for blood, but his hands didn't work, and he eventually found that black pool in his mind and sank and sank until he drowned. The water was warm and thick with debris.

It felt like dying in a pool of wet soil.

43

Michael is aware of the deep history between these folks, but he's never seen it in motion until now. However, there's no reason for them to protect Eddie like they are. Maybe they're doing it solely to keep Sharon free of suspicion, but would she face punishment for being a passenger? Alcohol was involved, and the reason the two of them went out together, while drinking, could be pretty fishy given the outcome, accident or not.

He examines the group. "So, one way or another, you eventually get Lydia back home last night, she falls asleep, and wakes up this morning with no memory of what happened? Just a big reset and everyone goes back to normal? She didn't realize she had a gap in her memory?"

"We tried to explain that." Eddie nods to the others. "We made up stuff about drinking Fireball and blacking out just to give her enough reason to doubt her memory and not think too hard. I mean, can you remember what you ate for lunch two days ago, especially if there's no reason to remember it?"

Michael laughs. "Sure, Eddie, but I think I'm missing the point. So Jack and Lydia wake up this morning without remembering anything after the event two nights ago, I got that right?"

They all nod along.

"Then what was the point of letting Lydia go her whole day today as normal? Just to see if you could get away with it and move on like it never happened?"

They're quiet for a minute. "We didn't know what we were dealing with," Eddie says.

"I'd say that's a huge understatement. What do you mean?"

"We didn't know if *Lydia* was actually back from the dead."

"As in, if Lydia was alive or not? You couldn't accept the possibility that you might've made a mistake and buried her alive?"

Eddie frowns. "She was dead, Pastor. We know that. We were there. But we had to be sure." He looks at the others, mostly skipping over Sharon, which is interesting to Michael. Why has he largely ignored the presence of his partner in crime?

"So we all decided," Eddie says slowly. "That before we made a final decision, we would conduct an experiment on her. And we did that today. We tested her memory of old and new events. We asked a lot of questions. Sharon and Kathy took her into the woods near the grave to see how she'd react. Some of us were worried about demonic influence or possession." Eddie tips his head at Michael. "That's why we needed to do this in a church with a pastor present. We need to know what we're dealing with."

"You think there's a chance she's possessed?"

They look uncomfortable. "Those woods aren't safe," Kathy says. "Have you heard the stories?"

"A little bit," Michael says. "Though I'd argue it's mostly folklore. What happens if you decide that Lydia never came back to life? That something else took over her body. What then?"

No one wants to say it. Michael knew they were heading this direction the whole time, but it only now dawns on Lydia, and she starts screaming into her gag and contorting her body.

"Nothing's been decided." Eddie raises his voice. "We'll look for the signs, right Pastor? If there are no signs, how can she be dead? Look at her!"

"She was dead," Alex says. "People don't come back to life for no reason."

"She's not a zombie." Eddie keeps pointing at her like it proves something. He knows they don't agree with him. "Will you look at her!?"

"That's why we're doing this, Eddie," Kathy chimes in. "To determine what she is. But we need to do this now. We can't wait anymore."

They're going to kill her, Michael thinks. *It's not trial, it's a sentencing. They already believe she's dead and that she needs to be put back in the grave. That's all this is: a confession. They aren't justifying what they did, they're justifying what they're about to do.*

44

Lydia's been here before.

Not in this exact circumstance, of course, but her body has been *here* before.

Trapped. Hopeless. Broken.

Time's running out. They'll kill her if she doesn't escape now.

She snaps her head back, rocking the chair. Leaning forward, she tries again. This time the chair falls backward and breaks against the stage. She doesn't feel the whiplash or the sharp jab in her spine because as she struggles to raise her arms and legs, a suffocating déjà vu overwhelms her.

The body remembers.

When Alex tied her to the chair, he didn't plan on it falling over. Maybe he didn't care. Maybe he knew she could fight all she wanted and it wouldn't matter. It's five to one.

The rope slips off the chair legs and uncoils around her ankles. She spins out of the broken chair, her hands still tied behind her back, and backpedals onto the stage. No one's made a move to stop her. She can't scream with the gag in her mouth, and they locked the door, so what would they worry for?

Eddie approaches her with his palms open, his voice low. "Lydia, it's not worth it. Let me fix this."

YOU HEARD THEM, she wants to scream. THEY'RE GOING TO KILL US.

Kathy stands. "We're wasting time."

Lydia sprints down the right side of the sanctuary, and still, no one stops her. Eddie and Alex wander down the center aisle like they're chasing a rowdy toddler. They think she's going for the front door, but they aren't thinking big enough. She's spent the last hour scouring the church's interior for anything useful. It's what kept her sane during that... *story* Eddie told.

Instead of running to the front door, she stops in the narrow foyer, spins around, and grips the hanging rope with her tied hands. She drops to one knee, bringing the rope down. Above her, the bell tower explodes with a reverberating ring.

Alex dashes toward her.

She jumps and pulls the rope again, forcing another thunderous ring as Alex finally rips the rope away. He shoves her body against the front door and draws his fist back.

Eddie comes from the side and deflects the punch. Alex's fist clips her ear instead of cracking her skull open. Everywhere, people are yelling. Eddie tries to tackle Alex, but he shrugs Eddie off and draws his gun. Kathy and her mom are waving their arms, shouting for them to stop, and Michael's somewhere in the background, crossing to the other side of the room. Lydia can't see what he's doing. Her view is blocked by Eddie, who's agreed to calm down if Alex will.

Alex retrieves a fresh chair from the back room and ties Lydia to it all over again, this time ensuring the rope won't slip off the front legs.

Michael is back in his corner with a stupid, satisfied smile on his face. She's not sure what he did during the commotion, but maybe it'll help save their lives.

"We need to hurry," Kathy says. "Great idea boys, putting a bell in here."

Alex is breathing hard. He adjusts his belt with both hands and nods at the others. "Let's be quick, before someone comes. This is the kind of shit we can't predict! It's exactly what I was afraid of!"

Kathy stands at the podium. The only person she seems to make eye contact with is Sharon.

She clears her throat. "My time with Lydia was unique. I spent most of yesterday with her. And I noticed some disturbing signs. Lydia was physically ill, which may have been a side effect of, well, coming back from the dead. She also told me extensively about a vision she kept seeing, regarding a solar eclipse in her mind, which is important, I believe. When I brought her home, my cat, Tiger, wouldn't leave his spot under the couch, and I know, I know that's not proof—"

Eddie stands up. "This isn't a joke."

Kathy waves him off. "He was scared of her! So was I. Then the crows in the front yard, you should've seen the way they reacted to her—"

"We're not accepting this," Eddie hisses. "Birds? You're trusting some fucking crows to tell you whether or not Lydia's her normal self?"

"Let her talk," her mom says.

"I could tell from the moment she stepped in my house, something was wrong with her." Kathy takes a breath. "In my opinion, we don't know what she is, but I stand by what I said. Nothing good can come from those woods."

Kathy rushes away, and all Lydia can do is imagine these stories as the truth. Was Tiger scared of her? Did crows treat her differently? It sounds truly insane, but here she is. If everything they're saying is true, shouldn't she at least consider the possibility that she returned from the dead?

And what about the eclipse? Lydia closes her eyes briefly. It's the first time she's kept her eyes closed all day, and to her surprise, the shadows in her mind morph into great black plumes against a navy-blue sky. She doesn't see an eclipse, but maybe it's hidden. The clouds are frightening enough; she opens her eyes and blinks the smoky tendrils away.

Her mom stands up but does not use the podium. She intends this to be quick.

Lydia wishes they'd kill her now. Just shoot her and be done with it. She's more scared of what her mom is about to say than she is of dying.

"I had three important conversations with Lydia today," her mom says. "One about Eddie and their relationship, and two about Sammy."

At the mention of his name, the room grows quieter.

"Lydia used to be such a cute little girl," her mom says. "She would draw pictures for me, even into her teen years, and if we had a fight, or she was upset with me about something, she always found a way to make it right, and more often than not, she used her drawings to tell me she was sorry. That little girl is long gone, and I know kids have to grow up, but I miss her so much."

Lydia already knows what's coming, and the sad part is, her mom is partly right.

"I didn't recognize her today. She's not the thoughtful, kind girl I know. She's closed off. She's secretive. And when I brought up Sammy earlier, there wasn't a shred of kindness or empathy in her heart."

That's not true, Lydia thinks. *I tried to hold your hand, Mom, remember? It was you who pulled away, not me. It wasn't me this time.*

Why is her mom lying? Why is she so convinced her daughter is actually dead? Even though her mom's right: Lydia *has* been closed off, and in her own world, and selfishly trying to live an impossible life that didn't start today. It's been happening for a year. That's what a secret does. It slowly hollows you out. Lydia knows that now; now that it's too late to change. Looking at her mom, she has an idea of what secrets can do to a person. There's another reason why her mom believes Lydia is dead. Why won't she say it?

"I loved Lydia," her mom says, her closing statement. "We all did. And we tested her all day, hoping to find that spark of who she really is. But we didn't find it. That *thing* in the chair is not my daughter."

Whatever is left of Lydia's heart disintegrates inside her chest. A final heartbeat. A whisper in her ear, saying, *No one can come back from this. You can die now or live forever as a walking, heartless corpse.*

Strangely, Kathy doubles over in the pew and grips her hat with both hands and clenches her teeth so hard Lydia hears them grinding. Kathy rocks back and forth. Her eyes are blood-red and wet, and she keeps looking at Lydia like she's seeing someone else.

Under different circumstances, Lydia would feel bad for Kathy, but she's reminded of the way her mom tore up her garden earlier, and she wonders if either woman truly feels any guilt over what they're doing or what they're about to do.

Eddie wipes a trickle of sweat from his face. "Pastor, you be the judge. You know the signs, right? You know what evil looks like. Can you see it in this room?"

All eyes turn to Michael, but he's mulling over Eddie's words.

Lydia waits with the rest of them.

Is she the inhuman creature they're making her out to be? She's partially curious now, but she doesn't like the way Michael's heavy gaze settles on her, or how he turns to everyone in the church and says, "I'll know if there's an evil presence here, but I need to do it my way. And I have to talk with Lydia alone."

45

Kathy's mind is a melting pot of memories, smells, and sounds. There are footsteps in the hallway, and they echo throughout the quiet house.

After leaving the gravesite, Kathy went home and hid the shovel beneath her bed in the corner of her room, and not long after, her phone rang.

She answered to Alex screaming, "SHE'S FUCKING ALIVE, KATHY! WHAT THE FUCK DID YOU GUYS DO WRONG?"

"Slow down, slow down."

But Alex kept going, "She's alive, she's alive!"

Kathy shook and trembled in her living room and the footsteps started to creep down the hall and listen to her cry.

"How do you know what happened?" she asked.

"Sharon called me and asked if I'd keep an eye on things."

Of course, Sharon would refuse to take the fall for this, and she was shoring up her defenses, starting with a man who could divert the law if needed. A man they knew well. A man easily manipulated. Kathy could almost hear Sharon's sad purring voice through the phone, and how easily Alex would've come alive for her again, the way he did after Sammy, always helping out at the bakery and telling Will his best jokes and playing Yahtzee with Lydia to prove he was more than a man who wanted to get laid.

"I saw her, Alex. She was dead!"

"Well I just drove past her, and she looks totally fine to me. What are you going to do about this?"

"I'll take care of it. Did you call Sharon?"

"She didn't answer. Holy shit." Alex honked his horn. "There's a guy in the middle of the road. He looks completely lost." The horn blared again. "What the hell is going on?!"

"Alex." Kathy's chest started to hurt. The footsteps were behind her now. Patter-patter. "Is the guy wearing gym shorts and a shirt with a front pocket?"

"Well, yeah, but how did you..." Alex punched something. "No, come on, no! Fuck! He's covered in dirt."

Kathy moved out the door, away from the patter-patter. "You have to take care of him."

"I am not killing someone for you!"

"You don't have to. See what he knows, keep him busy, and I'll take care of it."

"What will you do?"

Kathy started her SUV and peeled out of the driveway. "Find Lydia."

***

Kathy watched Lydia stare at the dirt road. She was trying to work out the tire tracks, bless her heart.

She approached slowly, carrying her fishing rod and tackle box to appear at ease. It worked. When she called out to Lydia, the young woman leapt into her arms, and Kathy couldn't bring herself to put the girl down, no matter how important it was, to all of them, for her to do just that.

There was a twinge of sadness in that embrace, making Kathy think of her baby girl, and how she would've given anything to hold her one last time.

And Lydia couldn't remember anything. How could she be a threat if she had no memories?

So Kathy took her home.

While Lydia showered, Kathy called Sharon and told her what happened: Lydia and her lover, Jack, were both alive. She had Lydia and Alex had Jack. What should they do?

***

Sharon came over and Lydia hid in the spare bedroom. Kathy pretended like she didn't know this was going to happen. She met Sharon outside.

"How's she doing?" Sharon asked.

Kathy explained the memory loss, Tiger's bizarre behavior, and her fear that Lydia's going to remember something. "How's Jack?"

"He's okay. Alex is keeping him at his apartment. He's giving him something to keep him under control."

"What do we do about this? Lydia doesn't remember."

"She doesn't remember yet," Sharon whispered. "We have to put her back."

Kathy inhaled sharply. "She's mostly normal, Sharon. You should see her."

"You saw them last night." She gripped Kathy's shoulder. "You know they were dead. How can they be alive if something didn't bring them back?"

"The Bible is full of miracles—"

"What miracles have you seen? Where were the miracles when our babies were taken from us? What miracle would restore Lydia's body and not her head? Don't you see it yet? There's something wrong with the woods, and it's gotten into my daughter."

Kathy had no answers, only more questions. Until now, she hadn't considered the nature of Lydia and Jack's resurrection. But she saw it now, the dead light in Lydia's eyes.

Sharon instructed her to bide time without giving herself away, so she could call Alex and Eddie and come up with a reasonable solution.

"What if she remembers something?"

"There's only one way we get through this, do you understand? It doesn't matter what she remembers or if the Devil himself brought her back to life. You and I are walking away from this." Sharon looked Kathy in the eye. "Eddie raped me last night, after we went home."

Kathy's world was a strange place, growing stranger. She could nearly smell the sweat and uncertainty pouring out of Sharon's skin. "Can you prove it, if you have to?"

Sharon barely nodded her head, but Kathy felt a little better. Sharon always found a way to keep going.

"Do you still hear footsteps?"

Kathy wondered why she'd ask that. "Yes."

Sharon appeared satisfied and said, "I'll be calling you soon, but be careful around Lydia. That girl is dead. This thing is just pretending to be her."

Kathy thought about that over and over as she went back inside to find Lydia in her bedroom with the dirty shovel in her hands. Lydia was so angry, it was hard to see the young woman Kathy used to know. Kathy kept thinking about pretending and footsteps and after staring at Lydia for a while, she didn't look human anymore. Her eyes were full of dead light.

***

Kathy called Sharon's number, her hands trembling. She stood in the dark woods on the other side of Route 4. Across the clearing, Alex glared at her, his uniform drenched in sweat.

"Hello?"

"I tried to shoot her, Sharon. I don't know what happened, I swear, I thought she was remembering everything. I didn't know what to do!"

"Slow down, what happened?"

"I'm telling you she's going to remember!"

"Kathy!" Sharon yelled. "Where is Lydia?"

Alex shook his head at her.

"We think she's going home," Kathy said. "We didn't have time to tell you, but she forgot everything from this morning. It's like her memory reset when she fell asleep, but I don't think it's going to stay that way."

Kathy explained how it occurred. Jack's apartment, Lydia's answers to their questions. Had she truly forgotten everything? Or were the memories lingering?

"I'm sorry. I know I messed up," Kathy said. "I just got so scared. I know she's your daughter, I just... I don't know what to think anymore."

Sharon was silent on the other end.

"What should we do?"

Alex looked up. He would do whatever Sharon asked of him. It was his nature. He even had Jack stowed away at his own house, thoroughly drugged up, because she asked him to. He'd been using Jack's phone to text his wife, text Lydia, text whoever just to buy time.

"Let her come home," Sharon said slowly. "I'll put her to sleep, and we'll see if her memory resets again."

Kathy could almost hear the thoughts clicking like an intricate machine.

"I'll call you," Sharon said. "Once she's asleep, you, me, Alex, and Eddie are going to have a long talk."

"About Lydia?" Kathy felt the need to clarify, given she couldn't tell if Sharon was upset with her for shooting at her daughter.

"About how to finish this."

Kathy turned away from Alex, lowering her voice. "What about Eddie?"

"This only ends one way, Kathy. Do you understand me? Eddie will pay for what he did to me, and to Lydia."

Kathy ended the call and looked for the stars, but the dense foliage blotted out the sky.

It was going to be a very long night.

46

Michael thinks back to what Eddie said after they found the bell: *If there is an evil thing in Hope, and if you see it tonight, can you kill it for me?*

Eddie wasn't talking about Lydia; he meant the others. He doesn't believe their motives, and Michael now understands why.

Because if hitting and killing Lydia and Jack were truly an accident, then why aren't they trying to amend their mistakes and still get away with it? Surely, with the broken memories, there's a good chance neither of them will ever remember the accident or be able to prove it ever happened.

When Lydia and Jack came back to life with their memories wiped, it should've been met with life-changing relief, not a cause for panic. Why spend two days in constant fear, scheming, and communication? Why create a makeshift trial to prove if they are human or not? It's like they *want* Lydia and Jack to stay dead.

Michael's missing something obvious. He keeps wondering why these people would put their necks out for someone like Eddie. But what if they're not?

He looks at the sanctuary, the candles, and the two prisoners bound and gagged. Unfaithful lovers, their sins exposed.

They won't let me leave this place, he thinks. Even if he agrees with them, there's no chance they simply let him walk away.

That's why he needs to stall. Something will happen—it always does.

"You have two minutes, Pastor," Alex says. "And be careful. We don't know what she is."

Michael tries not to laugh. "She's only human, I'm afraid. We *all* are."

Alex grins. "You're not thinking big enough. What happens if anyone finds out about these woods, and their... power? I know it's crazy, but if we accept that these two were dead, and the woods brought them back to life, then it can be replicated. Imagine a secret like that getting into the wrong hands. People digging up their freshly buried loved ones and giving them a special plot by the river. Hasn't anyone considered the implications of this?"

Michael wonders, *Can it be replicated?* "I don't know, Alex. No one knows. That's fine if you see it as your duty to guard this secret from the hounds of this world. But it's my duty to address evil where I find it. I need to speak with her."

He walks toward Lydia and ignores the others. They huddle near the back, their voices rising and falling nervously. Michael really might only have two minutes to save Lydia's life, and his own.

He spins Lydia's chair around so she's facing the cross on the back wall.

"Mike!"

"Acknowledging the cross is a good idea, sheriff, you should try it sometime," Michael calls.

Alex mutters something very profane for a sanctuary, but Lord knows, this church has seen its share of hell today.

Michael sits on the stage and leans close to Lydia. "I want to say that I'm incredibly, deeply sorry for what's happened to you."

She blinks. She doesn't trust him.

"There's no excuse for this, I don't care how scared they are," he says. "Eddie brought me in, as you've gathered, to consult on demonic possession. You and I both know that's not what this is."

Her eyes widen and she dips her head, mumbling into the gag. It sounds like a prayer for help.

"I know, I know. I'm on your side, Lydia. You've done nothing wrong. In fact, I think you're a miracle. If it's all true, if you died and came back, then you must be important. You know what I'm saying? Your life *means* something. Isn't that wonderful?" The thing in his stomach is swelling, inching closer to his skin, as if it can smell her. "I'm a little jealous, actually. I've been a bit of a cynic myself, all my life, because more than anything, I want to believe in a higher power, but I can't. I refuse."

She's confused now, but he's getting to it.

"*You* are my proof, Lydia. I'm starting to believe their story, but not the part about possession. I think you're dealing with traumatic circumstances, and anyone would've acted the same as you have. There's nothing suspicious about that. Now, we don't know each other very well, but I've wanted to get to know you for a long time, and I hope that will change. It's nice to meet you, finally. But I wish, of course, things were different, because I have to tell them what they want to hear."

The light starts to drain from her eyes.

"Hold on, wait. I think you're incredible," he whispers. "You're my little miracle. I won't let them hurt you. Jack's hands are untied. I did that while you rang the bell, which was very clever of you, I should say. That bell might be the miracle we need."

Alex is inching closer to the center aisle. Michael needs to hurry. "I need you to lash out, right now. We need to sell this to them, all right? Wait for my signal. I'll get you and Jack out of this. I know you don't want to give them the satisfaction, but it's the only way they'll trust me long enough to make my move."

"Pastor?"

"One second, Alex." Michael bows his head and places his hand on Lydia's shoulder. He pretends to pray and waits for her.

Sure enough, she lurches in her seat. The chair rattles on the old wooden floor and Michael scrambles backward on the stage.

"What'd you say to her?" Eddie runs toward them.

Michael glances at the cross and then back at Lydia. "It's real," he sputters, finding his feet. "You were right; she's not herself."

Eddie kneels beside Lydia, who's breathing heavily and straining against the rope. He looks at Michael. "You told me you knew the difference!"

"I do. You're the only one who can't see it, Eddie."

It's no surprise when Eddie leaps onto the stage and shoves him. He collides with the back wall, knocking over several candles. "Eddie, stop, you don't know what you're doing!"

Eddie swings his right fist and Michael ducks, kicking more candles aside.

Alex grabs Eddie and drags him away. He's nodding at Kathy, who nods in return. They're about to do something irreversible. Why has it taken Michael so long to understand? Of course they'd never keep Eddie's secret! That was never their plan.

"I believed you!" Eddie screams. "I was with her today! You don't know a fucking thing about her."

Michael watches the loose candles slowly roll along the uneven stage, leaving trails of hot wax. He knows why they chose this church, why they decorated it like this. It has nothing to do with whether Lydia and Jack are genuinely themselves or not. This was designed to look like a ritual, because when two secret lovers are found by the police, tied up and executed, every piece of evidence will point to Eddie and his radicalized, scheming pastor. All the others need to do is kill Lydia and Jack with an unregistered gun, maybe the one strapped to Alex's ankle, and the rest will take care of itself.

The problem is that Eddie doesn't realize this, and Michael has no way of telling him without tipping off the others. Although in a few moments, it may not matter. Everyone's on the same page now.

All that's left is the killing.

47

Still tied to this chair, forced to watch the chaos unfold, Lydia feels someone gently rub her shoulder. Kathy and Alex are on the stage, talking Eddie down. Michael's backing into the far corner, rambling because he can't tell Eddie what he's really doing and Eddie's too blind to see through it. Can't Eddie tell the others are not on his side?

The hand squeezes her shoulder and the chair spins around until she's facing her mom. Lydia doesn't want to hear a single word from that woman's mouth, but she has no choice. Her mom leans in close so Lydia has nowhere else to look.

Then she touches her forehead against Lydia's and places her hand on the back of Lydia's neck. What used to be a loving gesture is now a vice grip. Her fingers dig into Lydia's throat.

"You left the front door open," her mom whispers. "At the Fourth of July party, you couldn't find me, and you opened the front door to check outside. You left it open. And we lost Sammy."

The front door is perfectly alive in Lydia's mind. It's swaying in the hot summer breeze. The gravel driveway stretches out forever, and the night is filled with screeching fireworks.

"We never told you," her mom says, voice low. "We didn't want that burden on you. But I will never forget what losing my baby feels like. And I've spent the last twenty-one years looking at you and only seeing him. If you knew the things we hid from you all those years ago, you'd think we were crazy." Her mom smiles like she's in a daydream "And maybe we were. Maybe we should've told you the truth a long time ago."

Because of the gag, Lydia can't say what she wants to. *It's your fault,* she inwardly screams. *I was five years old. How can you possibly blame me for losing Sammy?*

Lydia tries to bend her neck, but her mom clamps down, her nails cutting through the skin. Lydia twists and strains, biting the bandana in her mouth. If her hands were free, she'd slap her mom's face. *Where were you that night?* She would scream. *Where were you?*

"Eddie didn't see you and Jack on the side of the road," her mom continues, saying each word slowly, like she's talking to a child. "He wasn't sober enough for that. I jerked the wheel from his hands and drove it off the road. He gave me an opportunity, and I took it."

After the things her mom said a few minutes ago, Lydia's heart is too far gone to damage further. Instead of shock and pain, she feels immense clarity. The possession scare is her mom's way of keeping Lydia dead, with her own hands washed clean of wrongdoing. It wasn't an accident after all, but a murder.

"You should've stayed in that grave," her mom says. "Then none of this mess would've happened." She turns her back on Lydia and sits down.

Lydia sees Eddie in the corner of her eye, storming off the stage with Alex and Kathy on either side. It all makes sense now. He's their scapegoat, and he really doesn't know, does he?

They'll get him for double homicide. Even Alex earlier, telling Lydia in the back of his SUV that Jack had said something about a "red truck" on the road. Or her mom and Kathy in the woods, making implications about Eddie's character. They were laying the groundwork. Perfecting their stories. Going through the motions of giving Lydia and Jack a fair "trial," even as they plot their murders. This would've been so much easier for them if Lydia had stayed dead because now they're forced to finish what they started. The worst part is, this seems painfully obvious to Lydia now, and to everyone else except Eddie.

His prints are everywhere, and with Lydia cheating on him, the motivation is too classic. Even if he tries to argue about their involvement, how much proof is available? They could spend days erasing everything that links them to Lydia and Jack. Even their numerous phone calls the last two days could be because they're old friends and were concerned about Eddie's post-marriage-rejection behavior.

Eddie truly never meant to hurt her, and if he's killed tonight or if he spends his life in prison, it'll be because of her mom. Yes, he's made countless mistakes, and he never should've listened to Kathy and her mom and participated in this fucked up experiment. Maybe he deserves punishment for his part, but he's going to take *all* of it while the rest get away.

Is there a way she can warn him? After what her mom said, there's no chance the gag will come off.

Michael seems to already know this will end horribly. Serves him right, after trying to save his own skin by lying about her—

Movement on the far side of the stage catches Lydia's eye. From the shadows, a black, double-barreled shotgun slowly emerges from the back room. Her dad lifts his well-oiled weapon, aiming it at the others.

"Step away from my daughter," he says calmly.

Everyone is stunned at the sight of him. "How?" Alex asks, reaching for his holster.

"Hands in the air, Alex," her dad says. "Right now!"

"Okay, okay." Alex raises his hands. "Was the back door *unlocked*?"

Lydia thought she'd lost everything, that things couldn't get worse. But seeing her dad face them down with only two rounds in the shotgun and no backup, she realizes how naïve she'd been. And to think, only this afternoon, she was afraid of watching her parents grow old.

Please no, please no, she tries to scream.

"You idiots," Michael says. "You didn't lock the back door?"

Eddie's shaking his head, raising his hands.

"How'd you know we were here, Will?" Alex asks.

"I heard the bell."

Michael looks at Lydia and smiles.

"But why were you looking for us?" Alex's voice is rising.

Her dad takes a deep breath. "We had dinner plans. No one was answering me, so I drove through Hope, saw Eddie's truck down the way, and walked around. That's when I heard it."

Lydia thinks back to that morning at the shooting range. A lifetime ago. Her dad offered to take her on a father/daughter date after her breakup with Eddie. How could she have forgotten?

"I've been listening," he says. "For a little bit, anyway, and I'm pretty fucking lost."

Sharon hugs herself, appearing small and helpless. "Will—"

"I heard what you all said!" He tilts the shotgun in her mom's direction. "I saw you whispering to her. What did you say? I don't know what you're doing or why, but I know it's wrong. You have our daughter tied to a chair. I don't need to hear the rest. Nothing you can say will change my mind. I've already called the police, and they're on their way. You have two minutes before they get here, so I suggest you all get to your knees and keep those hands high, and we'll let them sort this out."

No, no, no, Dad, Lydia thinks, *why didn't you wait? You've left them no choice.*

Kathy lifts her hands. "Will."

"SHUT UP AND GET ON YOUR KNEES!"

"I thought you checked on them this morning," Kathy snarls at Alex.

"I did!" he yells. "They were just shooting. How was I supposed to know they made plans!"

I'm going to lose them, Lydia thinks, *Oh God, I'm going to lose them.*

"I SAID GET DOWN, NOW!"

"We can't," Sharon says, barely above the noise. "No one can stop this."

Kathy's hands disappear inside her jacket, and she's suddenly holding a gun and squeezing the trigger. It takes a split second. Even before Lydia can scream or rattle her chair or do anything to prevent this, the candles flicker, and the air ignites with exploding cannons.

48

The moment Will Pratt magically appeared in the sanctuary, Michael knew someone had made a deadly, costly mistake. For all their scrambling, rushed plans, and cover ups, no one seemed particularly worried about Lydia's father. And considering the two of them made special plans at some point today and no one was around to witness it, only now do Sharon and her friends realize the true extent of their error. A stupid, careless mistake.

Will obviously loves his daughter, and his need to protect her is so strong, he came in before the police arrived. Also a stupid mistake. The day is full of them.

And when Kathy flinches and draws her gun, Michael knows the mistakes will go on and on and on until everyone is dead. Except him. He won't leave this earth without his miracle.

He drops behind the last pew as splintered wood and warm blood sprays over him. The little church rings with a thousand bells, joined by Eddie screaming beside him.

Michael crawls across the floor and peers down the center aisle, flat on his belly.

Jack has undone his ankle ties and is sliding along the floor *away* from Lydia, who is still tied to the chair. Michael wasted precious time helping him earlier. He won't do that again. But he can't get to Lydia without catching the crossfire.

He crawls to the right side of the room as silence falls. Or he thinks it's silence; he can't hear anything. Placing his cheek to the floor, he sees the opposite corner of the room, where Will should be dying in a pool of his own blood.

Except he's not there.

He looks behind him. Alex and Kathy are on their knees, reloading. Eddie's beside them, his face torn with tiger-like gashes.

Will must've retreated into the back room, either to reload or bleed out. Michael doesn't hear any sirens yet—how much longer do they have? Seconds? He doesn't want to be here when the police show up, but he's not leaving without Lydia.

On his left, Kathy and Alex raise their weapons.

"Look out!" he yells. It's enough to make Alex pause and duck his head, but it doesn't work on Kathy. She's probably deaf from the gunfire. Her hands are steady. She takes aim.

Michael sinks back to the floor as the *boom-boom-boom* of Kathy's gun rattles the windows.

The shotgun reappears, hovering in the back room's shadows. Will is still alive! Kathy slides to the floor; the shotgun roars twice, nearly disintegrating the last two pews. His little church will never recover from this.

Neither will this town.

While everyone reloads and holds their breath. Alex edges around the left side of the pews in a slow crouch, gun pressed to his cheek. Will is no longer visible, and Jack is still slinking away like a worm.

Michael doesn't trust himself to sneak up behind Kathy and stab her with the needle file. She keeps twitching like a bird, left-right-straight-back so she has eyes on every direction.

He can't save Lydia like this.

Sprinting past the hanging rope, he unlocks the front door and slips outside. There's a figure on the sidewalk across the street, who immediately dashes inside the nearest house and slams the door. Michael listens for sirens again and still hears nothing.

He could run away now and disappear. It worked with Darling; it can work with Hope. He would do it in a heartbeat, if not for Lydia. They have to escape now before Alex and Kathy murder everyone inside.

The path is very clear before him. Unlike that river in Darling and the old dying man, this path is his destiny. The miracle is here, and everything he's ever wanted is at his fingertips.

Miracles require action.

He runs down the front steps and around the corner, praying this works.

49

Lydia tries to keep track of everyone.

Alex is halfway down the left-side wall, close to the back room where her dad is hiding, and hopefully still alive. Jack is on the floor next to her, hands over his ears. It looked like he was crawling *away* from her before Alex started coming up the left side, forcing him to retreat. Michael unlocked the front door and ran out, so he gave up. Her mom has completely vanished, somehow. And Eddie...

He's crouched behind the pews near the center aisle, and he's looking at her with bloody streaks across his face.

No, she thinks. *I won't let him die.*

No one is dying today.

She shakes her head. She knows exactly what he's thinking, and she can't let him do it.

In the hushed room, Eddie's uneven voice seems to make everyone ponder, however briefly, if this could possibly be worth the cost. "I made you a promise," Eddie says, and charges down the center aisle, sliding at the end so he stays between the pews. He's now on the ground a few feet in front of Lydia, while on her left, Jack struggles to his hands and knees.

Alex leans against the wall where Lydia's dad can't see him. He tilts his gun toward Jack, gritting his teeth, but he doesn't fire. It'll give away his position.

Jack slowly stands up, raising his hands. But Alex doesn't move.

From the back, Kathy glances over the pews and settles on Jack.

"We can't stay," Jack says, turning toward Lydia, his lower lip trembling. He'd reopened the wound on his head, blood seeping through his hairline.

No, Jack, please don't, she thinks, scooting her chair forward.

But it's no use. Jack spins around and runs across the room. Lydia can't look away. There's a chance, if he can get down the right side and out the door—

Alex and Kathy take four shots each and half of them land. Red mist speckles the wall, and Jack is dead before he topples to the ground.

Alex doesn't see the shotgun peeking out of the back room. He stands against the wall again, goes to pull his pistol to his chest, and his hands are gone with a clap of thunder. A second shot follows, and he's thrown to the ground in pieces.

Eddie runs to Lydia and tears at the rope, freeing her from the chair when two shots ring out and he's knocked into her lap, his body limp. Two bloody bullet holes mark his back, and behind the last pew, Kathy lowers her gun.

Lydia yanks her gag off and tries to keep Eddie upright, but he slips to the ground and coughs, spitting blood down his shirt.

A shotgun blast fills the room, and Kathy immediately strides down the center aisle, sending a bullet into the back room with every step. Lydia dives for Alex's gun, slipping through his blood. She vaguely hears the back door crashing open; she turns, grasping the gun as a bullet lodges into the wall beside her head. Kathy's gun *clicks*, the barrel aimed at Lydia like a cold dark eye.

Lydia raises Alex's gun and squeezes the trigger. She's not holding on tight enough, and the recoil launches it out of her bloody hands. The bullet misses Kathy entirely, but it scares her enough to pivot into the back room and slam the door.

She retrieves the gun and aims it at the door, but it stays closed. Kathy's gone after her dad.

"Lydia!" Michael calls.

Rushing to her feet, she slips on Alex's blood and catches herself on the nearest pew. Outside the front door, Michael's backed his truck up and dropped the tailgate. He's waving both arms and jumping up and down. "Hurry!"

Kathy's outside, same as her dad, and a quick scan of the sanctuary confirms her mom isn't here either.

Fitting the gun awkwardly in her waistband, Lydia kneels beside Eddie. He's still alive, his eyes are open and alert, but his damaged face makes her want to cry.

"Why did you do that?" she says, finding an alarming amount of blood beneath him. "Why the hell did you do that?"

He chuckles. "I promised you, remember? I'm so, so sorry, Lydia." Blood leaks from the corners of his mouth. He's fighting for every breath. "We should've run away. I could've... I could've stopped this."

"It wasn't your fault," she says. "It was never you."

"I know," he smiles weakly. "I know you never loved me."

Lydia sits in his blood. "Eddie—"

"Please don't lie to me," he says, and it clicks in her chest—how much she's lied, controlled, and manipulated so she never had to lose anyone. Look where that got her.

"It's okay," he coughs. "I would do it again."

She smiles. "It's not too late, baby. We can still run. Just watch, it's not over."

"Lydia! We have to go!" Michael yells.

"Help me!" She slides Eddie's right arm around her shoulders. She can try and carry him without Michael, but if he slips off her, he could die when he hits the floor.

Michael sprints into the church. "There's nothing we can do—"

"*I said help me!*"

He squats and takes hold of Eddie's other half. They lift together; Eddie cries out.

"In the back, quick." Michael guides them to the bed of his truck, where they set Eddie down as gently as they can, even though he screams again.

Lydia flips the tailgate closed. "Take him away from here. I'll find you."

"Lydia—"

"I need to help my dad."

"Lydia—"

"Stop! I'm not leaving without him!"

Michael hugs her, picks her off her feet, and drops her over the tailgate. She lands next to Eddie and spins to her hands and knees as Michael hops into the truck and swerves into the street. The world is a spinning shroud of darkness and streetlamps, but Lydia can still see the lone figure standing beside the church, lowering a handgun.

Lydia drops down and hears a bullet zip overhead. Another shot rings out, even louder, and Lydia rises to her knees again in time to see her dad emerging from the shadows across the street.

Michael slams on the breaks and she reels backward, almost in a complete summersault. She sits up and looks through the truck's windows. In front of them, a car is parked diagonally in the street. Her mom is behind the wheel, her face hidden in the patch of darkness above white high beams.

The window beside Lydia explodes. Kathy's running toward the truck, gun outstretched.

Alex's gun! Lydia yanks it from her waistband, points, and pulls the trigger, even though it's happening so fast, she can't think or aim or breathe.

The shot misses. Kathy won't make that error. She lifts her gun, both eyes open.

"No!" Her dad fires. He's too far away, but Lydia crouches to avoid the volley of pellets. Kathy grunts and falls against the truck before slumping to the ground.

The truck lurches forward. Michael will have to go around her mom's car or ram into her. Her dad advances toward Kathy, who's still on the ground and motionless, even though the buckshot would've been too far away to kill her.

"Dad, stop, stop, stop!" she screams.

The truck hits something, presumably her mom's car. Lydia is thrown against Eddie, who doesn't cry out or move away from her. His body sways with the truck like he's in a deep sleep.

One shot rings out, and down the street, her dad collapses on the double yellow lines.

"*Lydia!*" he yells as they speed past her mom's car. He doesn't say anything else. Just her name. He knows that will be his final word, and there's no trace of fear or sorrow in his voice, only love; he *knows* who she is.

A second shot and her dad rolls over and doesn't move again. Kathy slowly stands, holstering her pistol, watching Lydia from the soft, orange glow of a streetlamp.

Lydia sits in the corner of the truck bed and gently lifts Eddie's head onto her lap. She smooths his hair down, but it keeps sticking up. "It's going to be okay, baby." Her dad saved her life twice, and now he's gone forever. He's gone and he won't come back.

If they turn around, Kathy will kill them. No matter how she looks at it, there's nothing she can do.

"No one else," Lydia says, tears blinding her eyes. Why won't Eddie's hair lay the way she wants it to? "No one else dies, okay? No more."

But Eddie's already dead, and she keeps trying to fix his hair like it makes a difference. "No one else, please, no one else."

"Lydia?" Michael calls through the back window. "What happened?"

"I can't lose anyone else," she says to herself over and over again. "I can't do it. *I can't lose anyone else!*"

Eddie can't hear her. He died trying to stop the horrific situation he helped create, and now he'll forever be known for murdering multiple people tonight. Alex, Jack, and her dad, will all somehow be Eddie's fault, even though he was the first to take a bullet, and he never fired a shot.

"No more, no more, no more," she whispers in Eddie's ear.

Four Blue Hill police cars zoom past them on Route 4. Their red and blue lights dance through the dark trees before fading into the distance. Kathy and her mom will either give up and get their story straight, or they'll pursue Lydia while the police are busy making sense of the bloodbath in Hope's local church. But will those women ever give up? What does Lydia do now if she forgets everything that happened tonight? Where does she go?

She won't be safe from them. Not unless she runs as far as she can. Or she removes the threat for good.

She leans into the open back window. "Michael, turn around."

"*What?*"

"Turn around." Lydia checks Eddie's pulse, even though she knows he's gone.

"And go where?"

"To the preserve," she says. "I know how we can save Eddie."

50

It's not going to work, Michael thinks.

He turns into the preserve and drives down the dirt road, stopping midway. "How do we find the grave?"

"It's between here and the river somewhere," Lydia says. "You have your phone?"

He shakes his head. It's still in the back room of his God-forsaken church.

Lydia hands him Eddie's phone. "Use the flashlight only if you have to, and keep it low to the ground. These woods are dense enough that it shouldn't give you away."

What is she talking about? "You make it sound like I'm doing this alone."

"Because you are." Lydia jumps out of the truck and drops the tailgate. "Carry Eddie. Remember, the river is the border. It might be easier to find the river first, then back up inside the tree line and work your way up and down, maybe thirty, forty yards total. I was here with my mom and Kathy earlier, and I obviously didn't know what they were doing at the time, but they went that direction," she points into the woods. "They wanted to see what I remembered. The grave is somewhere in there. You'll find it."

Michael can't suppress a smile. "Why does it feel like you've done this before?"

She tilts her head up like she's listening to something. "Because I have. A part of me remembers."

Well, that's interesting. Sadly, now is not the time for follow up questions.

They slide Eddie from the truck bed, and Michael tries to hold him gently, even though the kid looks dead. "You'll meet me there?"

"Let's hope so." Lydia grabs the handgun from the truck bed and checks the clip and chamber. Both empty. She tosses it in the woods and shuts the tailgate. "Can I have the keys?"

"In the truck. I'm guessing you have something in mind, Lydia?"

"I'll meet you there," she says, starting the truck and reversing down the dirt road.

Something's changing in her. How does it feel to be in her shoes? To feel perfectly like yourself, and then have your own mother claim you're a possessed, demonic thing? How does someone come back from that?

He activates the flashlight on the phone, trying not to drop Eddie at the same time. It's funny, Lydia didn't even mention calling the police. Kathy was a dispatcher, Will a paramedic. Between them, Alex, and Sharon, who hosted many parties throughout Will's career, calling the Blue Hill Police would be like calling a motorcycle gang and accusing their leader of murder. Michael has a high opinion of law enforcement, but they, like everyone else, cannot escape their own bias. It would be suicide and Lydia knows it. He suspects that if Kathy and Sharon happen to find them before the police, Lydia wouldn't want anyone to get in her way. She's not the same woman as when she woke up today.

Michael also thinks the police should be kept far away from this hallowed gravesite. He agreed with Alex on one thing: *the world should never know this secret.*

He pushes into the woods, constantly readjusting his grip on Eddie because his weight is awkwardly slack. The flashlight helps, but he still trips on every root and small rock. The woods are so compact, he's constantly twisting sideways to fit between trees.

How did he end up here, again? Bringing a dying man into the woods to save his soul?

Everything in his life had led him here, to this sacred land. He's approaching a river, again. He's going to pray for a resurrection, again. Where is the lighthouse in the trees, spinning darkly?

He's never been in the preserve before, but Eddie's stories and warnings of this place quickly come to mind. Nothing feels different. He waits for the thing in his stomach to respond, but it has gone quiet. Maybe it's bored of this development, or it's breathing in the forest air and testing the waters.

Or... it's afraid.

Michael pauses, adjusting his hold on Eddie again. Should he be terrified of this place?

He breaks from the tree line and finds the river. With Eddie's bloody corpse in his arms, he starts to understand what Lydia meant. Memory goes deeper than the mind.

Backtracking into the woods, he sets Eddie on the ground beside a large rock. It'll be easier to find the grave without carrying him.

He walks back and forth, keeping the flashlight low, slightly changing his direction with every turnaround. After coming full circle from where he started in Darling, he refuses to leave these woods without his miracle.

He will not walk away empty handed.

Headlights cut through the trees. He can't see the parking lot from here, but someone must've pulled in. Lydia plans to divert them from the grave, so where will they go? Is she leading them somewhere?

Turning off the flashlight, he walks toward the dirt road, taking each step slowly to minimize noise. A car door slams. Just one. A single car and a single door. So, who is it? Kathy or Sharon? And why are they alone?

He can't risk the flashlight. They have guns and he doesn't. Neither does Lydia, but he's not worried about her. They killed her out here once and she came back. Then they killed her soul in his church and here she is, surviving again. She won't quit.

"Come on, Lydia," he whispers. "What are you planning?"

There's a figure in the dark, on the edge of the woods, holding a shotgun.

Michael lowers himself to his stomach. *Any time now, Lydia.*

A bright white flashlight ignites and sweeps through the woods. He buries his face in his folded arms and watches from the corner of his eye.

The light drapes over trees and bushes, rotating above his head, and he can hear the *squeak-squeak-squeak* of the dark lighthouse going faster and faster.

If he's shot and killed in these woods, will he come back from the dead? Or does he have to be buried first?

The figure jerks the flashlight away and hurries toward the wooden bridge.

He jumps to his feet and rushes back to where the grave should be, the *squeak-squeak-squeak* cranking louder inside his head, making him giddy.

There *has* to be a true miracle tonight.

He may not get another chance.

51

After Lydia reversed the truck into the parking lot, she nudged it gently off the pavement and down the bumpy path to the wooden bridge. If Kathy and her mom see the truck over here, hopefully they'll check the bridge first. Would they even assume Michael and Lydia had gone to the grave? Maybe not. It's possible doing something as desperate as burying Eddie won't cross their minds, but she can't take that risk.

She parks the truck and runs across the wooden bridge. Up ahead, the Reaper watches her approach from under its dark hood.

The memories flutter around her heart: fireworks exploding above her; the red, white and blue sparks reflecting on the Reaper's knobby spine.

Ignoring the queasiness in her stomach, she steps inside the Reaper's shadow and finds the first hand and foot hold, the same position she's held a hundred times, except now there is no harness, no proper shoes, no rope. No one catching her if she falls.

Her shoes slip and she drops to the ground. It's not going to work like this.

Kicking off her shoes and socks, she buries them under a small mound of dead leaves at the foot of the cliff.

She starts again, barefoot. One step up, and her palms are sliding over the rock face, finding the ledges she can't see in the dark. She glances at the overhang, at the Reaper's swirling eyes and shark-like smile.

Don't look. Close your eyes. There's nothing to see.

With each step, she leans into the cliff, resting her cheek against the cool rock. She's only halfway, and this is the part she knows best.

The flutter in her chest has turned into a windstorm. If she looks up, she'll see the Reaper's wide-open mouth, waiting to swallow her.

Headlights briefly illuminate the rock, and a single car pulls into the parking lot.

You're out of time, she thinks. *They're here.*

She reaches for the next hold and pulls herself up, taking two steps and reaching again, her fingers finding the perfect grip, her toes scraping and straining to hold her weight. A car door shuts, just one.

She glances back. A lone figure leaves the parked car.

Why one?

They must've split up. One came here while the other searched her house, or the hospital, or stayed for the police.

Her arms are shaking, but she can't take a break. Holding still on a wall is exhausting. Too many pauses and she'll lose her energy.

The figure doesn't go to the truck or take the path. They walk down the dirt road.

"No, no, no," Lydia mutters, finding her footing. Her hand brushes the overhang and she stops.

So many failed attempts, what makes this any different?

There's no safety net, she thinks, her fingers exploring, finding the hold in the Reaper's mouth. *If I fall, I die.*

She climbs, her feet drifting away from the wall. Maybe Sammy's in these woods, cheering her on, and for once, thinking of him doesn't come with pain and emptiness.

She can't bring him back, no matter how badly she wants to. She can't go back in time and close the front door. She can't make her mom love her. She can't save herself from waking up in that grave. She can't stop her dad from dying in the road like an animal. She can't save Jack from getting shot in the church, or Eddie bleeding out in the back of a pickup truck.

Lydia slides one hand across the Reaper's mouth and finds a jagged tooth to grip. She lunges, grabbing the next hold with her fingertips. One hand over the other, her body dangling, she crosses the mouth and looks up. This close to the rock, there are no eyes or endless shadows. There's only a small cleft where her hand goes, and when she swings her other arm out, she barely grabs the edge. Then with both hands, she pulls herself up until she's on top of the Reaper.

She can't change what's happened, but she can still save Eddie and stop her mom and Kathy from hurting anyone else. They don't know what Lydia's capable of. Neither does she, but part of her remembers. The trauma she faced has shaped her body like floodwaters carving into a canyon.

She remembers what it's like to be terrified, and that will keep her alive.

Along the dirt road, a strong flashlight searches the edge of the woods.

Lydia checks her surroundings. She peels a heavy rock from the mud and rolls it over the edge. It crashes on the forest floor, breaking against the foot of the cliff and echoing through the woods.

The figure leaves the dirt road and starts down the path, washing the wooden bridge in white light.

If they come this way, they'll only follow the river and check the nearby trees and cliff base.

This is *Lydia* they're looking for.

They'll never think to look up.

52

On top of the Reaper, Lydia sinks to her stomach and watches the lone figure slowly advance over the wooden bridge.

It's Kathy. She has a tactical flashlight in one hand and a shotgun in the other. The shotgun is propped against her armpit, making it hard to shoot without dropping the flashlight. She must've run out of ammo for her own gun, having spent the last two bullets on Lydia's dad. Picking up his shotgun will be her final mistake. Before Lydia kills her, she will remind her why she never should've touched it.

Kathy slow walks from the wooden bridge to the Reaper's shadow, occasionally pausing to listen. The crickets and bullfrogs drown out all other sounds. Only once does she tip the flashlight upward, briefly scanning the cliff, before leveling it again and searching along the base.

Lydia smiles. She tried and failed to boulder the Reaper earlier, in front of Kathy. Why would tonight be any different?

Kathy turns right and hikes along the rock wall. It's one less side for her to protect.

Now that there's a river between Kathy and Eddie, Lydia plans to keep it that way.

She rises on her hands and feet and crawls over small rocks and roots to keep up with Kathy. The moon is barely bright enough to light the way, and with each step she feels herself teetering on the edge of the cliff, clinging to the jagged corner separating her from death.

Grabbing a small tree for support, Lydia picks up a rock the size of a softball. From this height, a direct hit will cave Kathy's head in. If Lydia misses, she'll have maybe another rock or two left to throw before Kathy gets out of range. Her chances of maiming this woman dwindle heavily if she screws up the first shot.

Rock in hand, Lydia resumes her precarious hike. She needs a clean open space over Kathy's head, and in another twenty feet, the cliff is sheer rock. A straight shot down.

Kathy pauses again.

No, no, don't turn around. You can't turn around.

Kathy checks every direction, especially the river.

Come on, Lydia thinks. *A little farther.*

Kathy moves forward again, ten feet from the smooth wall.

At the same time, Lydia trips over a root and lands on her side, still holding the rock. Kathy's flashlight jerks to the cliff, the white light hovering from tree to tree. Lydia holds her breath, feeling the night breeze run over her like a waterfall. Seconds pass. Then the air clears, the flashlight moves away, and the footsteps crunch onward.

Lydia rolls away from the edge, sighing deeply, and shuffles toward the sheer rock wall.

Why can't she hear Kathy anymore? She carefully peers over the edge. The flashlight is pointing at something on the forest floor, but she can't see what Kathy's looking at. She cranes her neck, setting the rock aside until she leans far enough over to see the flashlight all alone, resting in the center of a small bush.

She rolls backward as an explosion of rock chips and pellets shatter the night and ricochet off the Reaper. Even if Lydia can't see his expanding smile and shark teeth from here, she knows he's pleased to hear that sound.

How did Kathy figure it out? Now Lydia has no idea where she went.

She picks up the rock and silently backtracks to the other side of the Reaper. Looking down, she sees Kathy crouched by the cliff, aiming the shotgun skyward.

Lydia crawls on the Reaper's hood. With Kathy almost directly under her, Lydia shifts her upper body over the edge, lining up the rock as best she can in the dark. Whether it's a noise or instinct or a warning from the Reaper, Kathy flips around seconds after Lydia releases the rock.

What happens next is lost in the Reaper's shadow. Lydia's eyes aren't sharp enough, but the shotgun never goes off, and there's a distinct clank of metal and a thud. The shotgun spirals into view, and Kathy is face down on the forest floor, unmoving but probably still alive.

The shotgun is close enough for Kathy to lunge for, and she could be awake and waiting for Lydia to climb down. Lydia witnessed that trick less than an hour ago, and she won't be fooled by it. Unfortunately, she needs to get down somehow, and if Kathy's biding her time, she could shoot Lydia mid-climb.

Lydia can't wait forever. If Kathy's faking, Lydia will jump and hope for the best.

Swinging over the edge, she uses a tree root to lower herself down, finding the footholds with her toes and crossing beneath the Reaper to the route she's climbed down so many times, she can do it in the dark. Her feet are aching and starting to bleed, but soon she's halfway down and pausing to look beneath her.

Kathy's shifting her arms and legs on the forest floor.

She's alive, Lydia thinks. The rock hurt her, maybe knocked her out, but now she's waking up.

Her fingers slip, and she slides against the wall, catching herself ten feet above ground. She stops herself from crying out at the fresh cuts along her knees and stomach, but it doesn't matter. Kathy twirls around, sees Lydia coming, and scrambles for the shotgun.

Lydia jumps off the cliff, rolling to soften the impact and deepening the wounds on her knees.

Kathy grabs the shotgun but can't turn around fast enough or set her feet. Lydia hits her in the right eye as hard as she can. Pain shocks her entire arm, but she draws back and hits Kathy again, in the nose, and grabs the shotgun's double-barrel with her other hand. Kathy rolls to her side, her fingers on the stock, straining to reach the trigger.

Lydia yanks the gun away, curls up on the forest floor, and kicks Kathy in the chest with both feet, hard enough to knock her over.

Then Lydia shifts to one knee, presses the stock against her shoulder, and aims at the woman who killed her father.

Kathy stands up, blood streaming from her nose. She's too shocked to beg for her life.

"You know who taught me to shoot this?" Lydia says.

"Lydia—"

With a light squeeze and a deafening roar, Kathy becomes a dead thing scattered in the woods and river.

I didn't let her run, Lydia thinks, and sits on the forest floor, the ringing in her ears making her head hurt.

She struggles to her feet and finds her shoes. The shotgun is empty, and she doesn't want to search what's left of Kathy's remains, so she drops the gun in the bloody leaves.

In a few hours from now, they'll know the truth. If Eddie comes back from the dead, then she'll know what she is. Not something demonic or undead like her mom claims, but only herself, magically brought back to life.

What did Michael call it earlier?

A *miracle.*

53

There's *something* eerie about walking these woods at night. She's done this before. Exactly two nights ago, according to Eddie.

She knows he told her the truth; she can feel it in her footsteps and hear it in the crickets and bullfrogs.

How is she going to remember anything if her brain resets in the morning? And if Eddie doesn't come back? What does life look like after tonight? It's impossible to comprehend, so she shoves the thought away and forges into the woods on the other side of the river.

"Lydia?" Michael calls out.

"How'd you know?"

"I'm over here." A light flashes in the dark. "I found it! Just like they said. It's unnerving, isn't it? Being so close. I'm afraid of falling in."

Michael's looking at the grave like it's a long way down. Seeing it now for the first time, Lydia had imagined it to be bigger. The little patch of earth looks more like a quicksand trap than a burial ground, but what does she know? They must've stacked her on top of Jack. Had she been beneath him, she might have asphyxiated before he even woke up. But those memories belong to a different Lydia, the one who fought tooth and nail to stay alive.

She's grateful for what her past self did to survive and hopes to do the same for whatever version of her wakes up next.

Eddie's cold body is outstretched on the ground behind Michael, close enough to be stepped on if Michael isn't careful.

"I don't think it'll work," he sighs. He rubs his stomach with both hands, like he's about to be sick. "Conditions aren't right."

"Help me with him," Lydia says. She picks up Eddie's arms while Michael grabs his legs. "And what conditions?"

"I've been thinking. Wait, where's Kathy? I heard shots."

"She's dead." If Lydia closes her eyes, she'll see Kathy's scattered remains. Some things are better off forgotten.

They set Eddie beside the grave and stand at both ends of him, hands on their hips.

"I've been thinking," Michael continues, "that Eddie won't come back to life like you and Jack did." He rubs his stomach again, grimacing. "There's no way this grave, this arbitrary plot of earth, is a magical resurrection machine. That would be ridiculous. Even if it happened once, it won't repeat. It was a fluke, if it happened at all."

She kneels beside Eddie. "You helping me?"

He pauses, looks at the ground.

"Okay, I'll do it myself." She steps inside the grave, and the dirt seems to latch onto her shoe, tugging it downward. Keeping herself mostly on the edge, she leans over and starts digging out the excess dirt with her hands. A little help from the pastor would be the true miracle right now, but Michael seems like he's going through something.

"My point is, this is a waste of time," Michael says with a flick of his hand. "An utter waste. I mean think about it. Eddie didn't die in these woods like you did. If this plot of earth has rules, that could be one of them, right? What about old corpses? Does it bring those to life? Is there a timer before you're too far gone, and has Eddie surpassed it? You must have a million questions, Lydia. Don't you want to know how this works?"

She's creating sizeable space in the grave. The dirt's so loosely packed, she can reach far into it without hitting the bottom. Every time her hand goes down, she braces herself, half-expecting to touch something living or dead. She's not sure why. Another ghost memory, maybe.

"We don't know if it works or not," Lydia says. "We don't know anything."

"We know it may have happened once, and thanks to our friends, we know the exact, scientific conditions that made it happen."

Lydia sits up and wipes her forehead. "I don't think science is the answer here."

Michael's pacing now, holding his stomach like a pregnant woman. "I know, it's foolish. But we have one single shot at this. There's no do-over. After tonight, the police will take everything. Everything. Even us."

She kisses Eddie's forehead. If he comes back, will the gashes on his face heal? She has no obvious wounds from her scrape with death the other night, but she can't be sure about Jack. Surely, the grave has to heal what's damaged. Except her brain, apparently. But will time change that?

"If this doesn't work, Eddie will take the fall," she says. "He'll be branded as a murderer, and every death will be his fault because there's no one else to blame. My mom is the only other person alive who knows the truth, and she's going to paint a picture of Eddie that'll make him look like Ted Bundy." She runs her finger along Eddie's collarbone and over a long scratch on his chest. "She's already made sure of that. We know the truth, but does it matter? What good is our word against hers when she has an obvious scapegoat? Even if we attempt to make my mom a suspect, my broken memory will make me useless."

Michael's staring at her even though it's too dark to see his eyes.

"Eddie has to wake up," she says. "It's the only way he clears his name."

Michael kneels. "Let me help."

She kisses Eddie one more time, on the cheek. "Please wake up."

Together, they roll Eddie into the hole she dug. Then they use their hands to cover him with dirt until he's completely gone.

Lydia pats the dirt with one hand, smiling for some reason. Maybe it's because she's confident it'll work. Or because smoothing the dirt over his grave isn't poisoning her heart like it would've two days ago.

A sharp metal splinter stabs into Lydia's side. Michael is next to her, letting go of a rusty file and stepping back. It's stuck in her ribs; she can feel it against her organs.

"I'm so sorry," Michael whispers. "I have to know. This is my only chance to get it right. You died in these woods two nights ago. Eddie didn't die here. It must be recreated as closely as possible for it to work."

He makes it sound like they're working together. Like she agreed to be stabbed with a rusty tool.

"You'll come back," he says, grinning with excitement. "You'll be back so soon and perfectly healed."

Lydia stands, gasping for air, the pain nearly crippling her.

"I'll bury you with him. You'll be together." Michael lifts his hands as if to push her backward. "Just get in the grave, Lydia."

Then she manages to surprise him, and herself, by taking off into the trees. She's not sure how. She's not thinking at all, just running like a headless chicken stubbornly clinging to a few final moments of life.

Her body is its own creature; a survivor. She barely manages to stop herself from running off the riverbank and plunging into the water. She teeters on the edge, gently tapping the file protruding from her side.

Michael breaks through the trees behind her. "Lydia, please, let me save you. I can bring you back."

She wonders if he'll underestimate her like everyone else.

"Lydia?"

"Carry me."

"What?"

She starts to fall backward and runs into him. His reflexes kick in, and he catches her, his arms preoccupied. Then she rips the file out of her and drives it into his stomach.

He screams, or rather, a strange voice screams inside of him, and he starts to twitch and spasm uncontrollably. Why is he in so much more pain than her?

He squirms on the ground, wailing like a dying animal. "Please, please, please, help me. I can come back, I can be the miracle," he shrieks.

Falling to her knees, she crawls to Michael and yanks the file out. The voice inside his throat is so dark and angry, it scares her.

"Please," he seethes. "Help me. I can finally see it—everything I've been missing my whole life, it's all about this grave. I was born to die in it, to be resurrected. Lydia!" His eyes flash brightly. "We can fulfill this miracle. If you help me, please, we can show them what we are, what this place really is."

Lydia nods slowly. She picks his arm up and slips it around her shoulders. "Thank you, thank you."

With a groan, she helps him to his feet, his stomach bulging out through his shirt. She steadies herself, holds his shoulders with both hands, and shoves him down the riverbank. He lands head-first in the shallow water, his neck snapping, his body bent in unnatural ways. She's afraid he'll come back, somehow. She's afraid of what's inside him. Before he sinks to the bottom of Moon River, there's a flash of white teeth grinning up at her, reflecting the moonlight. And then he's gone.

The night is quiet again, like it was after Kathy's death. Lydia falls to her knees, alone in this world. There's no one left, except her mom.

Where is Sharon? Shouldn't she be here already? Lydia examines the bloody file in her hand, covered in blood. She's certain she'll die from the stab wound, but if she lives through it and wakes up with no recollection of what happened, how will she protect herself from the only other survivor of this night?

She grips the rusty file and holds her left arm up into the weak moonlight. Shaking, fighting to steady her trembling hand, she carves a memory, slicing a symbol into the tender skin inside her wrist. Trails of black blood drip down her arm and elbow. It's over in a moment, and she nearly faints from the pain. If she's lucky, the wound will turn into a scar, a permanent message for her future self. She can't imagine what will happen to her if this fails. Because of the symbol, maybe she'll finally remember something.

She drops the needle file and rolls to her side, grinding her teeth to keep from screaming. She's never broken a bone before. Never had surgery, or even stitches. She's escaped any major physical injuries in life, and the last two days must be God's way of catching up to her.

What do I have to do to get your attention? she imagines Him saying.

"I'm ready," Lydia whispers. "I think I'm ready this time."

With a clenched groan she crawls into the tree line, hugging the earth like she did the Reaper, one handhold at a time.

She kicks and scratches her way to the grave, slowly dragging herself back into the soft earth. There's nothing left in her bones. She's out of energy, out of life. But the grave seems to sink and swallow her until the dirt is spilling over her stomach and legs. Eddie's beside her, and she lays her arm over his chest and rests her head against his shoulder.

"I miss Sammy," she says to the grave. "He needs to know that I'm ready."

The grave says nothing.

"Why did this happen? What was the point?"

Again, the grave is quiet.

"If You don't need me here, I'd like to go," she tells God. "But if You want me to stay, can you give me a reason? Because I don't know what to do."

She drifts into a deep sleep, wading into an ocean of clouds in her mind, surrounded by floating bodies. In the sky is a dying sun nearly eclipsed by a black moon. There's a sliver of sunlight left. Lydia can feel it on her face. But before the moon can block the sun, she hears someone behind her.

"Lydia."

54

Lydia's lying on a bed of clouds next to Sammy, staring up at the starry night with wonder.

"Can I stay here?" she says. "I just want to stay with you."

Sammy tilts his head. His eyes are moons eclipsing suns, dark orbs with gold rings. "You're not finished," he says.

"But there's nothing left for me."

He snuggles against her and kisses her head. "Don't worry, I'll be here, waiting for you."

She smiles. "I won't forget you. Even after I wake up, I'm going to remember *this*."

He hugs her tightly, but he's starting to fade. The clouds and stars grow dim, and before Sammy disappears from her arms, she hears him whisper: *I know.*

The world is dark and cold.

Far above her, red and blue lights flicker through the forest. A bright star shoots through the sky, then stops, hovers, and grows larger. The sound of helicopter blades echo off the Reaper. The spotlight drifts away.

"Lydia?"

Sitting up, Lydia stares at the dark woods around her and at her mom standing beside a nearby tree. She looks like she's been crying.

"Mom?" Dirt spills and sifts around her. She's sitting in a sunken pit, alone, somewhere in the nature preserve. "What happened, Mom?"

"Oh baby." She helps Lydia stand. "Oh baby, I'm so sorry."

"What happened?" There are voices nearby. The flickering lights are coming from an army of emergency vehicles.

Her mom looks away, sniffing. "What do you remember?"

She thinks back to last night, to... Eddie's proposal? No. Yes? That's not right. There's something bleeding through her mind like a freshly painted canvas in a rainstorm. Colors are running everywhere. Blood, water, light. Eddie! Where's Eddie?

"I know you don't remember, dear," her mom says, patting Lydia's hand. "It's okay. It's for the best. The things you went through tonight, no human being should ever endure that."

"What are you talking about?"

"You know Pastor Michael, right, from church?" Her mom wipes her eyes again, trying to hold it together. The voices are getting louder. It sounds like someone's stomping through the woods. Or a lot of people. "Well he and Eddie... it's so awful, I can't say it."

"Mom, what happened?" In the distance, the helicopter blades are coming back this way.

"Oh Lydia, they tried to murder you. They were planning this... ritual, and I was so worried, your dad and I went looking for you, and Kathy and Alex helped, but when we found you in the church, they attacked us."

"Where's Dad?"

Her mom tells her what happened: Eddie and Michael shot and killed Jack, her dad, and Alex in the church. Then they took Lydia and drove off. Kathy and her mom tried calling the police, and she wanted to wait at the church, but Kathy pursued them. She took her dad's shotgun and found them in these woods, where Michael and Eddie overpowered her and used the shotgun to end her life. Then Eddie and Michael must've had a dispute because Michael's gone, possibly dead, and Eddie buried himself alive in the grave with Lydia. A final act of psychotic belief.

Her brain isn't functioning. Her dad is dead, and it feels so dream-like and unbelievable that she can't process it. None of this is real.

But she knows Eddie. And she knows he would never hurt her. Is that why it feels like her mom's telling a story about someone else? If he discovered her secret life, he would've been shattered. But that's all. He's not a killer.

"So you really don't remember anything?" Her mom says, still holding Lydia's hand in a death grip. Flashlights cut through the trees behind her, almost upon them.

Lydia shakes her head, even though that's not the truth. She doesn't know what she remembers. The colors are still running. "Why did you say, 'I know you don't remember'? I never said that."

In the dark, it's hard to read her eyes. "You kept asking me what happened, Lydia, so I assumed you didn't know. That's all." She leans closer. "You're going to be all right. I promise. We'll get through this together."

"Where's Eddie?"

Her lower lip trembles. "In custody, where he belongs. They found him wandering the street, incoherent."

"We were both in a grave, and we weren't hurt?" Lydia looks down at a jagged and bloody hole in her shirt. She feels her side, finding a small lump of mangled skin, both tender and coarse to the touch.

"No, baby, you're just fine. It's a miracle."

She holds Lydia close, their foreheads touching. Then she places her hand on the back of Lydia's neck and rubs it like she used to do when Lydia was little.

"You're going to be okay," her mom says, and kisses her forehead.

Her lips burn Lydia's skin, and the heavy hand on the back of her neck makes her queasy.

"How did you find me?"

A dark cloud passes over her eyes. "You're my daughter. I knew I would find you."

Voices echo all around them.

"I found her!" Her mom shouts. "Over here!"

Lydia notices the dirt packed beneath her fingernails; the feeling of crawling through the mud and digging with her hands. It's coming back like a thought she can't quite remember; a shadow, a ghost of what it should be.

"Lydia? Are you sure you don't remember anything?"

It's all there, humming under the surface: the feeling of her mom's hand on her neck, their foreheads touching. "No. Nothing."

"You're safe now, okay? No one will hurt you."

People and lights converge on Lydia. It's too much at one time, and it's easier to close her eyes and pretend it's only a nightmare. They ask her to open her eyes, and she sees gloved hands, stern faces, and an anxious German shepherd. Police stand guard with their radios buzzing and let the paramedics move her to a stretcher, where they carry her through the woods and toward an ambulance.

Her mom never releases her hand.

Before they load her into the ambulance, her mom brushes the hair from Lydia's forehead. "I'll stay with you. You're going to be okay. They'll need to run tests and make sure you're all right, but it won't be too bad."

Lydia doubts that. There's a nagging feeling deep inside her chest; something she's supposed to do.

"I'm ready," she whispers. Those words echo in her mind like a song.

"I know you are. Let's get you taken care of."

She smiles at her mom, somehow the only other survivor on this horrific night she can't remember.

They ride in the ambulance together, away from the Reaper, away from Hope.

And under the lights Lydia finds a freshly healed scar on the inside of her wrist. It's a small squiggle, barely noticeable; a scar she doesn't remember earning and a shape she can't make sense of.

It looks like a crooked M.

ACKNOWLEDGEMENTS

After I attended Cincinnati's Books by the Banks festival in the fall of 2024 (I went as a reader), that very night, I had a dream I was the guest on a podcast (my subconscious brimming with aspirations of literary grandeur, no doubt).

The host asked me what my next project was, and I didn't have one lined up. So in my dream, I made up a premise on the spot. I said, "My next book is about a woman who wakes up in a grave in the woods, and she doesn't know if she's alive or dead."

Four months after that dream, I started the first draft of *Goodnight Lydia*.

I'm hardly the first person to be inspired by a literal dream, but I do think, in general, we tend to undersell what dreams are capable of.

As someone who is obsessed with wind patterns and coincidences and all manner of supernatural elements, I believe dreams are more powerful than most people assume. Maybe it's due to my faith as a Christian, and the importance of dreams throughout Christianity, but this is the first time I've ever taken action based on a dream, and I'm really, truly glad I did. The project appealed to me instantly, and I knew the idea never would've left me if I'd stubbornly refused to write it.

This book was elevated tremendously by my editor, Laura Joyce. She is absolutely brilliant and lovely to work with. Tiffany Avery does my copy editing, and every collaboration with her so far has been magic.

My early readers were endlessly helpful and guiding. We have long discussions about every project, and they remain my closest allies as an author. So thank you to my sisters, and to Aaron Bogan, Bayleigh Horn, Jesy Boales, Kennedy King, and Michaela Woods.

Thank you to my wife, Caitlin, for supporting this journey every step of the way. Without her, none of this would've happened.

Thanks to my brother, Matthew, who gave me plenty of good advice throughout.

And finally, a note on this story:

I've been calling this project my "love letter to psychological thrillers" because it contains many of the tropes and aspects that I love about thrillers. I may never again write a book that hinges on such a pivotal twist, and so I hope I've done this story justice and brought something fresh to the genre.

I've traditionally been a discovery writer and would never outline a story before writing. With *Goodnight Lydia*, I outlined the first 25%, and I knew the twist from the get-go.

However, you may be surprised at how much freestyling happened after the first few chapters. Much of the middle and the end of this story was written in the moment; I forced myself to improvise along with the characters, and I hope you had as much fun reading this as I did writing it.

em jones